The Poisoner of Ptah

Paul Doherty

headline

First published in 2007 by
HEADLINE PUBLISHING GROUP

First published in paperback in 2007 by
HEADLINE PUBLISHING GROUP

1

Cataloguing in Publication Data is available
from the British Library

ISBN 978 0 7533 2887 1

Typeset in New Century Schoolbook by Palimpsest Book
Production Limited, Grangemouth, Stirlingshire

Printed and bound in Great Britain by
Clays Ltd, St Ives plc

Headline's policy is to use papers that are natural, renewable and recyclable products and made from wood grown in sustainable forests. The logging and manufacturing processes are expected to conform to the environmental regulations of the country of origin.

HEADLINE PUBLISHING GROUP
A division of Hachette Livre UK Ltd
338 Euston Road
London NW1 3BH

www.headline.co.uk
www.hodderheadline.com

From Martin Zealander, with love, to his sister Ruth Robbins who sadly passed away on 8 December 2004, aged 45.

List of Characters

THE HOUSE OF PHARAOH

Hatusu:	Pharaoh-Queen of the XVIII dynasty
Senenmut:	lover of Hatusu: Grand Vizier or First Minister, a former stone-mason and architect
Valu:	the 'Eyes and Ears' of Pharaoh: royal prosecutor
Omendap:	Commander-in-Chief of Egypt's armies

THE HALL OF TWO TRUTHS

Amerotke:	Chief Judge of Egypt
Prenhoe:	Amerotke's kinsman, senior scribe in the Hall of Two Truths
Asural:	Captain of the Temple Guard of the Temple of Ma'at in which the Hall of Two Truths stands

Shufoy:	a dwarf, Amerotke's manservant and confidant
Norfret:	Amerotke's wife
Ahmase and Curfay:	Amerotke's sons

THE TEMPLE OF PTAH

Ani:	High Priest
Maben:	Assistant High Priest
Hinqui:	Assistant High Priest
Minnakht:	Chief Scribe
Hutepa:	a heset

THE HOUSE OF THE GOLDEN VINE

Ipuye:	merchant
Patuna:	Ipuye's first wife
Khiat:	Ipuye's second wife
Maben:	Ipuye's brother-in-law
Meryet:	Ipuye's sister-in-law through Patuna
Hotep:	Kushite, captain of Ipuye's bodyguard
Saneb:	Kushite: member of Ipuye's bodyguard

THE UNDERWORLD OF THEBES

Churat:	'The Eater of Vile Things': gang leader
Skullface:	one of the Churat's standard-bearers
Bluetooth:	a member of the Amemets, a guild of assassins in Thebes
The Vulture:	a member of the Amemets
The Gerh:	Lady of the dark

THE LIBYANS

Naratousha:	leading chieftain
Themeu:	Naratousha's kinsman

OTHER CHARACTERS

Nadif:	standard-bearer in the Medjay, the Theban police
Huaneka:	widow of the author of the Ari Sapu – the Books of Doom

HISTORICAL NOTE

The first dynasty of ancient Egypt was established about 3100 BC. Between that date and the rise of the New Kingdom (1550 BC) Egypt went through a number of radical transformations which witnessed the building of the pyramids, the creation of cities along the Nile, the union of Upper and Lower Egypt and the development of the Egyptians' religion around Ra, the Sun God, and the cult of Osiris and Isis. Egypt had to resist foreign invasion, particularly by the Hyksos, Asiatic raiders who cruelly devastated the kingdom.

By 1470 BC, Egypt, pacified and united under Pharaoh Tuthmosis II, was on the verge of a new and glorious ascendancy. The pharaohs had moved their capital to Thebes; burial in the pyramids was replaced by the development of the Necropolis on the west bank of the Nile as well as the exploitation of the Valley of the Kings as a royal mausoleum.

I have, to clarify matters, used Greek names for cities, etc., e.g. Thebes and Memphis, rather than their archaic Egyptian names. The place name Sakkara has been used to describe the entire pyramid complex around Memphis and Giza. I have also employed the shorter version for the pharaoh queen: i.e. Hatusu rather than Hatshepsut. Tuthmosis II died in 1479 BC and, after a period of confusion, Hatusu held power for the next twenty-two years. During this period Egypt became an imperial power and the richest state in the world.

Egyptian religion was also being developed, principally the cult of Osiris, killed by his brother Seth but resurrected by his loving wife Isis, who gave birth to their son, Horus. These rites must be placed against the background of the Egyptians' worship of the Sun God and their desire to create a unity in their religious practices. They had a deep sense of awe for all living things: animals and plants, streams and rivers were all regarded as holy, while Pharaoh, their ruler, was worshipped as the incarnation of the divine will.

By 1470 BC the Egyptian civilisation expressed its richness in religion, ritual, architecture, dress, education and the pursuit of the good life. Soldiers, priests and scribes dominated this civilisation and their sophistication is expressed in the terms they used to describe both themselves and their culture. For example, Pharaoh was 'the Golden Hawk'; the treasury was 'the House of Silver'; a time of war was 'the Season of the Hyaena'; a royal palace was 'the House of a Million Years'. Despite the country's breathtaking, dazzling civilisation, however, Egyptian politics, both at home and abroad, could be violent and bloody. The royal throne was always the centre of intrigue, jealousy and bitter rivalry. It was on to this political platform, in 1479 BC, that the young Hatusu emerged.

By 1478 BC Hatusu had confounded her critics and opponents, both at home and abroad. She had won a great victory in the north against the Mitanni and purged the royal circle of any opposition led by the Grand Vizier Rahimere. A remarkable young woman, Hatusu was supported by her wily and cunning lover Senenmut, also her First Minister. She was determined that all sections of Egyptian society accept her as Pharaoh Queen of Egypt.

In foreign policy Hatusu had to face three great threats. The first was from the Libyans who prowled the western desert. The second was from the southern province of Kush, a source of great riches. Kush was ever ready to rebel against a weak or distracted pharaoh. A third source of danger were the tribes generally classed as 'the Sea People', who prowled the Middle Sea. Egypt had to defend the delta in the north, and the long river Nile, which was the life blood of Egypt; if that was cut or cities along it seized, a major threat was posed. Successive pharaohs were always determined to confront such dangerous threats whenever they emerged . . .

EGYPT c. *1478* BC

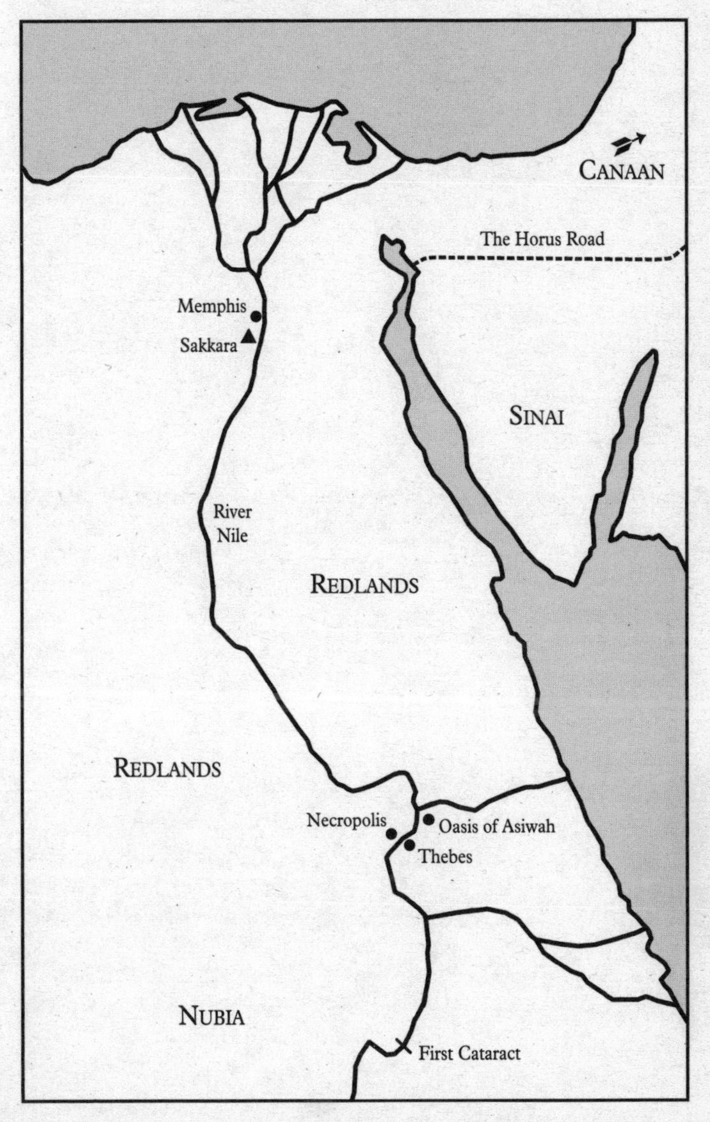

TCHETHU-I: ancient Egyptian, 'prison'

PROLOGUE

'Pay now devotion to the god with the face of a dog and the brow of a man. He who feeds on the slain, who keeps guard on the shore by the Lake of Fire, who devours the bodies of the dead, who tears out hearts and yet remains invisible.' The strident voice of the prison chaplain paused. 'Let us seek him who drinks the blood of the dead, who supplies the blocks with slaughter and lives on intestines. Let us remember him who herds the doomed to their death, stabs their bodies and smashes their skulls. Curses on them whose bodies are cut to pieces, spirit and souls severed from their shadows, driven far away, their skulls battered in, hearts plucked out.' The chaplain's voice echoed through the heat-laden air like the sound of a trumpet; it beat upon the high palisade, returning to ring through the enclosure of the Oasis of Bitter Bread, a hellish hole surrounded by burning sands a hundred miles out in the Redlands west of Thebes.

The prison chaplain, clad only in a loincloth, stirred restlessly on the makeshift wooden platform erected in the middle of the enclosure, the only shade against the burning sun a thin awning of striped cloth which drooped inertly in the heat. He paused, glancing quickly to his right then to his left at the Guardian of Shadows, the prison keeper and his standard-bearer, squatting on reed mats either side of him. He blew out a breath, hoping to cool the sweat on his face, and stared across at the execution stake, which soared at least five yards high. From it the dying prisoner hung head down, blood pouring from his wounds. The chaplain fingered the bracelet specially smeared in the hair, fat, gall and excrement of an ibex and prayed for release against the oppressive heat. He wondered when the prisoner would die, when the fiery sun would dip and the cool night breezes rise. Not for the time he deeply regretted his own indiscretions, the theft of sacred scarabs from the sanctuary of his temple back in Thebes. Such disgrace had led to his exile as a prison priest in this boiling antechamber of the Underworld. He just wanted to escape the fierce heat as the hapless prisoner hanging before him had tried to do. Escape brought no hope, not from the Oasis of Bitter Bread, where fiends roamed and the power of Seth the Destroyer was all-pervasive. The condemned man had been recaptured, then whipped and lacerated before being hung upside down in full view of the prisoners and their guards, a dire warning to all. The Oasis of Bitter Bread was their world, guarded by all the monsters of the Am-duat, the Underworld, and to escape meant certain death.

The unfortunate prisoner now swayed lightly, arms and head hanging down; the leather thongs around his ankles rippled, causing the victim to bounce eerily up and down. The chaplain continued his chant a little faster, fingering the *al-haggar-al-hurra*, the white cat's-eye stone which he wore on a cord around his neck for protection against nightmares. He stared around the compound, at the reed-topped huts, the palm trees clustered around the precious waterhole, the guards in their leather kilts and baldrics, shaven heads protected against the sun by striped head-dresses. The prisoners, some forty in number, were not so fortunate. Clad only in loincloths, they had all been manacled to goree sticks fashioned from tree branches. These were forked at one end and fastened around the prisoners' necks by a strip of leather.

The prison chaplain licked his dry lips; aware of the growing frustration of the Guardian, he gabbled his prayer to a finish. Immediately the Guardian rose, grasping his metal-studded mace, and started across the compound to the condemned man. All fell silent; there was nothing but the buzzing of flies, and the occasional dust devil, spurts of sand lifted by the hot wind to sting the eyes and clog the throat. Above them, black wings spread against the deep blue sky; the vultures circled as if Nekhbet, Mistress of the Scavengers, had summoned them to the impending bloody banquet. One of the guards hastened to hold the swaying man still. The Guardian approached, cheap bracelets and finger rings glinting in the light, oil-drenched thighs brushing against each other. He stopped before the prisoner, now held still by the guard, then grunted and drew back the mace. The condemned man whimpered a prayer or plea, but no one cared; even the gods had deserted this place. Only Seth, red-haired and green-eyed, together with his legion of demons, visited the Oasis of Bitter Bread. The Guardian brought the mace down, shattering the prisoner's skull, the bone cracking like a dusty jug against a rock. The man jerked a little, then hung still, blood and brains soaking the hot sand beneath. A collective moan rose from the prisoners. The Guardian waddled back to the makeshift dais and, taking a ladle of water, splashed his face and wetted his lips, provoking more groans from the watching men and women baking under the relentless sun.

'Know you,' the Guardian shouted, pointing at the dead man, 'the sentence for escape! The Guardians of the Fiery Lake prowl this oasis, Pharaoh's justice on you, filth under her sandalled feet.' He paused, relishing the thought. He had never looked upon the face of Hatusu, the She-King, Pharaoh of Egypt, but he'd heard about her beauty and terrifying majesty, as magnificent as an army in battle array. He took another sip of water, aware of the excitement in his loins, the usual effect of any execution, then threw the ladle down.

'Demons with deadly claws ever ready to slay,' he continued, his words rolling out across the dusty compound, 'watch you day and night. The slayers of souls and the boilers of flesh will trap you in so many ways.' He flung up a hand, pointing to the circling vultures. 'They watch and they report on any living thing which crawls on the sands beyond. They decide who shall be your executioners, the lions, the hyaenas, the snakes . . .' He paused for effect. 'Or the Libyans, sand-dwellers, desert wanderers . . . or the followers of Seth, outlaws and bandits who show no mercy. And if they do not dog your heels, the Devil of Thirst, the Demon of Hunger, the Fiend of the Sun, or the Terror of Icy Nights will surely trail your every step. Be warned!' He gestured at the dead prisoner. 'No burial rite for him! No help with his journey through the Am-duat, where Apet the Great Snake awaits him. Cut him down! Leave his corpse out on the sands.' He lifted his hands dramatically, and pointed once again at the vultures. 'The watchers await their banquet.'

The Guardian slumped down on to the cushions, congratulating himself on a job well done. Two prisoners, trusted ones, hastened across with fans to cool his sweaty face and body. The Guardian grunted with pleasure and slurped another mouthful of water, then he turned to his standard-bearer. 'The master of prisons will be pleased: no escapes, no mistakes!' He closed his eyes, which were almost hidden in rolls of fat. He could just imagine the report he would dictate to his superiors in Waset, the City of the Sceptre, Thebes. Perhaps that would secure him promotion. The custody of a greater prison, closer to the city, away from this dunghole, which was at least a week's march from Thebes. Nevertheless, there were still comforts. The Guardian moaned quietly with pleasure. Tonight he would eat fresh meat brought in by the hunters, spiced quail, and, perhaps, a juicy melon purchased from a passing Kushite merchant. Afterwards he would relax with that female prisoner so desperate to earn his favour.

'Master?'

He opened his eyes.

'The prisoners?' The Guardian's standard-bearer gestured across the compound.

'Ah, yes.' The Guardian mopped his face with a wet cloth. He felt magnanimous. 'Release them from the yoke, no manacles; a stoup of water, a bowl of bread and dried meat for each one.'

He stared across at the cowed, huddled group of men and women, herded here from all parts of the empire. He searched out that pretty, long-haired Memphite woman. She was gazing longingly across at him. At last she had succumbed!

'Two stoups of water.' The Guardian clambered to his feet.

'Even the Rekhet?'

'Yes,' the Guardian smiled, 'even the Rekhet.'

The prisoner known as the Rekhet, or Number Ten according to the prison roster, sat by himself on the collection of dry rags that served as his bed in the shadow of the palisade. Glad to be free of that hideous yoke, he lifted the cup of precious water, sipped carefully, then chewed on the piece of dried antelope meat the guards had flung at him. He lifted a hand against the dust and flies ready to cluster around his mouth or coat his cracked fingers, then stared up at the sky. The heat was dying. At last the sun was beginning to slip, the air was cool, the night winds offering some relief. He drew in a deep breath and gagged at the fetid smells. He had to escape! He had witnessed the execution, yet it had not deterred him. Tonight the Guardian would celebrate. The guards would drink until they dropped. He would never have such an opportunity again.

The Rekhet fingered the rough placard fastened around his neck bearing his name and his number. He was now known to everyone by that name, as if those crimes he'd been accused of in the court of the Temple of Ptah had, like Hags of the Night, clung to his very soul, following him here to this prison oasis. To be free of his manacles was a rare event, whilst the other prisoners always kept well away from him. It mattered little what he said or did; they believed in his reputation, whatever the truth of the matter. Even these malefactors and brigands regarded him as an evil man. He had scarcely been in the prison compound a month when six prisoners had died. He'd vainly pleaded that the cause of their deaths was foul food or brackish water, but he had still been singled out as responsible, and if it had not been for the prison chaplain, he would have been torn to pieces. In a sense this had been transformed into a blessing. He had been left well alone, and so he could plot. He'd now collected all the things he needed, hidden beneath his collection of rags: a waterskin, reed sandals, some grains of silver, a piece of cloth for his head, a pack of dried meat, a dagger, a piece of flint, some twine, even a crude map. Now he squatted and reflected. He'd not decided who in Thebes was responsible. Hutepa the heset? Or someone else who'd bribed the passing sand-dwellers and desert wanderers to visit this oasis, secretively seek him out and pass these forbidden items on to him? Somebody wanted him to escape, though who it was remained a mystery.

Once again the Rekhet stared up at the sky, longing for night to fall so he could go. No more days in this desolate place of torture with its cruel tedium, the petty brutality of its jailors and the cold ostracism of his fellow prisoners. At night, his dream-soul floated out back to Thebes, to walk in the flowered gardens of the Temple of Ptah, to savour their perfumed breezes, revel in the sheer beauty of the elegant columns washed by the moonlight, the sacredness of the sanctuary, the all-inspiring beauty of the Palace of a Million Years. In his dreams, he visited the library, smelt the fragrance of sandalwood and frankincense, scrubbed papyrus, thick ink and rich leather. In other dreams he sat by the pools of purity and watched the lotuses open. On such soul journeys he passed through the soaring pylons fronting the temple with their gorgeous standard poles, elaborate inscriptions and vivid drawings either side of the huge bronze doors. Other scenes would come swirling in. Heset girls in their gauze-like veils and robes, perfumed, oil-drenched wigs framing pretty faces, beautiful limbs moving sinuously to the clatter of the sistra and the beat of the tambourine. Fresh food piled high on platters, finest wines slopping in jewel-encrusted goblets. But his dreams often turned to nightmares. The arrival of the Medjay at his lodgings, his arrest, the vision of his comrades' corpses, foully poisoned, sprawled on the floor of that chamber. The horrific accusations had been hurled thick and fast: that he was a professional poisoner responsible not only for these deaths but for many more throughout Thebes. They claimed to have found his secret cabinet of powders and potions. The indictment had been drawn up damning him, leaving him no choice but to either throw himself on the mercy of Pharaoh or face immediate trial and summary execution.

The prisoner closed his eyes. He sat for a while rocking himself backwards and forwards humming a tune, as he always did at this time of the day, his only prayer that the gods would once again turn their faces to him and smile. When he opened his eyes, the sky was beginning to redden, the sun turning from a molten gold to a fiery disc, slipping quickly into the west. The prisoner recalled his days as a priest physician; how he would prostrate himself and pray to Osiris, Master of Yalou, Lord of the Evergreen Fields in the Eternal West. Until he escaped, *if* he escaped, there would be no more gods, no meadows of heaven, nothing but this hideous hell of a prison oasis.

The darkness came flowing in like a cloak. The heat cooled. The noises of the oasis changed as prisoners and guards relaxed, ready to enjoy a night of pleasure. A woman screamed, the sound broken by the raucous singing of the guards. The prisoner waited. The moon, the Khens, the Great Runner of the Dark Sky, rose full and clear. The stars, the flowers of the night, gleamed like precious jewels against a dark velvet background. The night air echoed with the howls of the night prowlers beyond the palisade. The prisoner, however, was not worried. He had studied the star maps at the Temple of Ptah; he had his own illicitly acquired crude diagrams. He could recognise the position and shape of the blossoms of the night: Sothis the Dog-Star; Mesekhti shaped like the Great Bear. He would use all this knowledge to plot his way out. He dug into the folds of rags and prepared himself. The drunken chanting of the guards was abruptly interrupted by a clear voice breaking through the strident din.

'How soft your hands, petals of your skin . . .'

The prisoner smiled to himself. He recognised that hymn, sung so delicately in this hellish place: it was a heset psalm from his own temple. The words and the melody were the prisoner's final spur. He would go tonight or die here in this place of horror, even if he had to use his skills to concoct some potion so that his *ka* could break free from his body and begin its awesome journey into the Eternal West. Whatever happened, he would escape or die in the next few hours.

The prisoner left in the third quarter of the night. He scaled the palisade, no real obstacle; the real keepers of the oasis, as the Guardian had proclaimed, lurked in the blackness beyond. He dropped into the hot, soft sand and stared up at the sky, recalling those star maps and the desert charts he'd consulted at the Temple of Ptah. From these he had learnt where the Oasis of Bitter Bread was situated. He would use this information to travel north-east, and break out of the hot sands on to the hard gravel land that stretched up to the tributaries of the Nile. Once there, he was safe.

The prisoner made his way carefully forward, a dark shape flitting across the sand. Roars, coughs and the growling of night prowlers rang out, though these were now busy tearing the flesh of the felon executed earlier. The prisoner didn't fear any pursuit, not yet. The guards who walked around the palisade would be slumped down in beer-drenched sleep or hiding in the shadows ready to be pleasured by the prisoners they'd selected. It would be at least noon tomorrow before the Guardian and his guards realised what had happened; early in the evening before they organised any pursuit. The prisoner slipped across the sand. Now and again he'd stop and stare upwards, studying the blossoms of the sky. The desert air was freezing cold but at least he was free. Somewhere to the east lay Thebes and the Palace of a Million Years. Only when he arrived there could he seek out Hutepa, demand justice, and take vengeance for what had happened to him.

MEN: ancient Egyptian, 'poison'

CHAPTER 1

'Ptah, Man God, when you show your face all the birds which were as dead spring to life. The beasts browse content in their pastures! Trees and plants grow luxurious. The birds fly and wheel under the sky, wings uplifted in worship of you. The deer spring up at the glory of thy power. Life-giving Ptah, turn your face towards us . . .'

The temple choir of Ptah, clad in brilliant white robes, paused in their paean of praise. The cymbals clashed to the rattle of the sistra and the joyful blaring of trumpets. The vast crowd gathered in the great precinct below the steps of the temple sighed in astonishment at the hundreds of pure-white doves that burst out from the massive pillared front of the building. These fluttered in a snapping of wings, joyful to be free, then turned and whirled like the innocent souls of the dead beneath the blue canopy of Nut the Sky God, soaring and dipping over the towering walls, pylons and broad bronze gates of the temple. Finally they flew out across the sacred complex of chapels, courtyards, sanctuaries, shrines, statues and gardens of Ipet-sut, the Most Desirable of Places, the temple city of Karnak in Thebes. Once they were gone, the choir continued their hymn:

'Fair of face and lovely of form are you . . .'

The crowds waved fans of palm fronds to cool their sweaty faces, and strained to stare up at the sacred precinct of the temple. Dazzling in the sun, this beautifully exquisite facing of pillars and columns of honey-coloured sandstone and pink sculpted limestone overlooked the broad, sweeping steps leading up to it. Maryannou and Nakhtu-aa now guarded these steps, an elite corps of the Imperial Army resplendent in their blue and gold headdresses and linen kilts of the same colours. From the belts of these soldiers dangled the *khopesh*, the killing sword; their right hands grasped blue and gold shields displaying the Horus hawk, while in the other was a long spear with a pointed barb. Beyond these guards, at the top of the steps clustered the leading priests of the temple in their gauffered robes, shoulders draped in the glossy, gleaming skins of leopard and panther. The celebrants moved in clouds of the most fragrant incense, curling up in prayer to the Man God Ptah, whose gigantic statue stared stonily down at them.

To the right of the priests sat Hatusu, the Glory of Egypt. She was garbed in the jewel-encrusted vulture headdress of Nekhbet, the lunging Uraei, the Spitting Cobra, around her brow. Her lovely shoulders were draped by the Nenes, the Coat of Glory, her long legs swathed in a long linen kilt. She sat on the Throne of Majesty, its golden arms carved in the shape of leaping lions, its silver legs ending in the sculptured heads of Egypt's enemies, the vile Asiatics, the Prowlers on the Great Green, the rebels of Nubia, and other foes amongst the People of the Nine Bows. Hatusu, her beautiful long face exquisitely painted, sat elbows resting on the arms of the throne, sandalled feet pushing against a footstool of silver and gold. She gripped the flail and rod and suppressed a smile. She only hoped the Libyan war chiefs, squatting on cushions on the other side of the precinct, did not notice the carvings on the front of the footstool: they depicted their warriors kneeling in submission, arms bound behind them, tufts of hair specially tied up so that Pharaoh, Horus in the North, the Mighty Bull of the South, the Glory of Amun, the Living Incarnation of Montu, might smash their skulls.

Hatusu wetted dry lips, and her sloe eyes, ringed in black and green kohl, glanced across at the five living sacrifices awaiting their fate. They knelt at the top of the temple steps like the carvings on the footstool, garbed only in loincloths, arms bound behind them tied at the elbow, shaggy heads hanging down, their faces hidden by bushy beards. Hatusu stilled her own qualms. Across the forecourt of the precinct squatted Naratousha, the principal war chief of the Libyan tribes who roamed the Western Desert, the disputed Redlands. She had to demonstrate to him and his council that the power of Egypt was invincible. As the hymn proclaimed: 'She is like the hawk lord on the wing who takes what pleases her at a glance of an eye, like the Jackal of the South, Lord of Quickness, the runner who crosses over the Two Lands, like the War God Montu who crushes the furthest perils . . .' The Libyans and others must accept the message of the paintings, carvings and inscriptions on the walls, columns and pillars around them, all summed up in one line of hieroglyphics edged gloriously in gold: 'Egypt will set its boundaries where she will. Pharaoh will crush the people of the Nine Bows.' In other words, squadrons of imperial war chariots must go where they wished in the western Redlands. Egypt's merchants and traders and those of its allies must trade unmolested as far west as the Mountains of the Moon and north to the coast along the Great Green.

Hatusu felt beads of sweat prickle her brow. She glanced quickly to her right but her Grand Vizier, First Minister and lover, standing behind her, the shaven-headed, craggy-featured Senenmut, had already anticipated her. He raised a hand and the fan-bearers to the left and right moved a little closer. The huge flabella they carried – ostrich feathers fluffed and dyed many colours before being soaked in cassia and kiphye – gently wafted away the hot sandy air and the ever-marauding flies. Hatusu felt Senenmut's fingers brush the skin at the back of her neck. He was encouraging her, telling her to be strong. Again she glanced to her right at her row of ministers, her secretary, chamberlain, Keeper of the Cabinet and, next to these, in his blue and gold head-dress and gauze-like robes, the Chief Judge in the Hall of Two Truths, Lord Amerotke, adorned with the necklace, pectoral and rings of Ma'at, the Goddess of Truth. It was Amerotke who had condemned the five sand-dwellers to be sacrificed. Marauders, murderers and thieves, twice warned, they had still attacked and captured an Egyptian merchant. Today these five condemned men would die as a sacrifice to the righteous anger of Pharaoh, a public warning to the enemies of Egypt and a grim reminder to the Libyan war chiefs. Hatusu breathed in. The moment was approaching; the choir was drawing to a close.

'We sing thy praises in the House of the Double Doors. We lift our hands in the Mansion of a Million Years. Glorious are you, Ptah . . .'

The choir finished. The Keepers of the Stake, the executioners, clad in red, faces hidden by Seth masks carved in the form of a dog, moved out of the shadows of the pillars. The chief executioner carried the sacrificial apron; his assistant the gold-handled war club of Pharaoh. Horns rang out, cymbals clashed, trumpets bellowed. The captives, despite the drugged wine they'd been given, moaned and stirred. The executioner's guards moved closer. Naratousha and the other Libyan war chiefs leaned forward, eyes glittering in their sharp, high-cheekboned faces. Hatusu rose. The chamberlains wrapped about her the thick, silver-edged apron embossed with the hawk head of Horus. Hatusu gripped the war club and, escorted by Senenmut, walked across to the line of captives. Again the trumpets shrilled, horns brayed, gongs boomed. Pharaoh walked carefully, slowly, wary of the lapis lazuli dust, glittering blue and gold, strewn on the floor. As she stood next to the first captive, her heartbeat quickened and she prayed quietly to Horus-Who-Burns-Millions. She must remember that these sand-dwellers had defied her, and murdered and raped her subjects. She was now Sekhmet the Lioness, the Devouress, the Destroyer. She ignored the stench of sweaty fear from the captive and grasped the specially prepared tuft of hair, then swung back the club, bringing it down with a hideous crack on the right side of his head. The sand-dweller collapsed, coughing on his own blood, body jerking, but Hatusu had already moved to the second captive. The eerie silence of the temple forecourt was broken only by the slither of her silver-edged sandals, the gasps and moans of the remaining captives and that hideous noise as war club shattered bone and brain.

At last Hatusu was finished, but instead of returning to the throne, she side-stepped the line of sprawled, bleeding captives to stand on the edge of the top step, her apron now bloodied, war club slightly raised, her left hand up, palm forward in blessing. Senenmut, who had been caught by surprise, gestured at the trumpeters, who blew a long blast, then his powerful voice echoed.

'Behold Hatusu, Red-eye Horus in the North and South. Beloved of Amun, Mighty of Montu, Glory of the Kingdom of the Two Lands, Possessor of Men's Necks, Protector of All, Sekhmet the Destroyer, the living incarnation of the God . . .'

For a few heartbeats the vast concourse simply stared up at this woman, queen, warrior, avenger and vindicator, then the silence erupted in a thundering wave of cheers, praise, paeans of victory and showers of flower petals. Where possible people prostrated themselves, noses to the ground, before this beautiful destroyer, fair of face and most fitting of form. Ministers and officials on the forecourt fell to their knees as Hatusu swept back round to allow the chamberlains to remove the apron, club and specially woven golden-edged red gloves from her hands. Naratousha and his chieftains were also on their knees. Hatusu, face impassive, winked at Senenmut and walked back to her throne. She glanced quickly down the line of ministers. Amerotke was kneeling, though lost in his own thoughts.

Once more there were clarion calls, and hesets sprinkled flower petals. The corpses were removed, the floor cleared and sanded. Hatusu made herself comfortable and the ceremony continued. A small *naos* was brought containing the treaty rolls, the freshly sealed peace terms between Pharaoh and the Libyan tribes. It was placed on the sacred table, its gold-plated doors of Lebanese cedar open, and flowers were arranged around it. Ani, the High Priest of Ptah, and his two assistants Hinqui and Maben incensed the scrolls. The three principal Libyan envoys came before the altar, and Ani handed them the beautiful bowl of turquoise faience threaded with gold holding the sacred wine. Each drank, then the bowl was given to the three Egyptian scribes who had negotiated the terms, leading figures from the House of Envoys, Nebseni, Menkhep and Kharfur. These too drank from the bowl, then knelt on cushions beside their new-found Libyan friends.

Hatusu relaxed; Senenmut beside her deliberately breathed out noisily. Fresh hymns were sung, flowers sprinkled, incense burnt. Hatusu was about to whisper, 'It is over . . .' when she heard a sound, a cough, strangulated and agonising. She glanced in alarm at the three Egyptian scribes. Kharfur was lunging forward, hands to the floor, coughing and retching. Nebseni and Menkhep were also in difficulties, as if each was choking on something. Kharfur was now convulsing, all ceremony forgotten. He lay sprawled on his left side, limbs jerking, white spittle bubbling between his lips. One of the assistant high priests had grasped the fallen man's hand. Hatusu watched in horror as Senenmut gestured for the trumpets to sound and a squadron of Silver Shields to deploy along the top steps to screen this abomination. The crowd in the concourse below sensed something was wrong, but only the former prisoner known as the Rekhet realised what was truly happening. He stood shaven and oiled on a plinth of a courtyard wall and stared at the chaos on the temple forecourt before the horror was sealed off by a phalanx of Silver Shields.

The House of the Golden Vine was an exquisitely stately mansion. It stood in its own grounds, protected by a high curtain wall and a massive double gate. It belonged to Ipuye, a leading merchant who imported spices from the land of Punt and whose fat, greasy fingers dabbled in so many pots. His house of dreams was the envy of his neighbours, even in that chosen spot amongst the lush vegetation which grew along the east bank of the Nile north of Thebes. The house itself was one storey with a rising middle section built on a solid brick platform. It stood on a slight mound, its walls gleaming white, the cedar front door screened by wooden pillars painted a cooling green as if they were rushes sprouting fresh from the Nile, their base coated a rich brown, the flowery capitals silver and gold. The gently inclined ramp leading up to these pillars was broad and sweeping. The lintels of doors and jambs of window grilles were of the best imported timber, decorated in malachite and painted a reddish brown to lessen the glare of the sun. Nevertheless, the real glory of the House of the Golden Vine was Ipuye's exquisite garden. Most of its soil was rich and black, imported from Canaan and watered by ribbon-thin canals brought in from the Nile. Along these sprouted every kind of herb and flower: poppy, cornflower, mandrake and fat water lilies nestling between their waxen green leaves. Throughout the garden many varieties of trees were specially cultivated: pomegranate, date palm, doum palm, castor oil, sycamore, oak, acacia and terebinth.

All these beautiful trees could be viewed from the finely decorated summer pavilions with their pillared porticoes and cool rooms behind. These were decorated, both ceilings and walls, with bunches of black-gold grapes, which sprouted amongst brilliant silver-green leaves. Other, smaller resting places nestled in cool arbours approached by arching pergolas, climbing plants trained across their latticed timbers. Birds of all kinds nested in the garden: rock pigeons, swallows, turtle doves, cuckoos, pied king-fishers, geese and ducks, as well as gloriously plumed birds from south of the Fourth Cataract.

Ipuye was very pleased with his garden. He had even imported frankincense and myrrh trees from the land of Punt. He was particularly fond of the latter, which grew like low spreading cedars with gnarled grey branches, their small tufted leaves and white and yellow flowers often proving a talking point with guests. Ipuye had developed his garden to include a whole range of different features:

orchards, brightly coloured paths, ornate flower terraces, rich vineyards, fountains and pools. It was a veritable paradise. He was always quick to remind his guests that the infant Sun God was first born as a lotus and daily reborn out of a water lily in a garden such as his. Nevertheless, pride of place went to Ipuye's lotus pool, as he called the T-shaped bathing lake he had constructed in the far corner of his garden. This was the heart of his paradise. Here the lawns rose slightly, giving way to luxuriant bushes and beautiful sycamores, placed so close together in the rich soil that their branches intertwined. These in turn surrounded a high trellis fence or palisade at least four yards high and fashioned out of blackthorn branches specially interwoven and painted a deep ochre. This exclusive bathing area could only be entered by a narrow double gate which opened up on to a carefully tended lawn, peppered with bushes and trees, which surrounded the pool, its brilliant ivory and rose-coloured stone specially imported from the mines of Sinai. It was edged with different-coloured tiles, on each of these a carving of some animal: porcupine, mongoose, dog, cat and red fox. The pool itself contained the purest water filtered from the channels dug in from the Nile. On the water floated ornate blue and white lotuses. Around the pool were comfortable stone benches with cushioned seats, and at each end was a garden pavilion, elaborately designed to represent a miniature temple, with steps and brilliantly coloured columns behind which stretched small halls constructed so that their window vents could catch the weakest breeze and cool the guests who might wish to shelter within. The lotus pool was a place of beauty.

Ipuye, a former sailor who'd even travelled on the Great Green, loved water, which he regarded as the greatest gift of the gods. He and his new young wife Khiat would often go swimming in the lake, eat, make love, sleep and swim again. He called his garden 'the Paradise of the Far West', and imagined that when he died, a very old man, his *ka* would go out towards the setting sun and enter the Green Fields of Osiris only to discover they were no different really from his own elegant garden.

Ipuye intended to leave his paradise to his heirs, not die barbarously in it. Yet on that unfortunate day, the seventh of the second week of the third month of the Shemshu, he and his young wife Khiat were found floating face down in the pool, lifeless as the plucked petals bobbing around them. Saneb, the Kushite guard who found their corpses as the sun began to set, believed it was no accident: his master and mistress had died suddenly, brutally. The red-haired God of Murder had passed their way, stealthily slipping through that paradise to snatch two souls in his pointed net, two lives plucked before their time . . .

'Great are you, Your Majesty, Lady of the Two Lands. Your sacred hands exude the divine essence; you exhale the sweetness of the divine dew. Your perfume reaches—'

'Oh shut up!' Hatusu tore the oiled wig from her head and shook her close-cropped hair free. She undid the necklace and pectoral from around her neck, plucked the rings and bracelets from fingers and wrists, snatched off her silver-edged sandals and piled all these on the table before her. Then she glared at the astonished face of the young acolyte priest.

'I am sorry.' The Lady of the Two Lands put her head in her hands and stared at the young man nosing the ground before her. 'I'm truly sorry.' She sifted amongst the jewellery and tossed a precious ring at the startled priest, who caught it nervously. 'A gift from your pharaoh,' she murmured. 'Even the gods become tired.'

Hatusu glanced quickly at the two men sitting either side of her. Senenmut, with his clever tough face, his cheeks slightly reddened, snub nose sniffing the air, aggressive chin jutting out, was doing his best to conceal the fury seething within him at the blasphemy that had occurred in full view of the Libyans and the whole populace of Thebes. Hatusu could not deal with that. She had her own rage to curb. She glanced at Amerotke sitting on her left, serene, detached, and still garbed in his judge's robes, though he'd removed all insignia of office. His face, she thought, could be described as harsh, with its deep-set eyes, sharp nose, and firm mouth and chin. Nevertheless, it was redeemed by those crinkle lines of laughter around his eyes and mouth, that soft, dreamy look, and the way his fingers kept touching the lock of black hair, oiled and plaited, that hung down the right side of his face, tied at the end with a piece of red-gold twine. Hatusu used to wonder why he grew that; most people regarded it as a sign of youth not appropriate for a mature man. She had learnt, however, that it was a fulfilment of a vow concerning some hideous tragedy from Amerotke's youth. The judge had never discussed it, so Hatusu had never questioned him. Now she turned back to the waiting acolyte priest.

'Tell my lord Ani and his assistants that Pharaoh will show her face to them.'

The acolyte scrambled up and, head down, backed towards the door. Hatusu moved her cushion deeper into the alcove. Senenmut arranged more cushions along the floor before the slightly raised dais. Hatusu pressed her hot, sweaty back against the cold limestone wall and stared up at the shadows sent juddering by the flaming pitch torches. She had stayed in the Temple of Ptah after the tragedy had occurred, while Senenmut found this chamber, a secure room in a building belonging to the House of Scribes. It could only be approached by an outside staircase now guarded by members of the Imperial Bodyguard; a place where no eavesdropper or spy could lurk.

The door to this simple, stark chamber opened and Ani and his assistants stepped in, approaching the circle of light where the cushions were heaped. They went to prostrate themselves.

'My lords,' Hatusu's voice was low and warm, 'welcome. No need for any ceremony, not now. I've had sufficient for one day.'

She pulled the thick drapes of her linen shawl closer around her shoulders, then leaned forward and gestured at the cushions. Ani and his two assistants, with as much dignity as they could muster, squatted down. The High Priest kept looking back at the door and the steps beyond. He was an old man, with keen eyes in a highly ascetic face, cheeks slightly sunken, his lower lip jutting aggressively out as if watchful for any insult, ready to protest his innocence at the horrors perpetrated in this temple earlier that day. Hinqui and Maben, his two nephews, adopted a more obsequious attitude. They were dressed elegantly in fine linen robes, gold-edged sandals on their feet, and they schooled their oiled fat faces into looks of sorrow. Hatusu studied these two carefully. In the main she did not like priests: ambitious, sly politicians with sanctimonious expressions that belied cunning ways and glib tongues.

'Your Majesty,' Ani bowed, 'it is good to look upon your face and my limbs exalt—'

'I'm sure they do!' Senenmut cut in drily, his harsh voice ringing eerily through that sombre room.

Ani blinked away the insult. He secretly regarded

Senenmut as a commoner, a peasant, a stonemason no less.

'My lord, what do you want?' Senenmut's voice turned gentle. He gestured at the door. 'There is someone else? You keep glancing back?'

'Yes, my lord, I mean Your Excellency.' Ani diplomatically added Senenmut's proper title as if he'd momentarily forgotten it. 'Your Excellency, I beg you to include Minnakht, Chief Scribe of Ceremonies, in our discussion.'

'But he wasn't involved in the treaty-sealing or the drinking of the sacred wine afterwards,' Senenmut snapped. He shook his head. 'Everyone knows Minnakht is garrulous.'

'He'll hold his peace,' Ani offered. 'He might be of use.'

Hatusu agreed, and Minnakht was ushered in. He was a smiling old man, sprightly in his walk, his moon-round face wreathed in good humour, merry-eyed, with a snub nose above slightly protuberant lips. He immediately prostrated himself. Ani pushed a cushion towards him, and Minnakht took his seat blinking like an owl startled by the light.

'My lords . . .' Senenmut paused to clear his throat. 'Three priest physicians were murdered during a ceremony here at the Palace of a Million Years. A heinous crime has been perpetrated, a terrible sin committed.' He glanced quickly at Hatusu, who sat staring impassively into the darkness. 'The Divine One speaks with Kherou Ma'at, True Voice, when she demands the truth be known.' He stared at Amerotke, who seemed lost in his own reverie. 'What are the facts, Lord Judge?'

'The facts?' Amerotke shrugged. 'We don't yet know all the facts, only what happened. A ceremony was held. A peace treaty with the Libyan war chiefs was sealed. We were present to confirm it. There were hymns, prayers, chants and incense-burnings.' He grew more decisive, as if clearing his own mind of distractions. 'A bowl of sacred wine was offered. The Libyans drank and suffered no ill effects, neither then nor since. Our scribes from the House of Envoys did likewise, and within a short while all were dead! From the symptoms, the little I know . . .' Amerotke paused, 'the cause of their deaths must have been the wine. However,' he chewed the corner of his lip, 'the Libyans suffered no ill effects, the bowl was examined afterwards, the dregs were not tainted. There is no doubt that our three scribes were poisoned, but how?' Amerotke nodded at Ani and his two companions. 'The bowl was passed between the Libyans, back to High Priest Ani, then handed to the three scribes . . .' His voice trailed away.

'Who served the bowl?' Senenmut asked.

'I did,' Ani replied. 'I poured the wine; I gave it to the Libyans, then the three scribes.'

'Could they have died from something they ate or drank beforehand?' Senenmut asked.

'Impossible!' Minnakht retorted. 'They had to

undergo the Holy Fast in the Chapel of the Divine Infant; that's an important part of the ritual. They were kept apart, and did not eat or drink anything for a day before they sipped from that wine bowl. True,' Minnakht spread his hands, 'one of them may have been hungry or thirsty, eaten or drunk something secretly, but I doubt all three would violate such a sacred precept.'

'I agree,' Amerotke replied. 'So the poison must have been put in by the Libyans.' He smiled thinly at Ani. 'Or by you.'

'Divine One,' the High Priest objected, 'may the Spirits of the Morning be my witnesses.'

'Why should Lord Ani even be suspected of such an abomination?' Hinqui protested. 'Maben and I were there, close to the bowl. We helped pour the wine in. We saw nothing.'

Maben, sitting on the other side of Ani, nodded in agreement.

'Both jug and bowl have been closely examined,' Hinqui continued. 'No taint, no potion or powder were discovered.'

'Silence!' Senenmut held up a hand. 'Are you certain the jug has been examined?'

'Of course!' Minnakht replied.

'I did that myself,' Amerotke intervened. 'The dregs were poured out and given to a dog mixed up with its feed; no ill effects were observed.'

'The Libyan chieftains,' Hatusu whispered, 'don't know which mask to hide behind.' She stared straight at Amerotke, her beautiful eyes, ringed with kohl, gleaming like those of a hunting cat.

'Divine One?' Senenmut spoke.

'Yes,' she murmured, 'and so I am. I do not think I should have to account to desert wanderers, sand-dwellers or Libyans, or be humiliated in their presence.'

'Hush!' Senenmut hissed, then abruptly recalled the presence of the priests and bowed in apology for contradicting Hatusu. 'If the Divine One—'

'The Divine One,' Hatusu retorted, 'was commenting on the Libyans. They do not know which mask to put on, that of victim or aggressor. Naratousha, whom I do not trust, claims that the poisoned wine may have been meant for him and his comrades. I pointed out that the wine was not poisoned, whilst others might allege that the poison came from him.'

'Did it?' Senenmut asked.

'It is possible,' Amerotke replied. 'Naratousha was the last to hold the treaty bowl before handing it back to Ani.' He pulled a face. 'A sleight of hand? The conjurors and scorpion men perform tricks just as skilful in the marketplace.' He paused. 'But if so, why? Why would the Libyans poison three scribes? To break the treaty? It was they who asked for it.' He shrugged. 'However, I fully accept the Divine One's suspicions: Naratousha cannot be trusted.'

Minnakht leaned forward and whispered in Ani's ear.

'There is one other possibility.' Ani raised his head. 'Your Excellency?'

'The Rekhet,' Minnakht grated.

'The who?' Amerotke asked.

'His real name cannot be mentioned,' Ani replied, frowning at Amerotke as if the judge should have been aware of that.

'His name is amongst the Kherit,' Ani explained, 'the damned.'

'Explain.' Hatusu's voice was clipped. 'Lord Judge Amerotke may not have been involved in that case.'

'It occurred during the reign of the—'

Hatusu didn't wait for Ani to finish. 'About four years ago,' she began, 'during the last years of my half-brother's reign . . .' Her words were rushed; few, including her, liked to refer to her husband–brother who had died abruptly in mysterious circumstances. 'At that time,' she continued, her voice rising, 'hideous poisonings took place throughout Thebes. Indeed, the number of deaths, especially amongst the lords, was scandalous. Ah . . .' She smiled coldly at Amerotke's look of recognition.

'Divine One,' he murmured, 'I now remember it well.'

'Tell him.' Hatusu waved to Ani.

'As the Divine One says, horrid poisonings took place. People wondered who the killer could be. He apparently dispensed subtle, secret poisons the like of which had never been known before.' Ani paused and Amerotke sensed the horror behind his words.

The chamber seemed colder, the juddering shadows more fearful, the flame and torches not so powerful. They were all, Amerotke reflected, despite their status and power, vulnerable human beings, gathered in this stark, ill-lit chamber to ponder and reflect on sudden and brutal death. He certainly recalled the case in question. Murder often stalked the stinking alleyways and broad avenues of the city. Husbands tired of wives, wives tired of husbands, business rivals turned on each other. Assassins could be hired to wield the knife, thrust the dagger, pour the poison or loose the arrow. The Rekhet was different: philtres and potions given to the powerful of Thebes, all of them dying in mysterious circumstances.

'The perpetrator of these abominations,' Ani explained, 'came to be known as the Rekhet, the Poison Demon. Who he was and how he dispensed his flow of death, no one knew. Rumours flew thick and fast like starlings, yet the truth remained hidden. People claimed it must be a physician, someone who knew the secret of the powders.'

'And so the finger of accusation was pointed at this temple,' Amerotke murmured, 'the House of the Man God Ptah, the Physician, the Healer.'

'Precisely!' Ani wiped his mouth on the back of his hand. 'A group of powerful priest physicians began to study the various deaths. People can and do die of a wide range of ailments; suspicions can be raised but proof is very difficult to find.

Nevertheless, they had their suspicions. One of them, Userbati, who was also Scribe of the Waters, a very ambitious man, came to me. He provided no names but he mentioned that this Rekhet, this Poison Demon, may have found the Ari Sapu.'

'The Books of Doom?' Amerotke questioned quickly. 'I thought they were fable.'

'So did we,' Ani confessed. 'They were supposed to have been written many years ago by a skilled master poisoner, a sorcerer. The Ari Sapu are a compendium of all the poisons known under heaven: potions, philtres and powders which could freeze a man's heart or send his soul into the desert of dreams. Userbati believed the Books of Doom had re-emerged and that the Rekhet,' Ani leaned forward, face glinting with sweat, 'not only owned them but was one of us. You see, my lord Amerotke, Userbati claimed the Ari Sapu had always been here, hidden in this temple. He was supported in his allegations by a few of his colleagues.'

'Be more precise!' Senenmut snapped.

'I will be!' Ani retorted heatedly. 'Userbati, a man full of his own importance, did not tell me much. Instead he invited his colleagues to a special supper in his priestly office to discuss the matter. The meal was cooked in the temple kitchens.'

'And all were poisoned!' Amerotke intervened. 'I remember the scandal.'

'The alarm was raised after a servant found them sprawled in the dining chamber,' Ani explained. 'I immediately ordered Userbati's possessions to be searched. A scrap of papyrus was found containing a curse: "Ama-asht – the Eater of Abominable Things". This was repeated time and again, and beside it was the name of a leading priest physician. We believed him to be the Rekhet. Our guards searched the man's quarters here in the temple, and a cabinet of poisons as well as pouches of gold and silver were found. More importantly a *sehura*, a curse dedicated to the Watching Faces, and invoked against Userbati, was also discovered. The priest physician was arrested by Nadif, standard-bearer in the Theban police. He and the Medjay conducted other searches. The priest physician could not explain the cabinet of powders, Userbati's papyrus, the curse, nor the wealth he'd so secretly amassed.'

'It was a great scandal,' Maben intervened.

'Confidence in our temple,' added Minnakht, 'would have been shattered.'

'More than that,' Maben retorted. 'Everyone now knew about the poisonings,' he shrugged, 'partly because my brother-in-law, the merchant Ipuye, had posted a great reward for the Rekhet's capture.'

'Why?' Amerotke asked curiously. 'I know of Ipuye, a leading trader who has done much to develop trade with Punt, even with the islands in the Great Green.'

'During the time of the poisonings, the reign of the Rekhet,' Maben replied, 'Ipuye's wife mysteriously disappeared. Some claimed she had run away;

she has never been seen since. Ipuye believed she was poisoned.'

'By whom?' Amerotke stirred, intrigued by this widening tale of death.

Maben simply shrugged.

'And the Rekhet?' Senenmut glared at Ani.

'He was arrested,' Ani sighed. 'The evidence was shown. He denied it at first, proclaiming his innocence. We had to . . .' Ani coughed to hide his embarrassment, 'we did not want the case to be brought to trial. As my colleagues have said, the prospect of scandal . . .'

'I see.' Amerotke scratched his chin.

'The Rekhet eventually confessed and threw himself on Pharaoh's mercy. We intervened and whispered in Pharaoh's ear. The Rekhet was sentenced to life imprisonment at some oasis far out in the western Redlands.'

'And what relevance has he to the deaths that occurred today?'

'The Rekhet,' Senenmut replied, 'escaped from the Oasis of Bitter Bread about two months ago. He was apparently seized by a band of sand-dwellers, five of whom were sacrificed early today. They captured him as well as a merchant from Memphis, a dealer in skins who also worked for me. The sand-dwellers, in turn, were intercepted by an imperial squadron of war chariots.'

'And?' Amerotke asked.

'What the Tedjen, the commanding officer, didn't

realise was that during the fight with the sand-dwellers, the merchant was killed. In the ensuing chaos the Rekhet assumed the merchant's identity. Most of the sand-dwellers were killed; the squadron returned to Thebes; the Rekhet slipped away. Only much later did the Mayor of Thebes, who dealt with the case, discover that the Memphis merchant had been killed whilst the impostor had disappeared. At the time little thought was given to him; he was just another prisoner who'd soon be captured.' Senenmut moved his head. 'Only after messengers were sent to Memphis and the prison oasis did we realise how important this escapee was. Even so, it did not directly concern us . . . well, not until now.'

'But surely the Rekhet couldn't enter this temple!' Amerotke protested. 'Reach the sacred wine, distil a potion?'

'A possibility,' Ani murmured. 'He had lived here for years.'

Amerotke stared into the middle distance and wondered idly what his wife and two sons were doing. They were probably in the garden of their mansion, bathing in one of the pools or nestling in the shade of a sycamore tree. And Shufoy, his manservant, that little dwarf without a nose? Amerotke smiled to himself. Shufoy was probably drunk, stretched out snoring in the servants' quarters, or was he trying to trade some—

'My lord?'

Amerotke startled from his reverie and stared at Hatusu. 'Divine One,' he bowed, 'now we are entering the Field of Dreams – what could be, what might be, what should be.'

Hatusu nodded in agreement.

'We have done what we can. One question.' Amerotke raised a hand. 'The peace treaty was sealed yesterday morning just after the dawn sacrifice, is that correct?'

Ani and the rest nodded in agreement.

'And then what?'

'The three scribes followed the ritual. They were confined to the Chapel of the Divine Infant Horus, to spend the day in prayer and fasting before the treaty was blessed, made sacred.'

'And who was in charge of them?' Amerotke asked.

'I was.' Maben raised a hand. 'Though Minnakht advised me on the ritual!'

'Did anyone else enter the chapel where the three priests were staying?' Amerotke asked.

'I was involved with the preparations,' Minnakht replied, 'but I dealt solely with Maben here. I never actually entered the room.'

'And you are sure,' Amerotke insisted, 'that the scribes ate or drank nothing tainted.'

'My lord,' Maben raised both hands, face beseeching, 'I would take the most sacred oath. No food or drink entered that room; nothing untoward happened. True, the three scribes were hungry and thirsty, but they were joyful at the treaty they had sealed on the Divine One's behalf. They were promising themselves the most sumptuous banquet and celebration—'

'Is there anything else, my lord?' Senenmut asked abruptly.

The judge shook his head. He had already decided what to do. When the meeting ended, he made his swift excuses and left, going down the outside staircase. He paused halfway and stared across the elegant temple precinct at the splendid array of beautifully coloured pillars, squares, fountains, sun pavilions, aisles and alleyways; flower-festooned walls, gold-capped obelisks soaring up against the light blue sky, the central temple itself and its surrounding chapels with their various stones, snow white, honey coloured or pink limestone. The late afternoon air was rich with the tangy smell of blood from the smoking sacrifices: this mixed with the incense fragrance rising from the miniature containers carved in the shape of boats, as well as the pungent farm smells from the stables and oxen sheds. Voices shouted. Cymbals clashed. The faint words of some hymn floated on the evening breeze. The sun was beginning to dip, the golden light in the sky turning red, coursing like lines of thread through white streaks of cloud. Acolytes and servants hurried by, chattering and laughing. Ipet-Sut, Amerotke reflected: a perfect place! Yet, he reminded himself, this was also a place of *behen*, murderous intent. The home of the Rekhet, the place of the Ari

Sapu, the Books of Doom, a temple of dread where three high-born Egyptian scribes had been murdered to the anger and shame of Pharaoh and the humiliation of Egypt.

MESETCH-I: ancient Egyptian, ‘hatred’

CHAPTER 2

Amerotke continued down the steps. He took directions from a passing servant and went down more stairs into the yawning caverns of the House of Death and its inner sanctum, the gloomy ill-lit Wabet, the Place of Purity. Once he had closed the door behind him, showing his seal to the guards, he realised how stifling the air was. Peering through the gloom, he could make out the sweaty skins of the Keepers of the Dead, who moved quietly through the murk, faces hidden by the jackal masks of Anubis. The bitter, salty smell of natron mingled with the perfumes distilled to conceal the ever-pervasive stench of corruption and death. Priests of both the chapel and the stole intoned prayers and psalms from the Book of the Dead: 'I have come to thee, my lord of the Far West, to adore thy beauty; I have not done evil . . . Open, Spirits of the Light, the Gates of the West . . .'

The corpses of the three scribes lay on the far side of the room, beneath a small window vent through which the only light poured. Their embalmment on the tilted slabs had already begun, stomachs slit with the sacred obsidian knife, entrails collected, heaped and slopped into the waiting canopic jars. The Keepers of the Dead had certainly been busy, working swiftly against the heat and the hideous effects of the poison the men had drunk. In the poor light, the faces of the corpses now appeared composed, as if comforted by the serenity of death, their limbs supple-looking and straight. Amerotke recalled their frenzied fits earlier that day.

'My lord?' The Overseer of the Dead came out of a needle-thin passageway to Amerotke's right. An old, gentle man, he carried an asperges rod in one hand, in the other a small stoup containing water from the Holy Pool. He gazed narrow-eyed through the gloom and recognised Amerotke. 'My lord?' He bowed.

'Can you tell me,' Amerotke asked, gesturing at the corpses, 'how they died?'

'How they died, my lord? Something very evil.' The Overseer took Amerotke by the elbow and led him closer to the three corpses. He removed the linen sheets exposing their stomachs, slit open, the skin thrown back like a flap. Amerotke put his hands to his face. Despite all the washing and the perfuming, there was still a horrid stench that made him gag. He turned away. The Overseer led him across to the other side of the room to stand beneath a window vent.

'I have seen many corpses,' Amerotke wiped his mouth on the back of his arm, 'but that smell – it is more than just the stench of death.'

'It is the rank odour of poison, my lord. Yet what it was or how it was administered I cannot tell. When the bodies were opened,' the Overseer tapped his own stomach, 'their innards were tainted and discoloured.'

'And what could have caused that?' Amerotke asked.

The Overseer laughed. Putting down the asperges rod and the water stoup, he rubbed his hands together. 'My lord, how many ways are there to kill a man?'

'Have you heard of the Ari Sapu?' Amerotke asked. 'The Books of Doom?'

'Of course,' the old man replied. 'I have been in this temple since I was knee high to a flower. I love this place. It is my home, my life. I . . .' He caught the flicker of impatience in Amerotke's eyes. 'My lord, I apologise. To you this is a great mystery, but for me death holds no mystery: just three corpses, the *ka* of which are already travelling into the Far West. I am simply here to ease their way, like a midwife at birth, but yes, I've heard of the Books of Doom. You do know,' he moved closer, 'that our library holds a fragment of them? It was found many years ago. My lord, it might be worth reading.'

'Anything else?' Amerotke asked, gesturing back towards the bodies. 'Anything you can tell me?'

'I washed the corpses,' the Overseer replied. 'I have searched for any symptom, but . . .' He shrugged.

'Tell me,' Amerotke asked, 'when you remove the entrails from the belly, you sometimes find the remains of a last meal?'

'Empty!' the Overseer replied. 'The organs were stained and discoloured, slightly swollen as if scoured by some vile powder.'

'And anything else?' Amerotke insisted. 'Anything on the corpses, their hands, around their mouths?'

The Overseer shook his head. 'Nothing, my lord; I mean nothing I could see.'

Amerotke thanked the Overseer, then left the House of Death and walked up the steps into the courtyard. For a while he just stood enjoying the rays of the dying sun, welcoming the breeze, trying to rid his nostrils of the stench of corruption and the salty tang of the embalming chamber. He had indeed seen many corpses, but each experience was unique, bringing home the hideousness of death. He moved out of the shadows and stared up at the sky, which was now changing colour. From across the temple conch horns wailed, gongs clashed, the music of cymbal and lyre rippled melodiously as the temple musicians and choirs rehearsed a hymn for the morning sacrifice. He passed through a garden where a servant poured him a cup of clear water from a gazelle skin slung on a pole by its legs, a small pipe in place of its head. The servant directed him to the House of Scribes, where the archives and library were situated. The lower part of the House consisted of a series of small chambers standing off a passageway decorated with the insignia and signs of Thoth the God of Words as well as gruesome scenes from the macabre stories and tales so loved by Thebans. Amerotke recognised many of the figures: Sha, the malevolent creature of Seth, whose glare turned men to stone; the Saga, a loathsome hawk-headed creature capable of indescribable horrors.

The priest librarian, the Overseer of Books, who came out to greet Amerotke, resembled an old peasant, with his leathery skin, and watery, evasive eyes in a crafty face. He reluctantly allowed Amerotke through the heavy cedar doors but kept staring at the water bowl in the far corner of the passageway, the trickle from which slowly measured the passage of time.

'The light is fading,' he grumbled.

'But I'm not!' Amerotke snapped. 'The Lord Senenmut . . .'

'Of course, of course,' the librarian murmured, ink-stained fingers to his face.

Amerotke told the old man what he wished to see.

'The Ari Sapu fragment!' the librarian gasped. 'Oh dear, I thought of that myself today when those scribes . . .' and, muttering to himself, he led

Amerotke into a square stone chamber with a window grille high in the outer wall. Shelves ranged round the chamber, and beneath these were linen bags and reed baskets for storing manuscripts; cavities had also been burrowed into the wall to hold small scrolls and rolls of papyri.

'A dusty place of forgotten memories,' the librarian murmured as he approached one of the wall cavities and drew out a copper tube. He pulled back the lid and shook out the document, a roll of papyrus about two hands long and the same wide.

Amerotke took this out to the west side of the library so as to catch the fading light. He sat on a limestone bench and closely studied the carefully drawn hieroglyphs. It was only an extract, yet as he read it, a deep chill of apprehension seized him. He had dealt with sinister sorcerers and warlocks, the lords of the secret powders and potions, Masters of the Dark. Thebes also abounded with apothecaries, physicians, conjurors and cunning men who would for a little wealth dispense the most deadly venom. There were even guilds of poisoners, professional assassins, but this? Amerotke continued to study the extract carefully. It provided detailed descriptions of certain poisons and how to create them, potions he had never encountered before: rare minerals extracted from rocks and crystals, plants and herbs not found along the Nile, the juices of certain snakes and insects which only thrived deep in the lush jungles beyond the cataracts hundred of miles to the south. The collection, distillation, symptoms and effects of these poisons were objectively described, in a way very similar to an architect explaining the cutting of mud bricks and the building of a house.

Amerotke startled as he heard a sound. He glanced up, shading his eyes against the light with his hand. 'What!' He got to his feet, aware of how cool the evening had grown.

'My lord, I'm sorry.' Minnakht stepped into the shade, the hunched librarian trailing behind. 'Lord Ani said you might wish to inspect the Chapel of the Divine Child, where the three scribes stayed until the ceremony.'

'Yes, yes.' Amerotke stared up at the sky. The streaks of coppery red had broadened, mingling with the wispy white lines of cloud. He stretched his neck to savour the evening breeze, then handed the papyrus back to the librarian, thanked him and followed Minnakht across the temple grounds. They walked along colonnades where servants of the Mansion of the Gods lingered to gossip, past shrines and statues, through gardens shaded by sycamore, fig, persea and terebinth. Willows were also plentiful, a cascade of greenery as if the trees were bending down to drink the glinting water from the canals which fed the pools, fountains and miniature lakes of the temple. In the shade of these trees stood cone-shaped beehives as well as elegant sun pavilions where drink was stored for those who sheltered there.

At first they walked in silence, Minnakht acting as if he was in total awe of the Lord Judge. Amerotke smiled to himself as the Chief Scribe's natural garrulousness emerged and he began to chatter about the affairs of the temple.

'How do you think they died?' Amerotke immediately regretted his harsh interruption.

Minnakht stopped his gossiping, his face puckered in surprise. 'Lord Judge, you want my opinion?'

'I'd value it!'

'Well,' Minnakht squinted up at the sky, 'it must be the Libyans.'

'But how?' Amerotke asked.

'The scribes were in good heart this morning. True, Lord Judge?'

Amerotke agreed.

'Well,' Minnakht pushed his face closer and whispered, 'it must be the bowl. Remember, my lord Amerotke, the bowl was held by Naratousha; he handed it back to Lord Ani, who gave it to our three scribes.'

'And?'

'I remember,' Minnakht continued excitedly, 'Ani and our three scribes held the bowl in the palms of their hands, but the Libyans, as is their custom—'

Amerotke caught Minnakht's excitement. He'd seen Libyans and desert wanderers drink; they'd often grasp the rim of the cup or beaker. Shufoy also did that. Amerotke closed his eyes. 'Naratousha and his colleagues held that bowl—'

'They did,' Minnakht broke in, 'they held it by the rim.'

Amerotke opened his eyes. 'You're sure?' he asked.

'Not only me,' Minnakht continued, 'but Lord Ani. He declares that when he handed the bowl back, Naratousha held the rim with both hands. So you see, Lord Judge . . . ?'

'He could have had his hands dusted with some venom, some evil potion, and coated the rim of the bowl,' Amerotke concluded. 'Something lethal, swift as a poisoned arrow. Of course that part of the rim held by Naratousha would then be offered to our scribes; to move it around could be construed as an insult, Egyptians refusing to drink from that part of the bowl held by Libyans. But is there a poison so powerful that a mere smear . . . ?'

'I do not know,' Minnakht replied, 'but there are mixtures, so the physicians tell me, where a small drop can kill in a few heartbeats. The Redlands hold scorpions and snakes that can kill in the blink of an eye.'

'Do you know anything about poisons?'

'A little!' Minnakht laughed. 'I'm more priest than physician. I also know something about the Ari Sapu.'

'What is their history?'

Amerotke took Minnakht by the arm and led him over to one of the sun pavilions decorated with blue and yellow climbing flowers. It was furnished with a bench along which a quilted flock had been stretched.

'The Books of Doom,' Minnakht began, making himself comfortable, 'are no legend. About fifty years ago a priest physician decided to go on a journey. He was a man of the night, a dark soul with a curious heart. He travelled beyond the cataracts, into the dense jungles south of Nubia. Many thought he'd died, but some years later he reappeared and resumed his duties as a priest, physician and scholar. He soon won a reputation for healing, but that was during the hour of Ra when the Eye of the God was upon him. At night, however, this creature of the dark would creep into the city with poisons he'd concocted and feed them to the Maar, the wretched ones. He'd then carefully observe the effects and symptoms of the various potions.' Minnakht paused, screwing up his face to recall this sinister history. 'Afterwards he'd return and make more entries in his great work, what is now called the Books of Doom.'

'And?'

Minnakht pulled a face. 'The poor always die like flies, but the number of poisonings amongst the wretched rose dramatically, their corpses found in the derelict huts and shabby tenements and slums. The Mayor of Thebes became concerned; riots were imminent. Eventually the murderer was captured. He was put on trial and buried alive with his books,' Minnakht waved his hand across the gardens, 'somewhere here in the Temple of Ptah.'

'On sacred ground?' Amerotke asked.

'Ah, my lord, remember this was many years ago. Since then the temple has been enlarged and developed, but the legends claim that somewhere here lie the Books of Doom alongside the corpse of their author.'

'You have read the extract?'

'Oh yes,' Minnakht replied. 'Most scholars in our House of Life have.'

'Have you been a devotee of this temple for many years?'

'Of course.' Minnakht smiled. 'Since I was a boy.'

'And you have family here?' Amerotke asked, curious about this benign-looking scribe.

'I am a bachelor, my lord, but I have lived a good and full life, merry as any sparrow that nestles near the altar of the Lord Ptah. I have,' he mused, 'been Assistant High Priest; held most of the high offices in this temple.'

'Did you know the Rekhet, the prisoner who escaped?'

'Oh yes, vaguely.' Minnakht paused, head cocked, as if listening to the songbirds in their silver cages as they began their liquid hymn to the approaching night. 'He was a scholar, a quiet man, no family. He was immersed in his studies. I would never have suspected him. Indeed, I still find it difficult to accept what he really was, but there again,' Minnakht shook his head, 'the waters of the Nile flow smoothly yet they still run very deep. My lord, shall we go on to the chapel?'

'No, no.' Amerotke rose and stepped out of the pavilion. 'You mentioned the Libyans. Come,' he smiled back at his companion, 'let us visit them.'

Minnakht reluctantly agreed. He summoned two acolytes, young men training for the sanctuary, to lead them across to the Mansion of Ease where the Libyan envoys were lodged. The surrounding garden was guarded by officers from the Glory of Amun regiment. They shared this duty with the Libyans' retainers, wiry, leather-skinned men dressed in loose-fitting robes and linen headdresses, the folds of which were brought across the nose and mouth to give them a sinister, rather secretive aspect. An Egyptian officer vouched for both Amerotke and Minnakht, and they were ushered up the steps and through the porter's lodge into the vestibule, which was lit brilliantly by oil lamps glowing in multicoloured translucent alabaster jars. After a short wait, they were led into the central room, a grand, elegant chamber, its slender columns carved at the top and bottom with golden lotus flowers, and lit by clerestory windows. The walls were covered with eye-catching designs of flower garlands: lotus, poppy and the yellow bloom of the mandrake. At the far end, on a broad dais under one of the windows, the Libyans lounged in a circle on cushions, the tables before them crammed with platters and goblets. Nearby stood wine jars on stands decorated with flowers. Somewhere in a shadow-filled alcove musicians played softly on mandolins, harps and lutes. The

Libyans were chattering amongst themselves. They fell silent as the officer hurried forward to announce the arrival of their unexpected guests.

'Come, my lords.' The Libyan in the centre stood up and waved them forward on to the dais.

Naratousha seemed taller than he had done on the temple forecourt. He was certainly most relaxed, wafting his sharp face with an ebonite fan covered with gold and spangled with turquoises and cornelian, a personal gift from Pharaoh. More cushions were brought, goblets filled with the best wines from Imit and Abesh. Amerotke and Minnakht were invited to sit, and the Libyan war chief gestured at the silver and gold platters strewn across the tables containing a range of different dishes: melokhia, aubergine salad, hamine eggs, fish in hazelnut and onion sauce, chicken, calf meat in pepper sauce, semolina cakes and honey slices.

'Eat, my lords?'

Both guests tactfully refused. The Libyans, Amerotke concluded, staring round, had certainly eaten and drunk their fill. The cakes of perfume placed on their cropped hair had long dissolved in rivulets of sweetness down their cheeks, necks and bare chests. Despite the windows and side doors being open, the dais seemed stiflingly hot.

'For the pleasure of your company, my lords,' Naratousha grinned round at his companions, 'we are truly grateful.' He slurped noisily from his goblet.

A mistake, Amerotke thought; a pretence to mislead

them. The other Libyans might be drunk, but Naratousha was as sober as he was; he could tell that by the clearness of the man's eyes and the preciseness of his movements. Yet that was Naratousha's nature, sly and cunning, dangerous qualities in an inveterate hater of Egypt. Not for the first time that day Amerotke wondered why this war chief, with the blood of so many Egyptians on his hands, had come in from the Redlands to smell the earth, as they put it, the rich, papyrus-filled banks of the Nile. According to Senenmut, the Libyan had agreed to become 'Pharaoh's dog' in return for gold, silver, precious stones and the right to trade with the great mines along the Horus Road through Sinai.

'My lord!' Naratousha broke off from chattering to Minnakht and leaned against the small acacia table in front of him. 'My lord Amerotke, are you tired of our revelry?' The Libyan spoke the Egyptian tongue with a clipped accent, using the lingua franca of the harbours along the delta.

'Yes, I am, my lord. I'm sorry,' Amerotke replied brusquely. 'The deaths of our three scribes this morning . . .'

The good humour drained from the Libyans' faces and the hum of whispered conversation died abruptly.

'You have found the killers?'

'Of course not!' Amerotke protested.

'So why do you come here? We are not responsible. You have not come here . . . ?'

'No,' Amerotke tactfully intervened. He watched as one of the Libyans grasped his wine cup by the rim. 'I have come to inform you that the deaths are still a mystery.'

'Ah, and you want to question us?'

'Yes.'

'And?'

'Do the deaths of the three scribes in any way interfere or diminish the peace treaty you signed with Egypt?'

'Of course not. Does the Divine One . . .'

'Of course not.' Amerotke deliberately echoed the Libyan. 'The treaty will be honoured, eventually.'

Naratousha's smile returned.

'One more question.' Amerotke picked up a beaker of cold water; he pressed this against his face and smiled at the Libyan.

'Yes, my lord?'

'Why the peace treaty?' Amerotke asked. 'I mean, why now?'

Naratousha spread his hands expansively. 'Egypt will set its borders where she will.' He intoned the phrase like some wandering scholar in a dusty square, almost chanting the words as if to convey his secret mockery.

'My question, my lord,' Amerotke insisted, 'was why now?'

'The Divine One's chariotry sweeps wider and further,' Naratousha snapped. 'We need to trade, to live in peace.' He waved around. 'To imitate the greatness of Egypt. Now, my lords, will you not drink?'

Amerotke sensed he would learn no more. He took a few sips of wine, toasted the Libyans, nudged Minnakht and made his diplomatic farewells. Once clear of the house, he paused under the stretching branches of a sycamore. Darkness had swept in. The temple paths were now lit by cresset torches. They could see the pinprick of flames as temple servants hurried to light more.

'I'm not sure,' Minnakht nodded back at the Mansion of Ease, 'whether Naratousha is as innocent and naïve as he pretends.'

Amerotke grunted in agreement. As they continued down the beaten sandy pathway, he became aware of how silent the temple grounds had grown. He also felt uneasy. He and Shufoy often had to thread their way through the foul, needle-thin alleyways of the Necropolis, the City of the Dead on the west bank of the Nile. Amerotke possessed what Senenmut called an almost animal sense of danger. The judge secretly believed this was the fruit of years of military training out in the great desert fortress at Buhen. Even in the peaceful Temple of Ptah, this awareness of danger could prick his heart. The night air was refreshing, the moon full, the stars hung like beautiful blossoms against the sky. Yet as Minnakht chatted about the Libyans, Amerotke felt his unease deepen. They left the shelter of the sycamores and were about to turn a corner when he abruptly paused and glanced round, startling his companion. Amerotke stared down the darkened path. Yes! He was sure he glimpsed a shadow, a fleeting figure, leaving the edge of the path and disappearing into the trees.

'What is it?' Minnakht asked.

'Nothing!' Amerotke turned back even as a night bird shrieked raucously from the trees behind him, and they continued on their way. He was certain that someone, soft-footed and watchful as a lynx, dogged their every footstep. But who? A priest from the temple, or one of the Libyans sent by Naratousha? Amerotke remained vigilant.

They entered the walled garden which stretched in front of the Chapel of the Divine Infant. Torches glowed in the sconces fixed along the colonnaded front of the small temple. They went up the steps, through the half-open door and across a moon-washed courtyard into the hypostyle, or hall of columns. In the poor light of lamps and lanterns, priests were busy in the sanctuary at the far end, a rectangular chamber with numerous rooms off each side. Minnakht explained how these served as vestries or storerooms. The *naos* on the sacred table was closed; heaped around it were garlands and wreaths of cut flowers, piles of ripe fruit and platters of freshly baked bread so the priest could offer the Divine Horus Child a meal during the morning sacrifice.

Minnakht led Amerotke across to one of the

chambers that faced the *naos*. A keeper of the shrine came hurrying up and unlocked the door, then ushered them in and hastened to light lamps and lanterns. The chamber was bare: a few sticks of furniture, prayer cushions, and a table littered with pots and scraps of parchments. Amerotke glimpsed the palliasses, makeshift beds along one wall beneath a stele of a naked infant Horus. The young god, standing on a crocodile, held writhing serpents; above him was the grinning figure of Bes, the ugly household god. Amerotke suddenly experienced a sense of unnamed dread as he stared at that stele. A similar one had been etched on the wall of his bedroom when he was a young boy, yet it had not protected him or his younger brother against horrific tragedy.

Amerotke steeled himself against the memories flooding back. He swayed slightly on his feet. He was tired, his belly nauseous; he could taste the acid at the back of his throat as if he had drunk poor wine or eaten tainted fruit. He should really go home. He wanted to be away from here. He forced a smile at Minnakht, then walked across to the table and stared down at the unguent, kohl and perfume pots standing next to a sheet of polished copper; this would have served as a mirror when the scribes prepared themselves for the ceremony earlier that day. He could see no sign of food or drink, nothing out of place. He picked up the various pots and sniffed at them, but detected nothing but the tinge of perfumed oil.

'Who came down here, apart from the scribes?'

'We did!'

Amerotke spun round. Lord Ani and his two assistants, Hinqui and Maben, stood in the doorway. Maben looked distinctly agitated, Hinqui rather ill. The High Priest swept in, eyes darting to the left and right.

'Lord Judge,' he gestured, 'this will have to wait. I have come from the Divine One. She has,' Ani pressed the palms of his hands together, 'retired for the night. My Lord Senenmut said you must be informed of what has happened. You must deal with it.'

'Must?' Amerotke queried. 'Must deal with what?'

'My lord,' Maben stepped forward, 'terrible news! It arrived late this evening. We've been searching for you.' The priest glared angrily at Minnakht, as if holding him responsible for the delay.

'What is it?' Amerotke demanded.

'My brother-in-law, the merchant Ipuye, a patron of this temple, he and his wife were found late this afternoon dead, drowned, face down in a lotus pool. They had been swimming . . .'

'An accident?'

'No, my lord. Standard-Bearer Nadif of the Medjay believes it was foul play.' Maben spread his hands beseechingly. 'That is all I can tell you. I'm going to the House of the Golden Vine myself. I wonder . . .'

Amerotke walked through the door and out into the sanctuary. He caught the stench of blood from a recent sacrifice. He rubbed his stomach and stared at the doorway. Darkness had fallen.

'The day's lamp is burnt low,' he murmured to himself.

'My lord?'

'Yes?'

Ani came into the sanctuary, sandalled feet slapping the floor, gauffered robes billowing out. He looked rather eerie, sinister, like something from a ghost story.

'My lord, your servant Shufoy, the Nemma . . .'

'Yes, he is a dwarf and my servant; he is also my friend. What is it, what's wrong?'

'Nothing.' Ani smiled. 'He's just drunk, fast asleep. Two of my temple servants have taken him in a litter back to your house. I thought it was appropriate.'

'Thank you.' Amerotke now regretted his earlier testiness. 'Maben,' he called, 'go to Ipuye's house. Tell Standard-Bearer Nadif that I shall be there early, at the brilliant hour.'

Amerotke made his farewells and left. He collected a walking cane from the porter's lodge and made his way down through the temple concourse towards the postern gate to the right of the soaring pylons leading into the temple. He passed the main building, which was shrouded in darkness except for the oil lamps burning before the statues, spreading pools of light in the blackness. He recalled the glorious ceremony that had taken place there earlier, and the abominable sacrilege that had brought it to an abrupt close.

A small boy holding a puppy scurried through the dark, shouting at his mother far in the distance. Amerotke watched him go and thought of Shufoy. He just hoped the little man had not been involved in any mischief here in the temple. Shufoy, despite his noseless face and wispy hair, always dreamed of becoming a powerful trader, which induced him to dabble his little fingers in all sorts of pots. Amerotke always wondered why. He just hoped Shufoy had not done the same today; he had a tongue more nimble than a scribe's pen. The judge was tired of pointing out to his servant that whatever wealth Amerotke and his family owned, Shufoy could share. The little man remained obdurate.

'Am I wealthy?' he'd declare, pointing to the scar where his nose had been. 'I lost that. I was sent to the village of the Rhinoceri and appealed to you, Lord Judge, who eventually saw justice done. You cleared and exalted my name.'

'But I never got your nose back!' Amerotke would joke.

'Not as important as my name, master. One day I must repay you.'

Amerotke smiled, lost in his own thoughts. He was halfway down the lane, thin as a ribbon, that ran between the various temple buildings when he heard a sound. He made to turn, only to feel a barbed blade prick the side of his neck.

'Lord Judge,' the voice hissed, 'I mean you no harm.'

'So why the blade?'

'Prudence.'

'Who are you?'

'Why, my lord, the one they call the Rekhet.'

'And you've come to proclaim your innocence?'

'Would that make any difference?'

'No.'

'Very good, Chief Justice in the Hall of Two Truths. In that case, just look, listen, recall and reflect.'

'On what?'

'The truth,' the hoarse voice whispered, 'the deaths.'

A sharp, shrill whistle pierced the darkness behind them. Amerotke was gently shoved forward; when he whirled round, there was nothing. He started back but glimpsed the slit-like alleyways leading off the lane to both right and left. The Rekhet could have gone either way. Amerotke breathed in deeply, calming his excitement, then turned and strolled down the lane to the postern gate.

The heset girl Hutepa, responsible for the shrill whistle, stayed hidden in the shadows and watched Amerotke disappear in the gloom. She wiped the sweat from her face. Only when she thought it was safe did she run back through the darkness to the House of Praise and the security of her own small chamber at the back of the building. As she closed the door behind her, she noticed the cup of wine she'd left. Absent-mindedly she picked this up and cradled it, smiling as she drank. She lowered the cup, stared at the dishevelled bed and went across to sit down. As she raised the cup for a second sip, she abruptly remembered: the cup had been empty when she'd left; who had refilled it? She rose swiftly to her feet, but the poison was already working within her. Violent cramps attacked her, hideous shooting pains. She dropped the cup and staggered towards the door, but the pain was so intense she collapsed to her knees. In her dying moments, Hutepa suspected who was responsible. Stretching out, she seized a pair of castanets from the top of a coffer, and held them tight even as she died.

THES: ancient Egyptian, ‘a tissue of lies’

CHAPTER 3

Amerotke stared round the beautiful hall of the House of the Golden Vine. Its floor was a polished glaze. All round were eye-catching wall frescos celebrating the life and legends of the Great Green, where sea monsters sported around fat-bellied ships gliding through gold-edged blue waves. Above these a relief done in light green depicted birds of every kind: lapwings, sparrows, green-ribbed siskin, grey doves with black collars, all wheeling and turning between coppery rays of sunlight. Amerotke stared up at the ceiling, which was painted a restful pastel shade. He certainly felt little serenity emanating from those sitting or kneeling on cushions around him. To his right was Standard-Bearer Nadif of the Medjay police, thin and wiry, with the sharp eyes and deft movements of a hunter. On Amerotke's left was a sleepy-faced, heavy-eyed Shufoy, who rocked on his cushions as he tried to disguise his rumbling belly. The others were members of the House of the Golden Vine. Meryet, Maben's sister and that of Ipuye's first wife, was a very pretty but hard-faced woman of slender build, lustrous eyed with a petulant mouth. Next to her sat Maben, then Hotep, the captain of the dead merchant's Kushite bodyguard. Hotep was black as night, tall and muscular, his oiled hair closely cropped, a cornelian necklace round his neck, bare chested with a fringed linen kilt; an ornamented war belt, holding club and dagger, lay heaped on the floor beside him. A former member of the Medjay police, he kept smiling at Nadif, though in truth there was little to smile about. The House of the Golden Vine was in mourning. Fires had been damped, lamps extinguished, stoves and ovens lay cold. Ipuye's household had enacted all the customary rituals: ash and dust strewn on hands and faces, no welcoming water for guests, beakers of drink or platters of food. Now that Nadif had delivered his sombre report, the atmosphere had grown even more oppressive.

'It must have been murder,' the standard-bearer declared. 'Ipuye and his wife the lady Khiat were excellent swimmers, and for both of them to be found drowned in the same place at the same time, face down in a lotus pool . . .' Nadif pulled a face.

'But how?' Hotep exclaimed. 'I and six other men circled the palisade fence around the pool. Two others guarded the gateway. We saw nothing; we heard nothing except for the sound of splashing, then silence.'

'And?' Amerotke asked.

'Well, the sun was setting,' Hotep replied. 'One of my guards, Saneb, became curious that there was no sign of Lord Ipuye or, indeed, any further sound. He opened the gate and went in.'

Amerotke held up a hand. 'Bring that man in,' he ordered.

Hotep rose to his feet and left. Amerotke heard him shout, 'Saneb!' and a younger man entered. A Kushite, he was as strong and muscular as Hotep, though softer faced and rather nervous in the presence of Amerotke. He simply repeated what Hotep had related: how on that fateful afternoon the sun was setting, the hour growing late. He'd become concerned and anxious so he'd opened the gate to the lotus pool and gone in to discover his master and mistress floating face down in the water.

'Were there any signs of a struggle?' Amerotke asked. The Kushite shook his head.

'No,' Nadif agreed. 'I arrived shortly afterwards. I could detect no sign or mark of violence on the corpses or round the pool.' The rest concurred with this.

'Food and drink?' Amerotke asked.

'A jug of charou wine and two half-filled goblets were on a table in the lotus pavilion,' Nadif replied. 'I was told they'd not been moved or touched once the corpses were discovered.'

'How can you be sure of that?' Amerotke asked.

'Lord, the wine was in the shade but still it had

begun to dry. I distinctly noticed that. I examined both jug and cups carefully, but there was nothing tainted.'

'Still, it could have been the Rekhet, the Poison Demon,' Maben spat out. 'He has escaped. My brother-in-law Ipuye posted a reward on his head. He has returned to wreak his revenge.'

'But how?' Amerotke asked. 'How could he get in, steal past the guards, climb that high fence and approach Ipuye and his wife without being detected or raising the alarm? If he was carrying poison, how could he enter that pavilion unnoticed by anyone and taint the wine? And if it was violence . . . well, Ipuye was no warrior, but he would struggle and resist. Khiat too, she would have screamed, run for help; such violence would be obvious both during and after the event. As to any potion or powder,' Amerotke continued remorselessly, 'you've heard Standard-Bearer Nadif. Nothing tainted was found, and the corpses betrayed no sign that they'd eaten or drunk something poisoned.'

'Both corpses,' Nadif replied, 'were taken late last night to the House of Purification at the Temple of Ptah. I asked the Overseer of the Dead for his opinion; he replied that he needed more time. The embalming might yield some truth, though a superficial examination showed that both Ipuye and Khiat had drowned. He too admitted he'd never heard the like before: two healthy people drowning silently, mysteriously in the same lotus pool at exactly the same time.'

Amerotke felt tempted to ask Nadif there and then why he was so insistent that both Ipuye and Khiat had been murdered, but decided to leave this until they were alone. Momentarily he speculated on the possibility that one of the victims had drowned and the other died immediately of natural causes, but quickly dismissed the thought: such a coincidence was virtually impossible. Moreover, he was aware of the agitation in Meryet's face, as if Ipuye's death was a matter of little consequence and she wanted to discuss something else.

'Why did Ipuye place a reward on the Rekhet's head?' Amerotke glanced at Maben.

'I have told you,' the priest replied.

'Then tell me again.'

'Ipuye's first wife, our sister Patuna, disappeared during the time of the great poisoning. Ipuye believed she'd been poisoned.'

'Why?'

'Ipuye liked the ladies,' Maben whispered, wiping a sweaty streak of dirt from his face. 'Perhaps one of them reasoned that if Patuna disappeared or died . . .'

'Ah, I see.' Amerotke smiled thinly; he'd heard of similar cases in the city. 'One of these ladies might have aspired to become Ipuye's second wife. Could Khiat have been one of these?'

'I doubt it!' Meryet scoffed. 'Khiat was only in her sixteenth year when she married Ipuye, twelve at the time of the great poisoning. I don't think she and Ipuye had even met. However, I don't believe,' she continued in a rush, glancing sideways at her brother, 'that Patuna ran away. True, she wasn't happy; who would be with Ipuye's womanising? Of course she protested about it.' Meryet ran a hand across her dust-strewn shoulder. 'Whatever,' she whispered, 'the judgment of Seth has been carried out, the day of reckoning, life for life.'

'What do you mean by that?' Amerotke demanded.

'Patuna did not run away!' Meryet's voice rose. 'She was murdered by Ipuye! She was even denied the right to go peacefully into the Far West; she lies buried somewhere here, in a hole, an unmarked grave.' She scrambled to her feet, knocking aside her brother's restraining hand. 'I shall prove that, Lord Judge.'

'My lady,' Amerotke also stood up, 'I must ask where you were when Ipuye died.'

'Lord Judge, I was with you at the Temple of Ptah. I saw those scribes choke to death. I went with my brother Maben to the ceremony. I was present as a special guest in the Pavilion of Restfulness to the right at the foot of the steps. Ask the royal chamberlains, they will attest to that.'

'Sit down,' Amerotke ordered.

Meryet looked as if she was about to refuse, dark eyes smouldering, her lips no more than a thin bloodless line.

'Please,' Amerotke added. 'I must know what you mean.'

'Ipuye liked the ladies.' Meryet slumped down on the cushions. 'I think he just grew tired of our sister and what he called her nagging, her constant remonstrations, her tantrums and her anger. He wanted someone young and fresh like Khiat, so he killed Patuna and buried her somewhere here in what he called his paradise.'

Maben closed his eyes, a sign that he was tired of his sister's constant ranting.

'But, mistress,' Hotep broke in, 'that cannot be true. Ipuye was away when the lady Patuna disappeared. He was doing business in Memphis.'

'Was he? Then he hired someone else!' she spat back.

'What exactly happened?' Amerotke asked.

'My sister was unhappy,' Meryet retorted, again knocking away Maben's hand. 'Ipuye had his mistresses, women of the city. Naturally, my sister was distressed. Ipuye ignored her. Anyway, he went off on business to Memphis, probably with a whore or two. A few days later Maben and I . . . I remember it well.' Meryet's voice grew strident. 'It was before the brilliant hour, the first light of day. We went on to the roof of the house because it was the height of Shemsu, the hot season, when Amun's breath is so pleasing.' She wiped her dusty face, as if imagining the cool morning breeze. 'We expected Patuna to join us, but she never did, so I went looking for her. I could not find her in the garden, so I visited her chamber.' She paused, fighting back a sob. 'It was clean and tidy, but on the floor were the burnt remains of her wedding collarette and marriage bracelet.'

'But that's what happens when a couple divorce!' Amerotke intervened. 'They declare their marriage vows null and void, and the marriage insignia are burnt.'

'Patuna must have done that before running away,' Maben hastily intervened.

'Was anything missing?'

Meryet shook her head. 'Nothing, nothing at all,' she declared. 'Oh, Lord Judge, others claim that Patuna ran away. That she must have had friends in the city, merchants and traders with whom she could have hidden money, which she then collected, swearing them to silence.'

'Did she leave anything else?' Amerotke demanded.

'A scrap of papyrus,' Maben declared, 'lines from a poem.' The priest closed his eyes. 'I have gone, I will not return. Think not ill of me, but let the memories . . .'

'Sweeten your soul,' Amerotke finished for him. 'A beautiful poem, I know it well.'

'We sent messages to the master,' Hotep intervened. 'I and others searched the countryside but there was no sign of the lady Patuna. The same was true in the city. Whatever anyone says, my mistress had not gone there. No shopkeeper, trader or merchant had any knowledge of her. My master hastened home. He too joined in the search, he was distraught. He hired the Scourers; my lord, you know who they are?'

Amerotke nodded. The Scourers were a guild of searchers who, for a price, would comb Thebes and its surrounding countryside for anything or anyone.

'Nothing,' Hotep declared in a deep, carrying voice.

'Now all this occurred during the time of the great poisoning,' Maben intervened. 'My brother-in-law eventually concluded that Patuna had been one of its victims.'

'But he had no proof of that?'

'None whatsoever, so he posted a reward, a lavish one, ounous of gold and silver and a pouch of precious stones for the person who trapped the Rekhet.'

'And when he was caught?' Amerotke moved on his cushion. His throat was dry, but he dared not break with etiquette and ask for a beaker of water.

'My brother-in-law,' Maben replied, 'gave the reward to Ani, High Priest of Ptah, as a gift to the temple, the fulfilment of his promise to the divinity of the Man God.'

'When the Rekhet was captured,' Nadif added, 'he was interrogated about Patuna. Of course, he denied any knowledge of her.'

'But you don't believe all this?' Amerotke pointed at Meryet. 'You maintain Ipuye was responsible, so I ask you again, where is your proof?'

Meryet tapped her chest. 'Just a feeling here, a suspicion. Patuna would not run away. As for the

Rekhet, my sister has disappeared, not been poisoned, there's no evidence for that.'

'You do Ipuye and his memory an injustice,' Maben whispered. 'My lord,' the priest leaned forward, 'Ipuye was undoubtedly a man of the flesh, yet he was kind. He offered rooms here to both Meryet and myself, and even when Patuna disappeared, he insisted that we stay.'

'So who will inherit this beautiful mansion?' Shufoy, who looked as if he had been asleep through the entire proceedings, now stirred, bright eyed and smiling as he looked round the circle.

'My friend,' Amerotke declared slowly, as if measuring his words carefully, 'asked an important question. Who does inherit?'

Maben coughed and cleared his throat. 'My lord, the Temple of Ptah does. In his testament, Ipuye willed that if he died without wife or heir, everything should go to the Lord God as an *atatau* – a divine gift to Ptah.'

Amerotke nodded understandingly. Such bequests were common; little wonder the temples of Karnak prospered like the cedars of Lebanon. By now his throat was so dry he decided to dispense with protocol.

'My lady,' he bowed towards Meryet, 'my throat is as gritty as a piece of sand. A little water, please.'

She smiled, her face becoming soft and pretty, then rose to her feet and scurried out of the hall.

Amerotke turned to Maben. 'What was the

relationship like between Ipuye and Meryet? I mean before Patuna disappeared?'

'They were friends.' Maben shrugged. 'Sister-in-law, brother-in-law, we dined and wined, we went into the city. Very friendly.'

'And afterwards?'

'Cool.' Maben chose his words carefully. 'Formal. They spoke, but in the main they tended to avoid each other.'

'Was there any violence between them either by word or act?'

'Oh no,' Maben shook his head, 'nothing like that. More like envoys who are enemies but have decided to hide it for the sake of harmony.'

'In between the disappearance of Patuna and the death of Ipuye, did anything happen in this house,' Amerotke pointed at Maben, 'that could have had a bearing on these dreadful deaths?'

Maben closed his eyes for a while, thinking hard. When he opened them, he was looking directly at Amerotke. 'Nothing, my lord. It wasn't the happiest of households, but after his marriage to Khiat, Ipuye seemed content enough.'

'And this occurred . . . ?'

'About a year ago. He and Khiat appeared deeply in love with each other, nothing else mattered.'

Amerotke fell silent as Meryet returned with a tray of beakers, each containing a little water. They all drank gratefully. Amerotke drained his and placed it back on the tray.

'So, my lady, you accuse Ipuye of being *behen*?' Amerotke used the official legal term for being murderous.

'Yes, I do.'

'But you have no proof?'

Meryet stared coolly back.

'Be that as it may,' Amerotke sighed, 'we have Ipuye's death in mysterious circumstances.'

'Perhaps it was dire accident,' Shufoy declared. 'An act of Shai the God of Luck.'

Nadif shook his head vigorously. Amerotke secretly wondered why the standard-bearer had decided to be particularly stubborn. Or was he, Amerotke, just trying to smooth matters over? The Divine One had sent a messenger who'd been waiting for him outside the House of the Golden Vine when he arrived earlier. The messenger had expressed the Divine One's deep displeasure at Ipuye's death whilst reminding Amerotke how Ipuye had been 'a friend of Pharaoh who had basked in her smile'. In other words, Amerotke ruefully concluded, Ipuye had supported Hatusu amongst the Powerful Ones of Thebes as well as donated gold and silver to the House of Treasure.

'Look,' Amerotke used his fingers to emphasise his points, 'first, the lotus pool is surrounded by a high blackthorn palisade, which even a skilled climber would find difficult to scale, yes?'

Nadif agreed.

'Second, the palisade and the gate were guarded

by Hotep and his men, yet no one reported anything untoward. Third, there was no one in the house apart from servants, Lady Meryet and Lord Maben being at the Temple of Ptah, and everything was quiet.' Again a low murmur of agreement greeted his words. 'Fourth, Ipuye and Khiat drank untainted wine, we've established that.' Amerotke felt flustered. Here he was in this beautiful hall trying to establish the truth of these abrupt, mysterious deaths. Nadif claimed it was murder, Meryet the Judgment of Seth, whilst Maben called it an unfortunate accident.

'I have questioned enough,' Amerotke abruptly declared. 'Let's go out and see for ourselves.'

They all rose and left by the main door out into the glorious paradise. Amerotke stood on the top step of the house and savoured the cool breeze. He stared around: the garden was a most beautiful place, a pageant of green grass and lush trees. Brilliantly coloured birds darted and swooped. Fragrant smells wafted across from the flowerbeds, fountains splashed, pools glittered. The garden still enjoyed the morning freshness, a refreshing, inviting place where it would be so easy to lie in the shade and forget the troubles of the world. Amerotke, lost in his own thoughts, walked down and stood beside the fishpond near to the house, where golden carp darted amongst the greenery. His sons would love such a place!

'My lord?' Hotep's voice was harsh. The Kushite pointed across the garden. 'I will take you there.'

They walked across the lawn, the grass still cool

underfoot, and entered a line of trees. Hotep paused and explained how these trees, clustered so thickly together, screened the palisade around the lotus pool. They threaded their way through, climbing the slight hill, then left the trees and crossed a green verge towards a soaring black fence. Amerotke reckoned it was higher than he'd thought, at least four yards. The blackthorn strips had been carefully woven and would provide no easy grip; as he had thought, even an experienced climber would find it difficult to scale. Hotep explained how the fence ringed the lotus pool and led him along the palisade towards the wicket gate. This was as high as the fence but of lighter wood and held shut by a clasp. Hotep undid this, swung the gates open and Amerotke entered.

Like the rest of the garden, the pool enclosure was exquisitely fragrant, a ring of green grass stretching to coloured tiles, then the pool itself at least three yards across and eighteen long. At either end of it stood a sun pavilion of dark wood painted to resist the heat and enhanced with climbing flowers. Hotep indicted the one Ipuye had used. Amerotke walked towards it, then paused, staring down at the clear water. The lotus pool was fed by a rivulet, the water being siphoned off through another canal, ensuring that those who swam there always did so in the coolest, purest pool. Amerotke noticed the lapis lazuli dust strewn on the tiles around the pool. He entered the sun pavilion: a small porch led into a luxurious inner room with vents in the wooden wall to provide fresh air and light. He sniffed carefully. Ipuye had cleared it of insects by grinding flea bane with charcoal, as Amerotke's wife did, then masked this with pots of perfume containing a mixture of frankincense, myrrh, cinnamon bark and other herbs boiled in honey. The furniture was simple but refined: folding chairs and stools; a couch; acacia-wood tables with ornamental tops; carved, gable-lidded caskets and coffers containing fresh linen cloths; unguents and phials of perfume with which Ipuye and Khiat would anoint themselves after their bathing, all neatly clustered on a table. Amerotke stared around. Had murder really taken place here? He told the others to stay outside the pavilion and invited Nadif in by himself, Shufoy guarding the door against any eavesdropper.

'Why?' Amerotke turned on the standard-bearer. 'Why do you think this was murder?' The judge paced up and down. He felt angry, yet at the same time guilty, as if he was forcing Nadif, for the sake of peace, to concede that these two deaths might be an unfortunate accident. However, he wryly concluded, that was not the same as the truth.

He paused and stared at Nadif. The standard-bearer was of medium height, his narrow face a mask of respect betrayed only by those eyes, sharp and full of questions. He stood fingering the chain of office round his neck, the Medjay bracelet and ring on his right arm and hand winking in the light, the coloured sash around his waist pulled tight. In one hand he held a walking cane, in the other his war belt. Amerotke could not sustain the standard-bearer's cool glance and turned away. Nadif, he knew, was an excellent officer, the pride of the Medjay, rigorous and incorruptible, thorough and painstaking. Amerotke closed his eyes and drew a deep breath. He must not irritate this man; he was an officer simply doing his duty.

'What do you think of Hotep and his guards?' he asked, not turning round.

'Good men,' Nadif replied calmly. 'They did excellent service in the Medjay before leaving some years ago. Once they wore the ring and the bracelet on their right hand; now, as retired veterans, they wear it on the left, but I would hope they have kept their integrity and served Ipuye well.'

'So why,' Amerotke turned, 'do you think, Nadif, that their master and mistress were murdered here, drowned in this pool?'

'Lord Judge,' Nadif took a step forward, 'I can see that you are angry and for that I apologise. I haven't the slightest shred of proof, the most meagre crumb of evidence to establish my case, except for one thing.' He lifted his walking cane, pointing it at Amerotke. 'I just do not, Lord Judge, believe in such coincidences.'

'Tell me,' Amerotke gestured towards the door, 'when you arrived here, what did you find?'

'Nothing really: some linen cloths, pots of perfume opened, a flask of oil, a lamp burning, one of those fragrant types that exudes perfume. The corpses had been taken from the pool and laid here on the floor. I questioned Saneb, the guard who found them; he said Khiat was floating at one end of the pool, Ipuye at the other.'

'So?' Amerotke asked.

'Lord Judge, let us say it was an accident that Khiat was in difficulties, or alternatively Ipuye; one or the other jumps in to go to his or her aid. Again an accident occurs, a seizure, I don't know what. To put it bluntly, Lord Judge, if that was the case, why weren't their bodies floating together? They were found apart. I just don't believe two people can accidentally die at the same moment in the same pool. Of course,' Nadif shrugged, 'if you write to the Divine One and report it as an accident I'll accept that, but I tell you this,' he stepped closer, 'if you took me to the Temple of Ptah and asked me to swear on its most sacred shrine that this was an accident, I would refuse. Lord Judge, I believe Seth, the God of Murder, visited this house. He swept through that beautiful paradise and visited this pool. Ipuye and Khiat were murdered.'

'Yet we do not know what happened here,' Amerotke retorted. 'The best we can do, Standard-Bearer Nadif, is try to re-create events, and that is exactly what I intend to do.' He patted Nadif on the shoulder and walked out of the pavilion. The sun was growing stronger, so he told Shufoy to open the parasol he carried, then he summoned Hotep and told him exactly what he wanted him to do. The Kushite gazed back in amazement.

'Are you sure, my lord?'

Amerotke beckoned Hotep's men to draw closer. 'Look,' he declared, 'you were all once members of the Medjay?'

They nodded in agreement.

'Once you wore the ring and bracelet on the right hand; now, as former veterans, you wear them on the left?'

Again they grunted in agreement.

'Well, what I want you to do,' Amerotke continued, shading his eyes against the sun, 'is to re-create what happened here. Two of you will swim in the lotus pool. You, Hotep, and one of your men will try to climb that blackthorn fence without being detected. The rest of you will occupy the same guard positions you did yesterday.'

At first this caused some consternation, even amusement. Nadif made to object, but Amerotke held up his hand. 'It's the least we can do,' he declared. 'We might find out exactly what happened.'

Amerotke went and sat on the lawn beneath Shufoy's parasol. Two of Hotep's men stripped and without any encouragement dived into the pool, swimming and splashing around. Maben and Meryet stood in the shade of the pavilion and watched the drama unfold. At last Amerotke imposed some sort of order. The two Kushite bodyguards swimming in the pool grew tired and waited. Beyond the palisade

Amerotke could hear Hotep and Saneb trying to climb the fence. Eventually the wicket gate opened and a shame-faced Hotep, followed by Saneb, came through.

'My lord,' Hotep stood at the edge of the pool, staring across at Amerotke, 'it's impossible.'

The judge got to his feet and came round the pool. 'What do you mean, it's impossible?'

'Come,' Hotep replied, 'I'll show you.'

They left through the wicket gate and went along the side of the fence to a place near the corner. Hotep nodded at Saneb, who tried to climb; however, the way the fence had been constructed, a latticework of intertwining branches, made any chance of securing a foothold virtually impossible.

'It's also prickly,' Hotep explained, 'and it bulges out slightly so you cannot get a grip. Lord Judge, nobody could have climbed that fence.'

'And if they had,' Amerotke mused, 'they would have had to drop to the other side, surprise Ipuye and Khiat, then kill them without raising the alarm.' He gestured at the trees. 'As well as make their way back through these without being noticed by any of you, which, by the Lords of Light, they would also have had to achieve before they even reached the fence in the first place.' Amerotke shook his head. 'Nadif,' he turned to the standard-bearer, 'unless you produce more evidence, this must be judged as an accident.' He made to walk away, but stopped when he heard the shrill call of a bell. He paused and glanced back. Nadif was holding a small handbell which he shook vigorously. Amerotke walked towards him.

'A tortoiseshell bell, my lord.'

Nadif turned the dark brown cup up so Amerotke could see the clapper inside.

'Khiat always carried it with her. I found it here next to the pool. Khiat was rather imperious; she rang this bell to summon servants. It never rang that day.' Nadif stepped closer. 'Think, Lord Judge,' he hissed fiercely, 'two human beings dying immediately in the water, impossible! If Ipuye had had a seizure, Khiat would have rung that bell. If Khiat had got into difficulties, Ipuye would have done the same or called for help.'

'Let us say,' Amerotke retorted, 'for sake of argument, that someone did scale that fence, though to do so they would have needed a ladder: they'd plunge into the pool, they'd become soaked, they would cause an affray which would raise the alarm. The bell would definitely have been rung.' Amerotke shook his head and stared across at the pavilion where Shufoy sat joking with one of the Kushites. 'Saneb!' he shouted.

The young Kushite rose to his feet and hurried across.

'Hotep.'

The captain of the guard, standing near the wicket gate, joined them. Amerotke beckoned them closer. 'On the afternoon your master died, what were you doing?'

Hotep shrugged. 'As always, Lord Judge, we took

up position in the trees around the palisade. Well, you've seen it; we watched that and the wicket gate. For the rest,' he grinned shyly, 'we drank our jugs of beer and gossiped. We drank again, dozed and rested. But there again, Lord Judge, this was my master's paradise, not some lonely outpost or a war camp in the Redlands. We relaxed, we heard nothing wrong. We saw no one we could challenge. Only when Saneb opened that gate and went into the enclosure did we even suspect anything was wrong.'

'My lord!' Maben and Meryet hastened across. 'What will you say to the Divine One?'

'What can I say?' Amerotke retorted. 'Before I leave, I must see Ipuye's private chambers.'

Meryet agreed. She led Amerotke back through the house and into Ipuye's quarters just beyond the central hall. Amerotke quickly appreciated the merchant's wealth; this luxurious enclave comprised a central bedroom with adjoining chambers for archives and stores, a bath place, toilet, everything being well furnished and clean. The central chamber, Ipuye's and Khiat's personal room, was tastefully decorated and filled with carefully fashioned furniture. Amerotke was immediately distracted by the frescos on the walls, which described a topsy-turvy world where donkeys dressed as priests sacrificed to gods; cats fanned mice at meals, served them food and carried baby mice in shawls; foxes and jackals played the double pipes: smiling crocodiles strummed lutes; lions herded geese: blackbirds gathered figs in baskets whilst hippopotami nested in the branches of palm trees. He studied these carefully and realised that he and Ipuye had a great deal in common. The dead merchant seemed to be mocking the gods and the Osirian rite of journeying into the Far West. Amerotke gnawed his lip. He'd secretly confessed to his wife Norfret how he believed that the stories of Seth, Amun, Ra, Horus, Hathor of the Sycamores and the other gods and goddesses of Egypt were just that, figments of man's imagination. Ipuye had certainly believed this.

Amerotke walked away from the paintings and began to study the chamber in detail. Nothing was out of place, it was all beautifully decorated and elegantly furnished. Ipuye and Khiat had lived a leisurely, rich life. He went into the archive chamber, a square, whitewashed room with two window vents high in the wall. He opened the linen bags and began to sift through the records. The day wore on. Shufoy came in and demanded to know when they were going to leave. Amerotke murmured his apologies, now fascinated by Ipuye's records and letters. He found nothing significant: bills of sale, agreements, purchases, a vast array of evidence to show how Ipuye was exploiting the markets to the east, opening a rich and prosperous trade with Punt and islands in the Great Green. One item caught his attention: Ipuye's movements four years earlier when his first wife had disappeared. Amerotke called both Maben and Meryet back into the chamber and interrogated them carefully on the date Ipuye was supposed to have left Thebes for Memphis. After some difficulty they provided this and Amerotke went back to the records. The more he studied, the deeper his unease become, because according to the itinerary based on purchases made and agreements reached, Ipuye had journeyed no further than Thebes. He had visited the Temple of Ptah, as his list of expenses showed, before moving to a dwelling he called his Place of Pleasure, very close to the precious stonemakers' quarter. Amerotke called Maben and Meryet back again and questioned them closely, pointing out that, according to the records, Ipuye had never journeyed to Memphis. Both seemed highly embarrassed by Amerotke's find, though he suspected they had known of it, regarding it as a family scandal, clear evidence of Ipuye's womanising.

'It certainly proves my argument.' Meryet rubbed her cheeks, eyes bright with excitement. 'If Ipuye didn't leave Thebes for Memphis, why did he lie? He stayed in the city to make sure his wife was dead!'

Amerotke could not answer her. They left and he continued his searches but found nothing else. He was about to call Nadif to meet him in the central hall when Maben burst into the chamber.

'My lord Amerotke,' he gasped, 'a messenger from Thebes sent by the Lord Ani. You must come! A temple girl, Hutepa, a heset, a former friend of the Rekhet, has been found poisoned.'

'When?' Amerotke asked.

'Late this morning,' Maben replied. 'She was supposed to attend a ritual in the temple but never appeared. Only later, when a servant went to discover why, did they find her sprawled on the floor of her bedchamber. My lord Amerotke, she's been poisoned! Minnakht himself has brought the news.'

Amerotke met the Chief Scribe out in the garden under the shade of a terebinth tree. Minnakht looked agitated.

'My lord Amerotke, you have heard the news? Hutepa is dead.'

'She was a friend of the Rekhet?' Amerotke asked.

Minnakht pulled a face. 'According to some evidence, a man was seen near her chamber late last night, but due to all the visitors to our temple, no one paid much attention to him.'

'Were they close friends?' Amerotke asked.

Minnakht shrugged.

'And why should he poison her?' Amerotke insisted.

'Perhaps he visited her to ask for help,' Minnakht offered. 'Perhaps she refused, so she had to die?' He nodded towards the house. 'My lord, my apologies, you seem to have troubles enough.'

Amerotke smiled grimly. 'That's the way of the world, isn't it, Chief Scribe? When your woes come, they tend to arrive in baskets rather than one by one.' He asked Minnakht to wait, hurried back into the house and told Nadif and Shufoy the news. They made their farewells of Maben and Meryet, then left the House of the Golden Vine, taking the route along the Nile which would bring them back into the city through the Lion Gate. Amerotke walked quickly; Shufoy was full of chatter and gossip, eager to question Minnakht about what had happened, and what was going to happen. Nadif kept his own counsel, whilst Minnakht, happy to find a fellow spirit, gossiped back as if he and Shufoy were old comrades.

SEBA: ancient Egyptian, 'to act as an enemy'

CHAPTER 4

The prisoner who had escaped from the Oasis of Bitter Bread moved from beneath the cluster of palm trees. He lifted the bundle of sticks on to his shoulder, then, head down, waited for Amerotke and his party to pass before mingling with the crowds streaming along the thoroughfare. On their right rose the mansions and palaces of the rich and powerful; on their left was the rich ooze of the Nile with its papyrus thickets, clumps of bullrushes and clusters of trees alive with the whirr of insects and the constant chatter of birds and monkeys. Now and again beneath all these the crash and roar of the hippopotami echoed like a roll of thunder, whilst the crocodiles, still sluggish, sprawled in the mud warming in the strengthening sun. The former prisoner watched his quarry carefully as they threaded their way through the crowds. Amerotke walked ahead, swinging his walking cane, Nadif slightly behind as if the two men had recently quarrelled. Minnakht and the dwarf Shufoy followed on, chattering incessantly without pausing for breath or really listening to what the other was saying. The escaped prisoner smiled grimly to himself. Minnakht hadn't changed, still as garrulous as ever! He wondered if he could approach him: the scribe had a kindly heart and was well known for his humanity, unlike the other arrogant ones, but not for now; he would simply follow Amerotke and see what path he followed.

The escaped prisoner adjusted the bundle of sticks on his shoulder and fingered the Canaanite dagger thrust into the cord that served as a belt round his waist. He kept a vigilant eye on those he passed. He carried a dagger and, thanks to Hutepa, something more deadly. He was determined not to be taken alive. Thankfully, it was an auspicious day, holy to Hathor, Lady of the Sycamores. The markets along the great thoroughfares and in the dusty squares would be busy. Everyone was going to Thebes. A group of Shardana mercenaries, armed with swords and clubs, swaggered by in their strange helmets, rough short tunics, and penis-sheaths, their feet and ankles protected by heavy sandals. These were followed by a group of Medjay police with their distinctive curled hairstyles, the jewellery of office glittering on their right hands and wrists, leather kilts flapping, studded baldrics fastened across their chests. Each man carried a club, which they were only too ready to use at any sign of disturbance. Carts full of produce lumbered slowly by, oxen straining at the yoke, the air above them infested with black hordes of buzzing flies which disappeared at the crack of the whip only to mysteriously gather once again. The litters and carriages of the rich desperately tried to push their way through only to be met with raucous abuse and outright defiance.

The air was stiflingly hot and reeked of ooze, dung, sweat, fish and cheap perfume. Children screamed and yelled. Water-sellers stood either side of the road with stoup and bucket promising 'the best and the coolest from a new spring recently found outside the city'. Barbers had set up shop beneath palm trees; these were quickly joined by fruit-sellers and cooks, their portable stoves already fired. Gazelle, antelope and quail meat was cut and sliced, doused in oil, chopped into manageable portions and placed across makeshift grills. The air grew thick with the odours of burning meat. People clustered hungrily around, mouths watering, waiting for the meat to be turned and poked before being doused in more herbs to hide its rancid taste, then placed in palm leaves. Other enterprising traders were also setting up business. Scribes touted for trade, nestled in the shade, ready to barter their services, be it drawing up a document or copying a letter. A group of priests belonging to some alien cult had erected a temporary altar around a grotesque statue that was half man, half monkey, and were offering it macaroons and strong palm brandy: they waved these before the sightless eyes of their god before eating and drinking them themselves amidst roars of laughter. The music of pipes played by a blind musician echoed stridently; his milky stare terrified some children, who ran screeching away. A scorpion man tried to sell the former prisoner an amulet and a scarab of Meretseger the Goddess of Silence, who watched from her soaring peak overlooking the Necropolis. Crocodile men from the City of the Dead had already swarmed across the Nile, offering visitors and pilgrims safe passage across the river to visit the embalming and coffin shops. City prostitutes, garish in their cheap flashing jewellery and ostentatious flowery wigs, bartered for custom. They offered to lie with clients under some shady awning, share wine and satisfy their customer's every desire. The former prisoner drove all these away, eyes intent on Amerotke and his group.

At last they reached the Lion Gate. Amerotke's pursuer kept his head down. Hutepa had already warned how his description had been posted and proclaimed all over the city. An imperial chariot squadron, the electrum of their carriages shimmering in the sunlight, horses restless in their gleaming black harness, sheltered under a cluster of palm trees. Nearer the gate, on each side of its approach, mustered the Medjay police and a cohort of auxiliaries in their garish armour. These proved no threat to the former prisoner, as they were more concerned with the clouds of dust, the hovering flies, the bray of donkeys, the din and clamour of hundreds of people eager to reach home, a market shrine, a temple, a shop or just to escape from the noisy hustle and bustle of the city. Amerotke and his party went under the great gate, their pursuer following, on to the broad, basalt-paved Avenue of the Sphinx. The escaped prisoner relaxed. The crowds were now fanning out, going off down roads leading to the various markets, where the perfumers, linen merchants, fruit-sellers and geese and duck traders plied their trade. Amerotke, however, continued on the avenue which would take him up to the Temple of Ptah. His pursuer stopped to shift his bundle from one shoulder to the other, only to realise that two men had abruptly flanked him. They were both dressed in the striped robes of desert wanderers, faces blackened by the sun, bushy haired, bearded and moustached. Their clothes were dirty but they were well armed: each carried a sword and a club, with a dagger thrust through his belt. They came in close, and their hot breath upon the prisoner's face reeked of onion and spiced meat.

'You don't like us?' one of the men growled, blocking his way, whilst the other slipped behind him. 'You don't like us?'

'I don't know you,' the former prisoner replied.

'But we know you,' the man behind whispered in his ear. 'You are the Rekhet. You can crop your hair, moustache and beard, but we've been watching you following the Lord Judge.'

'I don't know what you're talking about.' The escaped prisoner was aware of passers-by staring at them curiously.

'Don't you?' The one in front poked him in the chest, then, leaning forward, plucked the Canaanite dagger from his belt. 'We'll look after that. You must come with us.'

'I don't want to.'

'It's not a question, my friend, of wanting or not wanting. The Churat, the Eater of Vile Things, wishes to meet you.'

The prisoner closed his eyes. He'd heard of the Churat, the nickname of one of the gang leaders in the slums of Thebes.

'It's a good walk,' the man smiled, 'into the Abode of Darkness. That's where he rules, and he wants to talk to you. Now, you can either come with us, or I can,' he pointed to the Medjay police standing in the shade of one of the brooding Sphinxes, 'call them over and introduce you.'

The prisoner gripped his bundle of sticks tighter. He knew resistance was useless; they'd taken his weapon. Both men were armed and resolute, and there was only one way he could escape.

'Very well,' he sighed, 'I'm in your hands.'

'You certainly are,' the man behind him replied. 'Now come on.'

They walked a little further along the thoroughfare, one in front, the other behind, then turned down a street. The former prisoner knew where they were taking him. The Abode of Darkness was well named: a warren, a veritable maze of needle-thin alleyways, shabby housing and small dusty squares. Even the Medjay police and imperial troops were reluctant to enter that nest of vipers.

'Keep hold of your bundle,' one of the men joked, 'so we know where your hands are. Don't try to run away.'

The escaped prisoner looked around. He realised how any attempt to flee would be brutally stopped, but he resolved not to enter the Abode of Darkness. He pretended to stumble and crouched down.

'What's the matter?' The two men towered over him. 'Are you ill?'

The escaped prisoner shook his head and wiped the sweat from his brow.

'I'm not ill, just thirsty. I have not eaten and drunk for some time. For the sake of pity, I'll go faster, there'll be no trouble. Just a jug of cooling ale, that's all I ask.'

The men looked at each other and nodded. They went across to a wine booth, an awning attached to surrounding trees. It boasted a shady stall, some stained cushions, cracked stools and little tables. The former prisoner insisted on buying, offering the bundle of sticks he carried for a jug of ale and three cups. The wine master looked at the bundle, nodded and shrugged.

'Might as well,' he grumbled. He dipped a jug decorated with griffin heads into a barrel, drew it out and placed three beakers on the table. They were chipped and none too clean. The escaped prisoner picked up the jug, sniffed carefully, poured some of the contents into a cup and tasted it.

'You call this good ale?'

The wine master came back.

'What's the matter with it? It's freshly brewed. You don't like it, move on!' He kicked the bundle of sticks. 'But these are mine, you got what you asked for.'

Muttering and groaning, the prisoner indicated the far corner just inside the entrance. He gave the three cups to one of his guards, picked up the jug, swirled it around, sniffed, put it back on the counter and, picking up a piece of papyrus reed, stirred it. Then he took the jug over to the table, filled all three cups, lifted his to his lips and mockingly toasted his two captors.

'Gentlemen, I thought this was an auspicious day. What does the Churat want with me?'

'We don't know,' one of them replied, 'and we don't care. Drink your beer and we'll move on.'

The prisoner got up and moved to the entrance as if savouring the cool breeze.

'You'll not think of running, will you?' one of the men warned. 'There are others of us outside.'

The former prisoner looked to the left and right. He could see no one, but there again . . . He lifted the cup to his lips and returned to argue with the wine master as if still not satisfied with the quality of what he had bought. When he heard the first groan, he looked over his shoulder. Both of his captors had their cups back on the shabby table and were clutching their stomachs. One of them slipped off his stool, going down on one knee. It was enough.

'As I said . . .' The prisoner lunged. He pushed the wine master aside, scrambled over the counter and out of the tent flap. Behind him his two former captors writhed on the ground, legs kicking, mouths open in silent screams as the poison coursed through their bodies.

'May the Gates of the Far West be opened. May your journey through the Am-duat be safe. May the Divine Ones welcome you into the Halls of Eternity. May the eternal Green Fields accept your *ka* . . .' The lector priest's voice rose and fell. Incense swirled. The Anubis-masked priests moved like ghosts through the murk. The fragrance of myrrh mingled with the stench from the entrails slopped into the canopic jars. Amerotke kept staring at the painting on the far wall of the Wabet. On his arrival at the temple he had been immediately ushered down here to inspect the three corpses which were being prepared for burial. He found the atmosphere oppressive, so the wall painting was a welcome relief. The work of the artist quietly mocked the orderliness of life, reminding Amerotke sharply of the frescos in Ipuye's bedchamber. A small painting depicted a lion and an ibex playing *senet*; by the look on the lion's face, he was winning. Amerotke recalled where he was, dismissed the distraction and glanced down at the three corpses on the slightly tilting embalming slabs. Ipuye was thickset and muscular; Khiat's beautiful body was now slit open. Amerotke breathed his own prayer. Even though she was lovely in aspect, Khiat was nothing more than a child. Next to her lay the heset Hutepa, a comely woman, her finely etched face distorted by a hideous swelling which even the embalmers had found difficult to remove, the gruesome effect of the vile poison fed her. The others clustered behind Amerotke: Shufoy, ever inquisitive, head turning so he could recall everything he saw; Minnakht still whispering to the dwarf, despite the tut-tutting of High Priest Ani and the whispered pleas of Maben for silence. Hinqui was absent, Ani murmuring that his assistant was sickening though he did not know the cause.

At last the lector priest drew his prayer to a close. More grains of incense were burnt and the Overseer took Amerotke and his companions down a narrow, dark passageway, then up some steps into a surprisingly bright chamber which served as his office. The Overseer gestured at the cushions piled on the broad wooden dais beneath the high window vent, its grille now removed so that light poured through on to the vivid wall paintings of fishermen hunting herrings on the marshes or the brilliant pageant of a garden pool fringed with sycamore and date-palm trees. On a table in the centre of the room stood a statue of the Man God Ptah in its wooden shrine, fruit and flower petals heaped at its feet. The Overseer accepted his visitors' compliments on his good taste, made them comfortable and came swiftly to the point.

'Hutepa,' he declared, settling himself on his cushions. 'Well, only the God Man himself knows how and why she was poisoned or who was responsible—'

'The Rekhet?' Ani interrupted.

'Perhaps,' the Overseer continued. He paused as the door opened and a servant ushered in Nadif, who'd excused himself from visiting the Wabet. The standard-bearer sat down on a stool to the right of the dais.

'I tell you this,' the Overseer continued. 'Hutepa was killed by something as swift and as deadly as a bite from the most venomous snake, a potion that corroded her stomach. I've never seen the like before.' He fished in the wallet on his belt. 'I have something.' He handed Amerotke an oval wooden hand-clapper, the type used by temple hesets in their dances. Amerotke turned it over and inspected the rather faded painting of a dancer. 'She died with that clutched tightly in her hand,' the Overseer remarked. 'So tight I found it difficult to remove.'

Amerotke handed the item to Shufoy to keep.

'And Ipuye and Khiat?' he asked.

'Ah, well.' The Overseer spread his hands. 'The famous phrase: death is the brother of sleep. My lord, water filled their lungs and they drowned.'

'And you found no bruise or contusion, no evidence of poison or other violence?'

'None whatsoever.'

Amerotke, in his silent walk through the city to the Temple of Ptah, had reflected carefully on what he'd seen in and around that pool.

'Did you notice anything at all?' he asked. 'Dust on their hands or feet?'

'Nothing,' the Overseer replied. 'Why, what are you looking for?'

'I don't know,' Amerotke sighed, getting to his feet, 'I truly don't.'

Once they'd left the House of Death, Amerotke took High Priest Ani, Minnakht and Maben away from the rest into the shade of a holm oak. He took his fan from a pocket in his robe and wafted himself vigorously.

'Poison,' he began. 'Minnakht told me how a legend persists that the Books of Doom, together with their author, lie buried here in grounds now covered by the temple precincts.'

'A legend,' Ani scoffed.

'Minnakht?'

The scribe's jovial face broke into a grin. 'The High Priest may be correct, my lord. You see, when the author of the Books of Doom was punished and executed, his name was removed from every document, tablet and inscription. He was damned, and so was his memory. No trace of him remains. However, the legend persists that somewhere in an underground tunnel or cavern near here lie both the corpse and his damnable books.'

'And Hutepa?' Amerotke asked abruptly. 'Why should she be murdered?'

'She was apparently friendly with the Rekhet,' Minnakht declared. 'Isn't that correct, Maben?'

The priest, distracted by his own problems and grief, simply nodded.

'And?' Amerotke asked.

'According to one source,' Ani murmured, 'she directed the Medjay where to arrest him. Standard-Bearer Nadif would know more about that than us.'

'So,' Amerotke snapped his fan closed and put it back in his pocket, 'the Rekhet could have returned here and killed her as an act of vengeance?'

'Possibly,' Minnakht agreed, then shook his head. 'I have spoken to Lord Ani about this, we should all be very careful. I am anxious about Hinqui. Is he sick due to some contagion, something he ate? Is his heart troubled, or is it the work of the Rekhet? Has he decided to deal out vengeance in the Temple of Ptah?'

'Tell me something.' Amerotke put his face in his hands and thought for a while.

'Yes, Lord Judge?' Ani tapped his foot, impatient to go.

'According to you,' Amerotke replied slowly, 'the Rekhet was a priest physician whom some of his colleagues suspected. No, no, that isn't right. His colleagues suspected simply that the Rekhet was someone at the Temple of Ptah, correct?'

Ani nodded.

'Userbati and his colleagues were poisoned,' Amerotke continued. 'Then evidence was found that pointed to a certain priest physician being responsible. He was arrested, more evidence was gained, and he was condemned. Is that correct?'

Ani nodded.

'So why did those priest physicians suspect the Rekhet was someone at the Temple of Ptah in the first place?'

'Again, Standard-Bearer Nadif has more facts than we. One thing we did learn, my lord Amerotke, is that many of the Rekhet's victims were prosperous, patrons of this temple, visitors to our holy places. Now, as you know, there are criminals in Thebes who can be hired for a few grains of gold or silver to carry out a wicked deed. One thing became constant: most, in fact nearly all of those poisoned had had dealings with the Temple of Ptah. They had either recently visited here or were closely related to someone who had. As I said,' Ani pointed at Nadif, still standing at the top of the steps leading down to the Wabet, 'he can tell you more than I.'

'And we have your permission to search Hutepa's room?'

'Of course.' Ani pulled his shawl closer round his shoulders. 'My lord Amerotke, I have other duties.' He, Minnakht and Maben bowed and left.

Amerotke watched them go and waited for Nadif to walk across.

'Well, Lord Judge,' the standard-bearer stood hands on his hips, lips tight in anger, 'I suppose you are going to insist that Ipuye and Khiat died of drowning, an accident?'

'No, Standard-Bearer, I'm not!' Amerotke clapped him on the shoulder. 'I trust you, Nadif, you are sharp witted and keen eyed.' He tapped the policeman on the chest. 'I also trust your heart; it is pure, it speaks the truth. I believe you are correct: Ipuye and Khiat were murdered.'

Nadif gazed back in amazement, so startled that Amerotke laughed.

'Do you recall the lotus pool at Ipuye's house?'

Nadif nodded.

'What was scattered on the tiles around the pool as well as on the pathway between the pool and the grass verge?'

'Lapis lazuli,' Nadif replied slowly. 'It is put there for decoration, as well as to give wet bare feet a better grip on the tiles.'

'On those two corpses,' Amerotke asked, 'did you find on hand, foot or leg any trace of lapis lazuli?'

Nadif, eyes staring, mouth open, gazed at a point behind Amerotke's head.

'By the Lord of Light,' he breathed, 'no, I didn't.'

'And neither did the Overseer of the Dead,' Amerotke added. 'Standard-Bearer, think about that lotus pool. You went through the wicket gate and into the pavilion. Where were the corpses?'

'In the pavilion, lying on the floor, out of the heat of the sun.'

'What else was there?'

'The jug, the wine cups. I remember examining them first.'

'What else?'

'Some robes, jars of oil, linen cloths . . . yes, and reed sandals.'

Amerotke nodded. 'Ipuye and Khiat would have worn the sandals from the house to the pool. They had to cross paths which would have hurt their feet. Now think, Standard-Bearer, this is very important. I have asked this before. Did you detect any lapis lazuli on the feet of the victims or in the pool?'

Nadif closed his eyes, swaying slightly as if listening to the birdsong in the branches above him.

'No.' He opened his eyes. 'I remember distinctly looking for any discoloration of the skin, particularly on the fingers or the back of the neck, but I saw nothing. Both bodies had been taken from the water and placed in the pavilion.'

'And the water itself?'

'There was a little lapis lazuli dust floating on the top.'

'I saw that too,' said Amerotke, 'but we don't know if it was caused by the barefooted guards running across the path and plunging into the water to drag out the corpses.'

'But I'm certain.' Nadif raised a hand. 'I'm positive. I saw no lapis lazuli on the victims; in fact the soles of their feet were clean.' He scratched a bead of sweat from his chin. 'I follow your logic, Lord Amerotke. If Ipuye and Khiat took off their sandals and walked into the pool, some of that gold dust would have lodged in the skin of their feet. We found none. Consequently it's possible that they were dead before they ever entered the water, being simply carried there by their killer. Yet how he managed to climb that fence and gain entrance without being seen or raising the alarm is just as mysterious. But there again,' Nadif shrugged, 'perhaps they did enter the pool and the lapis lazuli was washed off.'

Amerotke nodded and glanced away. He felt as if such evidence was nothing more than straw on the water, yet he did not wish to alienate this sharp-witted Medjay. Amerotke himself secretly sensed that something was dreadfully wrong about those deaths. They weren't accidents. Nadif's contention that such a coincidence could ever occur was a powerful argument. But how could they prove that Ipuye and Khiat's deaths were an unlawful slaying?

'Nadif,' Amerotke decided to put on the bravest face possible, 'I need your help. First we should search Hutepa's chamber; perhaps we might find something.'

He walked across and crouched before Shufoy, who squatted on the grass half dozing. 'Little man,' Amerotke whispered, 'have you recovered from the wine you drank yesterday?'

Shufoy opened his eyes. 'Oh yes, master, I'm just thinking.'

'About what?' Amerotke asked.

'All this present business. What I think we should do is take our redoubtable standard-bearer of the Medjay for a few cups of wine and some tender sliced meat and fresh bread. Then perhaps we shall learn something.'

Amerotke smiled, patted Shufoy on the head and got to his feet. The dwarf rose and slipped his hand into Amerotke's. 'I'm sorry, master,' he murmured, 'I mean about yesterday. I drank too much.'

'Don't worry,' Amerotke replied. 'Yesterday was yesterday. Today is today. Let us do what we have to.'

A temple servant took them over to the House of Praise, then across a garden, though a door and down a passageway to Hutepa's chamber, a small room, sad in many ways, full of mementoes of the dead girl. Amerotke stared down at the bed: the whispery veils which protected the sleeper at night against marauding insects had been pulled back. He looked at the headrest mantled in blue and gold, the sweat marks on it still evident.

'Master,' Shufoy asked, 'what are we looking for?'

'Search this chamber,' Amerotke replied. 'Don't look for the obvious, but rather for something untoward that shouldn't be here.'

Amerotke sat down on the bed. The linen sheets over the broad flock mattress were rather grimy. This puzzled him. The rest of Hutepa's chamber seemed a very clean, neat place, its walls painted with tasteful scenes of hesets singing or collecting flowers beside a pond, the floor polished, the reed matting spotlessly clean. He noticed the dried onion placed against a small hole at the bottom of a wall as a protection against mice. Pots of herbs were also placed to fend off insects, whilst a net covered the window as further protection against dust and flies. Pegs on the wall held carefully draped clothes and ceremonial robes. On one side of the room were ranged caskets and coffers with gable-shaped lids and handles in the form of mushrooms, all painted a pleasing ochre and framed with black and white lines. Amerotke asked Nadif to empty the contents of these on to the bed. The room was rather narrow, so he sent Shufoy to the House of the Dead to make further enquiries. Clothes and robes were taken off pegs, a faded garland from a nail on the door. Nadif emptied the chests and coffers, their contents spilling out: a sistra, bracelets of cornelian, necklaces of jasper, rings, a cosmetic mixing dish, a pair of gazelle-skin sleepers, a polished bronze mirror, kohl containers, ivory combs, jars of unguents and perfumes. Nadif then lifted across a rather large jewellery box lined with strips of ebony to give it the look of darkish timber and decorated with small squares of ivory and faience. He opened the lid, emptied its few contents on to the bed, then weighed it in his hands. Amerotke, intrigued, edged closer. Nadif drew his dagger and prised loose the bottom of the casket to reveal a hidden cavity, from which he pulled out two small scrolls of treated papyrus. These he handed to Amerotke. The judge unrolled them quickly, reading from right to left the carefully formed symbols around the skilfully drawn maps. Then he moved to the narrow writing desk against the far wall. The scribe's tray resting on top was well stocked with reed pens, ink pots, pumice stones and small writing brushes. The inks were those of a scribe: green, black and red.

'A scholar,' Amerotke murmured. 'Hutepa was well versed.'

'Normal for a temple heset,' Nadif replied. 'Many of them are erudite, skilled in the arts of Thoth.'

'But what was she writing?' Amerotke asked. 'And why?'

The judge opened a folding stool and sat down so he caught the light from the window, then, with Nadif leaning over his shoulder, quickly perused both manuscripts. Hutepa had apparently written in a cipher known only to herself, but the maps she'd drawn were obvious. The title *Akhet, The Horizon*, written above one diagram, described the flatlands west of Thebes that stretched to the Place of Truth, the grey limestone valleys that housed the burial chambers of the pharaohs. Two great valleys dominated this area but there were other hidden, narrow ones. Amerotke knew the terrain very well. Hutepa had identified one of these, etching as the title the name Huaneka. Amerotke moved from scroll to scroll. Outside echoed the sounds of the temple, the lowing of cattle being driven to the sacrificial pens, the shouts of workmen, the faint singing of choirs, the chimes and melodies of practising musicians. He half listened to these as he studied the scrolls and realised that Hutepa hadn't so much written in a cipher or code as abbreviated certain words and letters. At first he wondered who this Huaneka was, until he came across the phrase 'widow of Ari Sapu'. It seemed Hutepa had been searching for the author of the Books of Doom, who'd lived in this temple some fifty years earlier and was apparently married to Huaneka. After he was caught and executed, his name damned for ever, his wife, apparently innocent of her husband's crimes, had been left to live out her life as an honourable widow, a pensioner of the temple. They must have had no children, for Huaneka had lived by herself, bereft of a family tomb. However, according to Hutepa, the widow had used all her remaining wealth to rectify this, purchasing a sepulchre in what was now known as the Valley of the Forgotten. Hutepa had clearly located this tomb, giving precise details of its position.

'But why?' Amerotke asked.

Nadif just pulled a face.

'And why was Hutepa poisoned?'

'Simple,' Nadif replied. 'She told me where the Rekhet was hiding. It was an act of pure revenge.'

'So,' Amerotke smiled at the standard-bearer, 'the Rekhet escapes from his prison oasis and returns to

Thebes bent on vengeance. But why should he kill three scribes, or even Ipuye and Khiat? We don't know. He also visits the heset who played a prominent role in his arrest and poisons her wine. She drinks it, so vengeance is carried out, yet . . .' Amerotke plucked at the linen sheets and, leaning down, smelt the sweat heavy on them. 'Did Hutepa make love to her killer? She was a graceful, sophisticated heset, an intelligent woman able to read, write and study. Look at her possessions: this chamber exemplifies her finesse, her elegance, yet this bed . . .' He grasped the grimy sheets. 'Undoubtedly someone lay here, dusty, sweat stained, tired. A man? Did he sleep? Did they make love? What sort of person, Nadif, would do that? When you and I return home tonight we will bathe, wash off the dust and anoint our bodies.'

'A fugitive?' Nadif asked.

'Precisely!' Amerotke agreed. 'Our escaped prisoner has to keep himself hidden. He cannot be glimpsed in galleries or passageways, out in gardens or crossing courtyards, so he slips in here. Hutepa must have allowed him in and offered her bed, either to sleep in, make love, or both. So why did the Rekhet kill her? Moreover, even more strange, why was this heset so intent on searching the history of the widow Huaneka? Finding out where her grave was? Did she go out there and visit that tomb? Nadif, we shall certainly do so.'

Amerotke paused at a knock on the door. Shufoy came in.

'I asked the Overseer of the Dead,' he announced. 'He assures me he found no gold dust on the feet, hands or corpses of Ipuye or the lady Khiat. He did add that it could have been washed off by the water. Having said that,' Shufoy continued, 'the Overseer says such dust often lodges between the toes, yet he found no trace of it whatsoever.'

'Thank you, Shufoy,' Amerotke replied absent-mindedly. 'Perhaps I'm clutching at straws; it's certainly not proof.' He glanced at Nadif. 'I still agree with you. The deaths of Ipuye and Khiat are truly mysterious—'

'Oh, by the way,' Shufoy intervened, 'Minnakht and Maben want to see you again. They said they'll wait for you outside.'

'No they won't,' Amerotke declared. 'Tell my lord Minnakht and Maben that I will see them later in their quarters. I have other business to attend to.'

'What business?' Nadif asked. Amerotke went across and opened the door; he looked out and came back to the bed.

'Help me to put these away.'

He took the small scrolls and put them in the pouch he always carried on his belt. The rest of the meagre jewellery was returned to the caskets, the clothes re-hung. As they tidied up, Amerotke told Nadif exactly what had happened the previous evening; how the Rekhet had approached him just as he left the temple. Nadif, squatting on the floor, heard him out.

'Tonight, Standard-Bearer, what are you doing?'

'Roast goose,' Nadif replied. 'My wife has promised to make me a dish I'll never forget.'

'Leave that.' Amerotke went over and sat down near the standard-bearer. 'Come for dinner at my house, I need to discuss matters with you. But first,' he helped Nadif up, 'we have a librarian for you to talk to.'

TEKHAR: ancient Egyptian, ‘frightening’

CHAPTER 5

They left the heset's chamber and went out into the busy temple grounds. Pilgrims were queuing up for various shrines and chapels. Visitors stood to gape and stare; acolyte priests moved amongst these trying to help. From the coolness of the colonnades, the temple police kept a watchful eye on the proceedings. A group of beggars, their thin-ribbed bodies clothed in rags, were being marshalled into an orderly line before the great double doors of the granary, where stewards prepared to deal out measures of free grain. The sun was now at its full strength, dazzling off the limestone walls and the red-basalt copper-tipped obelisks. Workmen balancing on planks were shouting as they worked on stripping the courses off a wall in preparation for new ones. They stopped to whistle and shout as four pretty temple girls, ankle bracelets jingling, walked saucily by, balancing on their heads plaited reed baskets containing offerings for some altar: conical loaves of bread, the dangling heads of dead waterfowl, and gleaming green vegetables. An overseer shouted angrily. The girls, hips swinging, passed on and the labourers resumed their work. The tap of mallet and copper chisel drifted out on the dusty air. Priests walked by, shaven heads gleaming, the skirts of their voluminous robes folded over their right arms; on their chests, the square pectorals of office shimmered in the sunlight.

Amerotke and Nadif fought their way through the throng. They became lost, and a servant had to take them over to Minnakht's office chamber, which was situated in a small, wall-enclosed courtyard, a soothing, pleasant place containing a fountain splashing merrily, surrounded by a grassy verge and flowerbeds rich in colour. In each corner of the courtyard stood a water clock: conical blue vases decorated with astrological signs and symbols with twelve red lines drawn around the outside. At the bottom of each vase was a carving of a baboon, sacred to Thoth, and between its feet a specially cut hole so the water inside could trickle out one section at a time to mark the passing of each hour. There were also sundials, as well as apparatus for measuring the time at night.

Minnakht met them on the steps to his chamber and apologised laughingly for his absorption with the measurement and calculation of time. Inside it was no different. The walls of the lavishly furnished room were decorated with symbols of Thoth and pictures of baboons squatting on cushions measuring out the skeins of time. At the far end of the chamber stood a row of tables, on each a cluster of beeswax candles, carefully ringed, to record the passing of the hours. Minnakht, still quietly mocking his 'hobby' as he called it, waved Amerotke and Nadif to cushions where a gloomy-faced Maben sat cradling a cup of wine.

'You asked to see me?' Amerotke settled himself. 'What is the matter?'

'Something Minnakht said we should have informed you about when you visited Ipuye's house.' Maben leaned forward. 'Four years ago Ipuye posted a reward for the capture of the Rekhet; the reward was later sent to the Temple of Ptah, but something else happened. Shortly after the proclamation was made, Ipuye – I believe it was during the hot season – decided to eat his evening meal on the roof of his house.'

'Long after the disappearance of his wife?'

'Oh yes, at least a month. Anyway, the servants poured out the wine, and one of them sipped at a goblet and immediately fell ill. The man was lucky: apparently he vomited whatever he'd drunk. When they tested the flask of wine they found poison mingled in it. At first Ipuye couldn't understand how that had been done: his mansion lies beyond the city walls, and only friends and servants were allowed in.'

'So,' Amerotke asked, 'how *was* it done?'

'It was pointed out,' Maben continued, 'that during the hot season Ipuye hired servants and gardeners, occasional labourers to do certain work in both the garden and the house. He suspected that one of these was the Rekhet, who, somehow, had slipped into the kitchen and mingled poison with the wine. After that, Ipuye was very careful. He actually said that he would eat nothing unless it was specially prepared by our sister Meryet. Ipuye always liked Meryet's cooking. Whatever their difficulties, he trusted her implicitly, and after that there were no further incidents.'

'The same happened to me.' Minnakht spoke up. 'As you know, gifts are sent to the temple. I was given a small jug of wine, covered and tagged, proclaiming the date and place of vintage.' He smiled. 'Any Theban would recognise it as the finest of a very good crop of grapes. Of course, I looked forward to enjoying it. Now such gifts are left outside my chamber.' He gestured at the door. 'I thought it was some pilgrim, or perhaps a colleague I'd helped. I brought the jug in here. I remember being absorbed with my calculations. I poured a cup of wine and drank some of it. I'd just cleansed my mouth with water, and although the wine tasted delicious, I caught a slight tinge. I looked at the jug. There was nothing wrong, but I did detect a slight odour beneath the wine fumes. I immediately threw the wine out, but a short while later felt nauseous. Of course at the time the temple was fully absorbed with the horrific poisonings in the city. I'd heard suspicions that the Rekhet might be a member of the Temple of Ptah. I panicked. I actually made myself vomit, but for days afterwards, Lord Judge, as the record attests, I was very, very ill.'

'And why are you telling me this now?' Amerotke asked.

'Two possible reasons: Hinqui has been moved to the temple hospital. Perhaps it is a contagion, perhaps something he ate. Or secondly . . .'

'The work of the Rekhet?' Nadif asked. 'Wreaking revenge as he did on Hutepa?'

'Precisely,' Minnakht replied. 'But also to give both of you a warning. If you are hunting the Rekhet, he may strike at you or yours.'

'He already has.' Amerotke swiftly told them about the confrontation the previous evening. Both Minnakht and Maben looked frightened.

'So he did get in here!' Maben exclaimed. 'Into the temple. No wonder poor Hutepa died.'

Amerotke felt tempted to ask them further about the Rekhet. He decided not to, he would trust no one except Nadif, with whom he planned to converse later in the day.

'Lord Judge?'

'Yes, Minnakht?'

'The three scribes who died, have you discovered anything?'

'Why should I?' Amerotke shrugged. 'How can I? Tell me who was responsible for the preparation of the wine.'

'Lord Ani,' Minnakht and Maben answered together. 'In fact,' Minnakht continued, 'Lord Ani supervised all the proceedings. I mean, the ritual is laid out but the wine itself was taken from the High Priest's store. He himself brought both jug and bowl into the temple. He insisted that he serve the Libyans and our scribes. Apart from that, Lord Judge, I cannot add anything.'

'And Hutepa's murder?' Maben asked. 'You searched her chamber?'

Amerotke chewed on the corner of his lip and stared up at the window. The sunlight was still fierce and strong. He felt very tired. He had not slept well the previous evening, his mind agitated, his belly upset.

'Hutepa?' Maben insisted.

Amerotke abruptly realised he could not trust this priest. In fact, he trusted no one in the Temple of Ptah. 'What we found was interesting but nothing remarkable.' He stretched and got to his feet. 'Well now, gentlemen, I bid you good day.'

'Where are you going?' Minnakht asked.

'To the temple library,' Amerotke replied. 'Standard-Bearer Nadif, will you accompany me?'

They made their farewells, left the chamber and made their way back on to the temple concourse. Once they were well away, Amerotke paused and gripped Nadif by the wrist.

'You're very quiet, Standard-Bearer.'

Nadif's thin face broke into a smile. 'And so are you, Lord Judge. Here we are in the Temple of Ptah, which housed the Rekhet. Fifty years ago another great assassin lurked here.' He sighed deeply. 'I don't know what to say. I feel that when I'm here I cannot trust anyone. I don't want to talk to anyone. I don't want to give them my opinion, speculate or reflect, and I suspect neither do you, Lord Judge. Oh, by the way, why are we going to the library?'

'You'll see.' Amerotke walked on.

When they reached the House of Books, the librarian was clearly not pleased to see Amerotke. Nevertheless, the judge took him into one of the reading chambers and sat him down on a ledge beneath a window.

'I don't need to see any manuscripts,' Amerotke began. 'I want to ask you some questions. A temple girl, the heset Hutepa, was poisoned last night; you must have heard?'

The librarian nodded.

'I know she came here,' Amerotke continued. 'She asked to see certain archives or records, is that correct?'

The librarian licked his dry lips and stared beyond Amerotke; Nadif stood against the door with Shufoy crouching next to him. In fact, Shufoy was sobering up, beginning to absorb what had happened, what concerned his master about this case. He had also heard the warnings delivered by Minnakht, and fully intended that once they returned to Amerotke's house, he would make sure no danger threatened.

'Hutepa,' Amerotke repeated. 'You knew her?'

'I met her here,' the librarian replied. 'A comely girl . . . I mean, she had no right to be here; the House of Books is meant for scholars.'

Just a shift in his eyes, his nervous gestures, made Amerotke suspicious. He studied the librarian carefully: a lecherous man, he thought, and wondered if Hutepa had bought his attention with her favours.

'You are Overseer of the Books?' Amerotke leaned so close he could smell the slight oily fragrance of the librarian. 'I'm asking you a question, sir. I do not want to bring Lord Senenmut down here or summon you into my court and put you on oath over the Sacred Books. So I want you to answer my question. Hutepa came here? Yes?'

The librarian nodded vigorously, eager to get rid of this inquisitive judge.

'And she asked you for archives you'd usually deny to a heset?'

'Histories,' the librarian conceded. He informed Amerotke in halting sentences how Hutepa was a constant visitor to the library. She had inveigled her way in with her winsome ways and asked to study histories and chronicles of the temple.

In the end Amerotke was satisfied. He thanked the librarian and, followed by Nadif and Shufoy, left the House of Books. They stood under the shade of a cluster of ageing holm oaks which looked as if they had been growing since the beginning of time.

'What was that about, master?' Shufoy asked.

'What was it about?' Amerotke retorted. 'I suspect

Hutepa spent most of her time searching for the identity of the author of the Ari Sapu, who worked here fifty years ago and wreaked such terrible damage. And this is the paradox.' He put one hand on Shufoy's shoulder, the other on Nadif's. 'According to you, Nadif, Hutepa actually directed you to where the Rekhet was hiding and you arrested him. However, she then spends considerable time studying the history of this temple as well as that of the author of the Ari Sapu. The mystery then deepens. Yesterday evening a man entered her room, slept in her bed; possibly her killer. So on the one hand we have Hutepa the traitor betraying the priest physician to you. On the other, Hutepa spent a great deal of her time, perhaps even trading her favours, to gain access to temple archives to discover the truth about the Ari Sapu. She then entertains the escaped prisoner only to be murdered by him. It's a riddle of contradictions and doesn't make sense.'

Amerotke left the shade of the trees and stood for a while easing the tension of his neck in the warmth of the sun.

'Where to now, master?' Shufoy called.

'Home,' Amerotke replied. He smiled at Nadif. 'I want to walk amongst lapis lazuli, paddle my feet in water and see what happens . . .'

Amenuefer, captain of the Glory of Sobeck, a cohort of the premier squadron of the Pride of Amun, had grown abruptly wary. He had, on his own initiative, decided to take his unit deeper into the western desert to establish if the peace the Libyans wanted was genuine. He and his superiors had discussed that very fact after evening sacrifice in their regimental chapel the previous day. They had squatted in the small garden courtyard, feasting on strips of well-cooked goose, leavened bread and dishes of vegetables. His superiors had unanimously agreed that the death of the three scribes during the peace ceremony at the Temple of Ptah was a judgement from the gods on an agreement that should never have been sealed in the first place. Amenuefer's colonel had slurped his wine, tapped the side of his fleshy nose and confided that General Omendap, commander-in-chief of Pharaoh's armies, had his own suspicions but what was the use? The Divine One's heart was fixed on peace, whilst Grand Vizier Senenmut was of a similar mind. No one in the mess had dared joke about when and how Lord Senenmut had provided such advice to the Divine One; that was a matter best left alone. However, Amenuefer had listened and reflected very carefully. If peace was established, where was the prospect of glory? Of promotion? Of winning the Golden Bees of bravery or the Silver Collar of Valour? Accordingly, he had decided to swing out along the hard shell of the desert edge and go further than his orders allowed. He'd discover what was truly happening beyond the Tuthmosis Line, the border defined by Hatusu's dead husband as the first direct sphere of Egyptian influence.

Amenuefer had led his twelve chariots deeper into the western desert. In fact, he'd really made the decision before he left the barracks, ordering the lightest six-spoked chariots, the strongest horses and twice the amount of provisions: black bread that could be softened in water, dried meat, and extra gazelle skins of water. He had not been disappointed. Something very intriguing was happening. At first they'd discovered the vast tracts of rocky desert quiet and empty until they began to intercept the traders: caravans moving across the desert to the north or the borders of the Great Green, merchants of every nation with their strange dress and outlandish ways. Amenuefer had questioned them and they'd replied how they'd been bartering with the mines in the eastern desert along the Horus Road in Sinai so that their panniers and baskets were crammed with uncut gold, silver and precious stones, items they'd bought with skins and other goods. Amenuefer, as he proceeded further beyond the Tuthmosis Line, had met similar caravans, bands of traders, groups of merchants all intent on reaching the Oasis of Khannu; this lay deep in Libyan territory, bestriding the main trade route to the Libyans' principal harbour on the Great Green. Amenuefer had never seen such trade before or men so keen to reach their destination. The single traders and solitary merchants provoked no suspicion. However, amongst the larger groups he had detected Libyans dressed in the striped robes of desert wanderers and sand-dwellers and, by their bearing and attitude, obviously soldiers.

Amenuefer now regretted his openness towards them. His questioning of the merchants had been too blunt; perhaps he'd aroused their suspicions. They had certainly aroused his. He had ignored the advice of his standard-bearer and continued to strike west to the Oasis of Plenty, a small but fertile plot with shaded trees, luxurious bushes and long spiked grass sprouting around a well which provided a never-ending supply of sweet water, a welcome relief after the rocky dust and constant glare of the sun. Evening was coming, darkness falling, the sun setting fast in a molten glow that changed the colour of both desert and sky. Already the silence of the day was giving way to the tangled noise of the night: the griping laugh of the jackal, the roar of lions, the coughing bark of the prowlers of the dark attracted to the oasis not only by water but by the sweet smell of food and the plump flesh of horses. Amenuefer was not concerned about these. During the last part of the march, as his chariots became clogged with sand so that they proceeded more slowly, his scouts had reported dark shapes in the rocks and gulleys. In the end they'd arrived safely enough, and the men were now settling for the night, the air full of the smell of sweaty leather, horses, dung and cooking. He'd arranged the chariots into a protective line, a barricade against surprise attack, and sent out scouts, but they'd not yet returned.

Amenuefer fingered his collarette and wondered if he'd made the right decision. He hoped to return to Thebes with news that would startle his superiors; now he was more concerned whether he'd be allowed to return at all. He looked over his shoulder at the welcoming glow of the fire, his men grouped about laughing and talking amongst themselves, his subordinates moving through the shadowed trees ensuring all was well. They'd caught their captain's nervousness. Amenuefer cursed. What could the Libyans be plotting, and why were those traders flocking to that oasis? If he could only discover the reason! If he did survive the night, he would not return to Thebes but would strike directly for the oasis of Khannu; perhaps under the semblance of friendship even approach the Libyan City of the Serpents. He stared up at the sky. The sun was slipping down like a coppery coin, the darkness swooping in, the sky turning blue-black, the stars hanging heavy. He heard a sound and looked up. Four figures were scrambling down a rocky face, stumbling towards the oasis. His scouts had returned! He recognised the headdresses, the glittering amulets round their necks. He looked back at the chariots, then, eager for news, walked swiftly towards the approaching figures.

'What news?' he called. 'What news?'

The scouts kept racing towards him. Amenuefer paused. There was something about them . . . he glimpsed a beard, a moustache. These weren't . . .

He turned, but all four figures suddenly stopped, their powerful Syrian bows drawn. Arrows whirled through the air; three of them took Amenuefer, one in the neck, the other two in his back. He staggered towards the oasis but found he couldn't speak. His breath wouldn't come, blood thickened at the back of his throat, then he collapsed.

Now the rest of the Libyans poured in. Armed with shields, spears, sword clubs and maces, they swept like shadows across the sand into the oasis, stabbing and hacking, showing no mercy. The Egyptian chariot squadron, caught by surprise, tried to fight. A few of the officers made a last stand near the waterhole, but just as the sun finally set, every Egyptian lay dead. The Libyan war chief walked through the camp, ensuring that no wounded survived, ordering the neck of each corpse to be hacked, searching the bushes and rocks for any survivors who might have crawled away. There was none.

The Libyans finished the meal the Egyptians had been preparing and drank their wine. Afterwards the war chief gestured at the corpses.

'Take them out,' he ordered, 'deep into the desert. Bury them in the sand, their armour with them.' He walked over to a chariot. 'Take all of these. Burn them completely, strip the horses of their harness. Let the Egyptians think this chariot squadron has disappeared from the face of the earth, for in truth, it has . . .'

* * *

'It's a game,' the judge announced as he smiled at his two sons, Curfay and Ahmase.

'Are you sure, light of my life?' Norfret, Amerotke's wife, teased.

The judge just winked at her and turned away.

'Nadif, Shufoy, we'll all take part. Now, Shufoy, do what you have to.'

Amerotke had returned home late in the afternoon. He and Nadif had been greeted by Norfret. They had washed their hands and feet, then eaten and drunk in the shade of the sycamore trees. They'd watched the brilliantly plumaged birds swoop low over the lake of purity, admiring the plants and flowers Amerotke himself had planted. Norfret was full of questions about what had happened in the city. She had heard about the poisonings in the temple and, of course, the escape of the Rekhet was common knowledge. Amerotke had kissed her tenderly and told her to wait. His two sons were growing older; both had a tendency to stand by doors and listen. He didn't want them frightened or to realise the dangers their father sometimes encountered. Moreover, Amerotke was uneasy. He'd listened very carefully to Maben and Minnakht's warning. They were correct. If the Rekhet had already approached him, why should he stop there? The judge's mansion to the north of Thebes was well known and the criminal had more than demonstrated his skill for inflicting sudden, brutal death.

Once Amerotke and Nadif had rested, they'd

organised this game; at least that was how Amerotke described it. Shufoy was now sprinkling lapis lazuli around the tiled edges of the pool, spreading it thickly. When he had finished, Amerotke took off his robe and, dressed in his loincloth, went and walked on the lapis lazuli, feeling it crunch under his feet. Norfret and his two sons joined in enthusiastically, Nadif more reluctantly, while Shufoy danced up and down making Amerotke's sons laugh even louder. Once Amerotke was satisfied, he then asked everyone to sit on the edge of the pool, feet in the water, to shake and kick to their hearts' content. For a while the garden echoed to the sounds of laughter and the shouted questions that Amerotke refused to answer. At last he announced that the game would continue. They would dry their feet and ankles with linen cloths, then each would take a small piece of papyrus provided by Shufoy and see if there was any gold dust either on their feet or between their toes.

Amerotke was intrigued by the conclusions. Everyone, somewhere, had traces of the gold dust on them. Even though they had washed their feet vigorously, it seemed to cling to the very skin, particularly between the toes and in the contours around the ankle. Amerotke, face now serious, experimented again, this time slipping into the pool and walking to and fro. Again, despite vigorous drying, traces of the gold dust remained. He quietly asked Norfret to take the boys away, then he, Nadif and

Shufoy retreated to the shade of the sycamore to discuss their findings.

'You are sure, Shufoy,' Amerotke asked, 'that the Overseer found no traces of lapis lazuli on the feet or ankles of the two victims?'

'Master, I went and searched myself. Something interesting, master: the Overseer also pointed out that both bodies had been well oiled, in other words—'

'In other words,' Nadif broke in excitedly, 'if the skin on the feet and ankles was oiled, the lapis lazuli would stick even more closely. Ipuye and Khiat entered that pavilion, but never went into the pool alive. Shortly after they'd oiled their skin against the sun, the assassin struck.'

'Could the oil have been poisoned?' Shufoy asked.

Nadif shook his head. 'I smelt the jug: nothing! Moreover, remember, I did not detect, nor did the Overseer of the Dead, any trace or symptom of poisoning.'

Amerotke closed his eyes and tried to recall what he had been told at Ipuye's house. 'The guards did not report anything untoward, though they heard voices and a little splashing. Was that when Ipuye and Khiat died?'

'Perhaps,' Nadif said slowly. 'We now have two reasons to consider their deaths mysterious. First that a vigorous man and a very healthy young woman both drowned in the same pool at the same time without any alarm being raised. Yes?'

Amerotke nodded.

'Second,' Nadif continued, 'if Ipuye and Khiat had walked into the pool and an accident occurred, some traces of the lapis lazuli would have been found on their feet, yet we found nothing at all, which means, Lord Judge, that either Ipuye and Khiat entered the pool and, most remarkably, managed to wash away all traces of the lapis lazuli . . .'

Amerotke stared gloomily back.

'Or they were carried to the pool,' Shufoy declared. 'In which case they must have been either dead or unconscious before they ever reached the water. Yet there is no mark of violence, no trace of poison, so what is the solution?'

KEFAI: ancient Egyptian, 'to be uncovered'

CHAPTER 6

A short while later, Amerotke, Norfret, Nadif and Shufoy sat down to dine on the roof of the judge's house. Darkness had fallen like a veil. The stars hung bright like blossoms against the heavens. A full moon in all its glory rode the night sky. Norfret had lit the lamps in their pure alabaster jars; they now sparkled like costly stones. It was a pleasant, refreshing night, with a faint breeze, like the breath of a god, that fanned away the pervasive heat which stifled the breath and soaked the skin. From the garden below rose a cacophony of sound, as nighthawks called and crickets chattered above the croak of bullfrogs. Norfret had prepared a tasty meal, nourishing but light: lamb tajine cooked in onions, olive oil, garlic, cumin and chickpeas. Amerotke had opened a cask from Imit; the wine was cool and delicate on the tongue. He waited until the goblets were full before describing the events of the day. He tried to minimise the danger, but Norfret was too sharp; she fully understood the threat facing her husband, and grew so agitated, she snatched the necklace from round her lovely neck and wiped the perfumed sweat off her throat.

'This is dangerous,' she whispered. 'Amerotke, you face a fiend!'

'And fiends can be trapped,' Amerotke retorted, breathing in the cool night air. He sat for a while, secretly willing that Norfret realise this was a path he must follow. It would bring them preferment, honour and riches, but also great danger.

'I have,' Shufoy abruptly spoke up, 'approached the Churat, the Eater of Vile Things in the underworld.'

Amerotke stared disbelievingly at his dwarfish friend.

'Well,' Shufoy shrugged, 'that's what he calls himself. He wants to meet. He needs to discuss a common problem with you.'

'Shufoy, when did you arrange this?'

'Today,' Shufoy replied, 'as I busied myself on my master's errands.'

Amerotke nodded understandingly. He was always fascinated by Shufoy's knowledge of the Am-duat, the seedy, violent underbelly of Thebes.

'The Churat,' Nadif spoke up, fortified by the wine, 'is a leader of a guild of assassins as well as a receiver of stolen goods. He is a man we much suspect though there's little evidence against him. Anyway, what in the name of Horus does he want?'

'I don't know,' Shufoy replied. 'However, while I was scurrying here and there in the Temple of Ptah, I saw one of his standard-bearers, Skullface, skulking in the shadows. He'd been sent in to find out what was happening. I told him as little as possible. Skullface declared that his master sent humble greetings to the Lord Judge and would His Holiness,' Shufoy laughed at the flattering title, 'graciously visit him around the fourth hour tomorrow? He asked me to tell you, Lord Judge,' he continued sarcastically, 'that he is unable to visit you as he prefers not to leave the Abode of Darkness.' Shufoy shrugged. 'I replied that you'd be most pleased to meet him; after all, he may have valuable information. But there again, master,' he added quickly, 'if you'd prefer not to go . . .'

'I will come with you,' Nadif volunteered. 'Lord Judge, the Churat is treacherous. Indeed, for a while people considered he might have been the Rekhet.'

'We'll go tomorrow,' Amerotke declared. 'Let's return to the business in hand. What do we have? Ipuye and Khiat drowned in that pool guarded by mercenaries: no violence, no potions, no intruders. We have two slender strands of evidence: the most remarkable and mysterious coincidence that they drowned at the same time in the same place, as well as the possibility that they did not walk into the pool because no trace of lapis lazuli has yet been found on them.' Amerotke sipped from his goblet. 'That's tenuous, to say the least. The water could have washed it off, especially as both corpses may have been floating there for some time. Ipuye did declare himself the public opponent of the Rekhet, but there is no evidence that their deaths were caused by poison. What else, Shufoy?'

'The business of his first wife,' the dwarf said between mouthfuls, 'who simply disappeared.'

'Yes, yes.' Amerotke squinted through the darkness. 'The woman simply disappeared, after burning her wedding collarette and marriage bracelet. Meryet believes Ipuye murdered her. At first a rather surprising claim, because Ipuye had left for business at Memphis. However, according to that merchant's own records, he did not. He stayed in Thebes at what he called his "Place of Pleasure", a room above a jeweller's shop in the precious stone market of the city, another place we'll visit tomorrow.'

'Why did he lie?' Nadif spoke up. 'He could have slipped back to that mansion and killed his wife; perhaps Meryet is correct. The grounds of the House of the Golden Vine should be searched thoroughly for her corpse.'

Amerotke nodded. 'Shufoy, tomorrow morning send a messenger to Asural, captain of my temple guard. Tell him to take a detachment of men out to the House of the Golden Vine. The gardens are to be scrupulously searched. They are looking for a shallow grave concealing the corpse of a woman.'

'You'll find her corpse.' Norfret spoke up, her voice clear and carrying.

Amerotke smiled at his wife. 'What makes you say that?'

Norfret tapped the side of her head. 'A woman's logic. Look, Lord Judge, if I was unhappy here . . .' She fluttered her eyelids. 'Let us say you were the most difficult man to live with, a lecher, a womaniser; why should that make me leave the luxury of this mansion to go wandering the streets of some city? There were other courses of action open to Ipuye's first wife. My dear, I doubt very much if any woman would leave such a beautiful house. I know the Golden Vine, I'd simply fight back. I doubt if Patuna ever left at all.'

Amerotke smiled to himself. He hadn't thought of that. He had simply accepted the logical conclusion that if a woman was unhappy, she would leave. Indeed, never once had Maben or the others indicated that there were other alternatives open to Patuna.

'Do what I ask, Shufoy,' he murmured. 'Tomorrow morning tell Asural also to take some labourers and gardeners from the temple. They must, literally, leave no stone unturned.'

'And so we come to the poisonings, Lord Judge.'

'Yes, yes, we do, Nadif. What do we know? About fifty years ago, the author of the Ari Sapu became an expert, skilled in poisons. He dealt out sudden brutal death in Thebes. According to tradition he was apprehended, tried and buried alive. Legends claims his tomb lies somewhere in the temple grounds, which also contain the Books of Doom, the Ari Sapu. Whether that is true or not, we don't really know. Nevertheless, about four years ago the Rekhet emerges and citizens are murdered. This is where I really want your help, Nadif. Who were the victims? What did they have in common?'

'I can only tell what you know already, Lord Judge. The victims came from every class, though most of them were merchants, nobles and officials. One thing they did have in common was that they, or someone related to them, had recently visited the Temple of Ptah.'

'How do you know that?' Norfret asked.

'During my enquiries I asked to see the records of all the various temple chapels and shrines. I soon recognised how the names of visitors were also the names of the Rekhet's victims. Of course, the temple authorities suspected something was wrong. Lord Ani often met with me to discuss the matter. Eventually he informed me that he'd been approached by a group of priest physicians led by Userbati. They maintained they were certain the Rekhet was a member of the temple hierarchy but they had yet to find firm evidence.' Nadif spread his hands. 'The rest you know. Userbati and his colleagues held a supper party at which they ate or drank some poison and died violent deaths. I was called to the temple. I viewed their corpses, then searched Userbati's dwelling, where I found references to the killer. We invaded his chamber in the temple, found powders and potions, as well as considerable wealth, and started searching for him. Lord Ani told us that the suspect was friendly with the heset Hutepa. We questioned her . . .' Nadif paused, as if listening to the bullfrogs croaking through the darkness. 'She told us that the Rekhet had fled into Thebes, hiding in a house near the coppersmiths' quarter. We arrested him there. Due to the influence of the temple, he was given a choice: he could go on public trial and plead his innocence, or he could admit his guilt and throw himself on Pharaoh's mercy. He chose the latter and was dispatched to the prison oasis.'

'You are sure you arrested the right man?' Amerotke asked.

'I think so,' Nadif replied slowly. 'The Rekhet remained quiet, assured, very calm. He gave no details; after a while he confessed and would say no more. I had my doubts, but there again, there was Userbati's reference to him in a document, the powders and potions found in his chamber, not to mention the curse he'd written out. More importantly,' Nadif continued, 'once he was arrested, the poisonings stopped.'

'Did he confess to discovering the Ari Sapu?'

'No, when asked that, he simply replied that there were many treatises on poison.'

'And how did he murder his victims?'

'Again he was enigmatic, pointing out that he had confessed and had little more to add.'

'And Hutepa?'

'She protested her innocence. She'd assisted us in the Rekhet's arrest; there was no reason to believe she was involved.'

'Did the Rekhet have any family?'

Nadif shrugged.

'And his escape?' Amerotke asked. 'How was that managed?'

'Sheer daring, cunning and courage: he apparently wandered off into the desert and was captured by sand-dwellers who'd also captured an Egyptian merchant. The sand-dwellers were jubilant; as you know, they sell their prisoners as slaves for great profit. This band were most unfortunate. They encountered an Egyptian chariot squadron out on the edge of the desert, the squadron attacked and the sand-dwellers resisted. In the mêlée the merchant was killed. The quick-witted Rekhet took his identity, so when the Egyptians questioned him they thought they were talking to a merchant whom they'd liberated rather than an escaped prisoner. When they returned to Thebes, of course the Rekhet disappeared. It was quite some time before the Mayor of Thebes realised the full truth of the situation, but by then, what could be done?'

'You have a description of the Rekhet?'

'Yes,' Nadif laughed, 'one which would fit half of Thebes: medium height, black hair, pleasant faced, but of course he is now probably disguised behind shaggy hair and a bushy beard. Lord Judge, I cannot provide you with a worthwhile description.'

'Nor can you give me any solution,' Amerotke replied testily. 'The Rekhet is back in Thebes. We suspect he visited Hutepa, possibly made love to her, then killed her, but why such cruel callousness? I cannot make sense of that, nor of Hutepa searching for the whereabouts of the tomb of the widow of the author of the Ari Sapu. Oh, by the way, that is another place we must visit, and very soon. Yet now,' Amerotke continued, 'we're faced with the Rekhet's return. Was he responsible for the deaths of those three scribes? They drank the same wine from the same bowl as the Libyans, who suffered no ill effects; the Egyptian envoys drank and, a short while later, all three fell ill and died in hideous circumstances . . .'

In the Silver Acacia Chamber which lay at the heart of the small imperial palace in the Temple of Ptah, Hatusu and Senenmut sat together like children, dabbling their feet in the Pool of Purity which the architect had cunningly fashioned at the centre of the chamber on the ground floor of the palace. The room was built so that three of its walls overlooked a rich garden filled with flowers, trees and shrubs from all parts of the empire. The perfume from the banked flowers drifted through the open window, filling the chamber with an exotic scent. In a pool of lanternlight in the garden, an orchestra of Mitanni musicians, a gift from a client king, heightened the rapture with melodious tunes on the lyre, harp and lute. Hatusu listened intently as she studied one of the small golden carp twisting and turning away from her painted toenails. She startled as a brilliantly plumaged bird fluttered through one of the windows, wings flapping frantically as it swooped, rose, turned and fled back into the starlit night.

'Hush now.' Senenmut pressed callused fingers against her smooth thigh. 'Sweeter than the honeycomb are thee,' he smiled, quoting from a poem. 'And your thoughts?'

'Murder!' Hatusu snapped. 'Murder and chaos on that temple forecourt. Naratousha grinning behind his hands, revelling in Egypt's discomfort.'

'He could be the one responsible,' Senenmut declared.

'I doubt it.' Hatusu splashed her feet noisily, then laughed. 'I feel like a little girl,' she murmured, 'having a temper fit because my father wouldn't see me. Of course this,' her lovely face hardened, 'is more serious. The murder of three scribes is Amerotke's business; the Libyans are ours.' She withdrew her feet.

'Why don't we eat?' Senenmut pointed to the dais in the far corner where everything was readied for the evening meal.

'In a while.' Hatusu was determined on her own thoughts. 'Why do the Libyans want peace? They've suffered no military setback. Until recently their tribes wandered the western desert, pillaging, plundering and robbing as long as they thought they'd escape unscathed.' She put her feet back in the water. 'We have agreed to respect their camps, merchants and traders. They have not asked us to withdraw our chariot patrols or small garrisons at certain oases. None of our troops have reported anything, and your spies . . . ?'

'Very little,' Senenmut replied. 'Libyan trade with the Sinai mines has increased but there is no report of the clans massing or organising. Strange,' he mused, 'that merchant the sand-dwellers captured along with the escaped Rekhet, whose identity the poisoner later assumed . . .'

'What about him?' Hatusu snapped, then sighed. 'My lord,' she leaned closer and kissed him lightly on the cheek, 'I apologise, but the heart becomes tired and the soul weary . . .'

'He was one of my best spies,' Senenmut replied, staring down at the water. 'He knew the desert tongue; he went deeper into the Redlands than any of the others. I wonder if he saw or heard something extraordinary. The Libyans do not concern me for the moment, except just before I came here,' he gestured with his head towards the door, 'a squadron commander in the Glory of Amun claimed a chariot patrol hasn't returned. It was led by one of our glory-seekers, a young captain. I just wonder. At first light, before the brilliant hour, I am going to dispatch two squadrons into the desert to investigate. Perhaps they might find something. What truly concerns me,' Senenmut withdrew his feet and stood up, 'is the Sea People. You know their warships have been seen off the delta, packed with men, painted, feathered and armed? Our ships have driven them off but they seem to be massing again, going back across the Great Green to small islands for fresh water before returning. It's as if they're probing for a weakness . . .'

'I'll give them weakness!' Hatusu stood up and went across to a beautiful stool carved out of acacia wood, its surface brilliantly cushioned in scarlet and gold. She picked up her robe lying next to it, put it around her and tightly tied the embroidered sash about her waist. 'Look, my lord,' she patted her stomach and gestured to where the oil lamps gleamed along the ledges above the eating tables, 'now we shall eat and drink,' she smiled mischievously, 'and who knows?'

Senenmut was about to engage in this teasing banter when he heard a hideous scream outside, followed by the crash of dishes. He hastened to the door and threw it open; down the painted passageway, a servant lay jerking on the floor, members of the Maryannou and Nakhtu-aa gathered about him. Other servants were screaming and yelling, pointing to a table where platters of food had been laid out in preparation for Pharaoh's evening meal. Senenmut hurried down, heart beating, sweat prickling his skin.

'Stand aside!' Officers and servants drew apart, and Senenmut stared in horror at the man jerking and kicking on the floor, mouth frothing. He gestured towards the platters of food. 'What happened?'

'My lord,' an officer replied, 'the cold meats and fruit had been left here, waiting for your summons. One of the servants became hungry.' He pointed to a dish of roast quail cut into neat pieces and covered with a delicious-looking sauce. 'We would have tasted the food anyway,' he continued, 'but he was so hungry he stole a piece, and paid for it . . .'

Senenmut stared down at the man. The hideous strangling sound had stopped; only his legs and feet jerked spasmodically. His face had turned a mottled hue, tongue popping, white saliva dribbling from his mouth. Senenmut pushed aside the officer and stepped around the dying man.

'How?' he demanded.

'My lord,' the chief cook came forward, 'the imperial kitchens are open; we had visitors, traders bringing in supplies . . .'

'In future,' Senenmut shouted at the cowed officers, 'the kitchens are to be guarded! Every jug of wine, every morsel of food prepared for the Divine One must be tasted.'

In the House of Books at the Temple of Ptah the librarian was also preparing for his evening meal. This was the hour of the day he liked most. He could lock the doors and sit here in his own private office: the lamps flaring merrily, a jug of wine, a platter of meat and fresh bread from the temple kitchens ready to enjoy whilst he pored over the delicious scenes of ladies making love in a book some long-dead merchant had bequeathed to the temple. The librarian treasured this manuscript above all others. He found certain scenes particularly delightful. He studied the pictures of cavorting young women, dressed only in oil-drenched black wigs, as they posed on the floor, stools or couches, he moaned with pleasure, hand slipping down to his crotch. He poured a goblet of wine and sipped from it carefully, then removed the linen covering from the platter and began to chew noisily on a piece of cooked quail in its tangy sauce. He was on to his second mouthful, pulling up the roll of papyrus so he could study one scene more closely, when he felt the first stab of discomfort. Others followed, as if his belly was on fire, the pain spreading up through his chest and round to his back. His legs felt as if they had turned to water. He tried to rise but couldn't. He doubled up in pain, pushing back the cushion, arching, trying to soothe the hideous tension. Even as he did so, he glimpsed the first brand drop through the open window and fall on to a stack of manuscripts. The flames, licking greedily, spread swiftly. The librarian opened his mouth to scream, but he couldn't breathe. He wanted to escape that pain even as his dying eyes glimpsed an oilskin hurled through the window to turn the entire chamber into a raging furnace.

* * *

Amerotke and Standard-Bearer Nadif, accompanied by two burly Medjay, bracelets and rings of office glittering on their right arms and hands, vicious-looking war clubs pushed into their belts, walked through the Lion Gate of Thebes and into the city. The brilliant hour had passed. Already the Breath of Amun, the refreshing dawn breeze, had disappeared. The sun was glaringly strong, the heat already making itself felt. The basalt-paved Avenue of Sphinxes was hot underfoot and a dusty heat haze swirled. Above this the gold- and silver-capped obelisks, temple cornices and malachite-edged gables of the palaces flashed back the light of the sun. Donkeys, strings of pack mules and carts were busy making their way down to the markets. Wine booths and beer tents were open, the air rich with cooking smells. Traders and tinkers with their makeshift stalls were shouting their calls, one eye ever vigilant for the market police. A group of priests garbed in saffron robes, oil gleaming on their shaven heads, hurried down to the river carrying the *naos* of their god on a reed-plaited punt. They chanted as they hastened along. Every so often they would stop, close their eyes, clap, shake their sistra and ring little handbells before continuing their procession. Through the morning air echoed the blare of temple conch horns, the clash of cymbals and the booming of gongs. A group of Danga dwarfs, dressed in multi-coloured rags, staged an impromptu play about Bes the Household God. Their faces hidden by grotesque masks, they jumped up and down much to the delight of a group of children on their way to some school under a tree in a dusty square, who shrieked like a gaggle of geese before being shooed on by their teacher.

Amerotke and Nadif left the avenue, going down side streets, the blind walls of the houses rearing above them. They passed merchants' warehouses under heavy guard, full of gold, valuable materials and precious vases, chests and coffers. The gates of some of these were secured by heavy wooden padlocks; others were open so carts could be loaded. The doorways to the adjoining stately merchant mansions were also thrown open. The mistress of the house was busy in one courtyard directing servants to draw water or help the baker to heap handfuls of grain on to the concave quern in order to grind flour to bake fresh bread for the day. Outside, more servants, armed with tubs, searched the streets for the dung of asses, oxen and sheep, so it could be later ground into a paste, dried in the sun and used for fuel. Doors slammed and opened, voices shouted, whilst in the shadow of all this wealth and business, red-eyed beggars quarrelled over favoured positions for the day's pleading.

Amerotke and Nadif eventually reached the jewellers' quarter, the market of precious stones, and the shop Ipuye had called his 'Place of Pleasure'. This was situated in a tree-fringed market square packed with booths and shops selling Hittite jewellery, sandalwood and gum from Punt as well as a range of fine linen, coral, gold, silver and precious stones. The owner of the shop was preparing his stall in front of the house. He pretended not to know what Amerotke wanted until Nadif pushed himself forward and whispered a threat. A key to a door was hastily produced and Amerotke and Nadif, accompanied by the Medjay, went up the outside staircase. They unlocked the door and went inside. Amerotke immediately whistled under his breath at the opulence of the room. The ceiling consisted of polished strips of timber which ribbed the painted white plaster. The walls were smooth and covered in a lilac colour on which the artist had described love scenes, men and women in various poses, temple girls servicing the god Min, the Lord of the Dance. The furniture was elegantly exquisite: reed matting covered the floor, and a huge bed stood in one corner, with cushions, small stools and tables crowding an eating area beneath one of the large windows. Nadif opened this, pushing back the shutters to allow in more light and air. Amerotke had seen similar rooms throughout the city, places of pleasure where a merchant could retire to be with his girls, prostitutes, whores or courtesans. The coffers and chests around the room contained precious jugs, goblets and platters. Amerotke realised that Ipuye, when he entertained his visitors, must have bought wine, meats and other delicacies from the local shops.

Nadif drew out a chest from beneath the bed, a

reinforced casket with two clasps each secured by a small wooden padlock. He broke these, tipped back the lid, took out two scrolls and handed them to Amerotke. The first was a book of love, full of erotic scenes describing the skills and devices a courtesan might use to please her customer. It was well thumbed and greasy. Amerotke tossed this on to the bed. Many temples in Thebes held such manuscripts describing the finer points of the art of love, the schooling of a courtesan. The second scroll was more surprising; Amerotke had never seen the like before. It was written in a neat hand which, Amerotke concluded, must be Ipuye's, and gave a graphic account of his encounters with various prostitutes, whores, courtesans of the city and other female guests: how they treated him in bed, their different specialities. In this detailed diary of love, Ipuye had given each of his lady friends a name as well as the dates and times they'd visited him: 'Shining Light', 'Betnu the Swift', 'Nebet Ankh the Lady of Life', 'Neshem the Precious Stone', 'Heriet the Terror' – Amerotke smiled at that – and 'Nibit Pi, Mistress of the House'. There were no physical descriptions but Ipuye described their charms and skills, what they preferred and how he had enjoyed them. The judge began to realise why, perhaps, Ipuye's first wife had fled, though the truth of that remained to be established. He placed both scrolls in his linen bag and stared round this chamber of love: at the paintings on the wall, the emblems of Ankh and Sa proclaiming life and happiness; the costly embroidered cushions, the polished furniture, the reed baskets and trays holding writing implements and papyrus, that large bed with its pure white linen sheets. Nadif was still going round the room finishing his own search.

'Every luxury,' he called out over his shoulder. 'Ipuye certainly was a man who loved the things of the flesh.' The standard-bearer came back and squatted before Amerotke. 'And the scrolls, Lord Judge?'

Amerotke quickly described them. Nadif grinned.

'Do you think they were all courtesans and whores?'

'Possibly,' Amerotke declared. 'I have some questions to ask the owner downstairs. Perhaps they might also have been the wives, daughters, sisters perhaps of other merchants, hence the names. Usually famous courtesans assume their own titles, but Ipuye was responsible for these, possibly to conceal their true identity.'

Amerotke paused as the door was flung open and Shufoy marched in. He was hot faced, wafting himself vigorously with an ostentatious fan, its handle carved out of gleaming ebony, the luxuriant folds a brilliant hue. In his other hand he carried a parasol, and he swung this backwards and forwards as if it was a symbol of office.

'That stupid owner!' he bawled, then fell silent as he gazed in astonishment round the chamber, distracted by the vivid, eye-catching wall paintings. 'By the Horns of Hathor, the Lady of Drunkenness,' he breathed. 'What on earth is this?'

'What it looks like.' Amerotke smiled, getting to his feet. 'A paradise of love, Shufoy. You carried out my instructions?'

'Asural, his temple guard and every idler he could collect are now searching the grounds of Ipuye's mansion. The lady Meryet is certainly pleased.'

'Good.' Amerotke smiled. 'Now I understand the Churat is awaiting us, but first, Shufoy, the owner of this establishment . . .'

Back in the street, the jeweller still seemed unwilling to talk. When Amerotke threatened him with the two Medjay standing on guard at the foot of the outside steps, the fellow became more cooperative, assuring the judge that as far as he knew, Ipuye had many lady visitors, though they remained a constant mystery.

'Veiled and masked,' the jeweller spread his hands, 'that's all I can say. Who they were?' He shook his head. 'They looked pretty: slim, elegant ankles, painted nails, rings gleaming, bangles jingling as they went up the outside steps. Ipuye was always waiting for them, but more than that, Lord Judge, I cannot say.'

Amerotke thanked him and walked away.

'Hardly courtesans,' Nadif murmured, catching up with him. 'Such ladies have no fear of exposing their faces. Indeed,' he laughed, 'that's part of the commodity on sale.' The standard-bearer turned and shouted at the Medjay to follow him, and they threaded their way through the stinking streets down to the Great Mooring Place on the Nile. This was busier than an anthill, with porters and servants carrying bundles, merchants and lords on their ornately harnessed donkeys, ladies in their palanquins and litters, sailors, burnt black by the sun, pushing their way noisily through the crowds desperate to reach the beer booths, wine shops and brothels along the quayside. Animal pens housing baby giraffes, monkeys, goats, sheep and geese gave off a rancid stench, which grew almost suffocating when it mingled with the tar and fishy smells of the river. Mountebanks touted for custom. Pimps darted in and out of the crowd whispering the delights of their beauties. Lizard and scorpion men looked hurriedly for easy pickings. Priests gathered to cross to the Necropolis. Three funeral parties stood waiting, caskets and coffers at the ready, choirs eager to sing, the Masters of the Tomb drilling the mourners on how to act.

Amerotke and his party shouldered their way through even as Shufoy rapped the wandering fingers of a lizard man. The judge made his way down to a small naval station and, using Pharaoh's cartouche, secured an imperial barge, *The Royal Horus*, flying the imperial standard. They clambered in and the marines shoved off. One sailor standing on the prow blew a conch horn, its wailing sound warning other craft to pull well clear of Pharaoh's messenger.

The Nile was sluggish; the air, even mid-river, reeked of cordage, pitch, tar and stale fish. Midstream, the waters became even busier with more funeral boats, their simple cabins draped in embroidered cloths or decorated leather. On deck the mourners faced back towards the slower coffin barge, built in the exact imitation of the mysterious craft which had taken Osiris across the Far Horizon. *The Royal Horus*, however, manned by master oarsmen, cut through the busy waters. Birds swooped and dived. Above these, circling like dark feathery shadows against the light blue sky, were the great vultures and buzzards floating in from the deserts to feed on whatever offal could be found. Amerotke, sitting in the stern next to Nadif, wondered what the Churat could tell them as the barge aimed like an arrow across the waters to the main quayside of the City of the Dead: the Resting Place of Osiris, whose soaring statue dominated the main entrance to the Necropolis.

Through the heat haze and clouds of dust, the judge could make out the various layers of the City of the Dead: lines of houses, cottages and workshops clustered together, a hierarchy of dwellings stretching up the side of the mountain, cut different ways by narrow winding lanes. He steadied himself as the barge swiftly turned to draw alongside the quayside. The manoeuvring was successfully concluded, and Amerotke and his party disembarked, moving through the milling crowd, wafting away the dusty clouds and myriad of flies. Shufoy opened the parasol but Amerotke declined it; he hadn't the heart to tell the little man he was too short. Instead he strode forward, the two Medjay going before them. They were now in the Land of the Dead, the Entrance to the Far West, the Threshold of the Far Horizon, beyond which lay the tombs, the Houses of a Million Years. The entire city was given over to death. Mourners were preparing to take the path up to the sepulchres, whilst a hired chorus rehearsed the hymn: 'To the West, best of men, even as the gods lament . . .'

Next to the funeral parties, those determined on earning a living bartered and sold everything from packets of fish hooks to measures of oil. Cooks offered food, bubbling in pots above beds of flame. Wine boys shouted the price of a goblet. Amerotke drove all these off as he entered the streets of the dead, along which stood the embalming and funeral shops, offering a wide range of services, from the raw gutting of the corpses of the poor, which would be cleaned in heavy baths of natron and packed with cheap sawdust and rags, to the lavish funeral arrangements for the wealthy, which provided everything necessary for a dead person's final, fitting journey. They left the main thoroughfare, turning right into the wretched, stinking maze of refuse-filled lanes, the dark tenements of the Ashu, the Outcasts, narrow tunnels harbouring every type of malefactor. Shadows emerged, menacing and dangerous, but these flitting figures soon melted away when they recognised Nadif and his Medjay. Amerotke and his companions were greeted with eerie shouts which echoed along the filthy alleyways, announcing who was coming, passing the information on deeper into those slums of hell. This truly was the Abode of Darkness, a maze of tunnels, rotting houses, derelict shrines and shabby shops. Amerotke felt as if the walls on either side of him were closing in when the tunnel they were threading through abruptly debouched into a broad, dusty square on the far side of which stood a derelict temple.

'The heart of the Abode of Darkness,' Nadif whispered. 'We will find the Churat here.'

They were hardly halfway across the square when from alleyways and doorways crept groups of men of every nationality: Khita, blond-haired mercenaries from the islands of the Great Green, Nubians black as night, Canaanites the colour of bronze, sand-dwellers, Libyans, all dressed in rags but very well armed. They moved quietly towards Amerotke with no sound, no murmur. The judge paused, opened the linen bag looped over his shoulder and took out the cartouche of Pharaoh.

'I am the Eyes and Ears of the Divine One,' he shouted, 'and this is Standard-Bearer Nadif of the Medjay.' The line of men paused; daggers were hastily hidden away, and they went down on their knees to respect the Imperial Seal. Amerotke was wondering how long this would last when a figure emerged through the colonnaded portico at the top of the temple steps. He was dressed completely in white gauffered linen, head shaved, his thin, ascetic face a mask of serenity.

'My brothers,' his voice was surprisingly strong, 'receive our guests kindly. Come, come.' He gestured at Amerotke. 'The Churat welcomes you.'

SKHINASHA: ancient Egyptian,
'to stir up, incite'

CHAPTER 7

The judge glanced at Nadif, who just shrugged. They made their way across the square, up the steps and into the coolness of the dark colonnade. The Churat looked and dressed as if he was a priest from one of the temples of Karnak, head and face perfumed and oiled, a peaceful-looking man with gentle eyes and smiling mouth. On closer inspection Amerotke realised the robes were of the costliest linen, the bracelets and rings on his wrists and fingers of pure gold.

'My lord.' The Churat came forward and grasped Amerotke's arms and they exchanged the kiss of friendship. He did the same to Nadif and bowed respectfully to the two Medjay. 'Come,' he repeated, 'you are my honoured guests.'

He took them into the Hall of Columns, where the pillars were peeling, plaster flaking from the ceiling, dark pools on the floor. He pattered ahead of them and turned right down a passageway into a surprisingly clean chamber. Its walls were tastefully painted, the floor scrubbed, the windows open; it was gracefully furnished with gleaming stools and tables. In the centre of the room, just near the hearth, was a raised dais on which everything had been prepared: low cushioned seats behind tables bearing platters of cooked meats and goblets of wine.

Nadif told the two Medjay to take their goblets, stand by the door and make sure that no one either entered or eavesdropped. The Churat smiled at that in a fine display of gleaming white teeth. He reminded Amerotke of some priest in a Chapel of the Ear, ready to listen to their confessions and offer absolution for their sins. At first the Churat talked about the day, the heat, the price of corn, how he looked forward to the Inundation, then, to the judge's surprise, he asked about Lady Norfret and Amerotke's two sons. He listened attentively to Amerotke's reply before turning to Nadif to talk about the promotion of the standard-bearer's nephew in the Medjay and what prospects further service held for him.

Amerotke, as he sipped from the bronze goblet and chewed carefully on the succulent meat, felt as if this was a dream. Here he was in the Abode of Darkness, in a shabby temple, yet at the same time he was sitting in a graceful room, drinking fine wine, eating food even Norfret would have relished. He broke from his reverie.

'Sir,' he bowed towards the Churat and gestured at the small tables and the platters of food, 'we thank you for your hospitality.' He glanced at Shufoy, who had fallen remarkably silent, just staring owl-eyed at this master criminal who controlled so much of the underworld of Thebes. 'You asked to see us, sir?' He decided respect was the best path to follow.

'Yes, I did.' The Churat put his goblet down. 'You see, Lord Judge, we all walk different paths. Indeed, our paths are mapped out before we are even born, and when we are, well, birth, status and family push us along that path. You follow yours, Lord Judge, I follow mine. The Rekhet has followed his. He has escaped from his prison oasis and is now back in Thebes?'

Amerotke nodded.

'And now the Divine One holds him responsible for the deaths at the Temple of Ptah?'

Again, Amerotke agreed.

'And you believe that, Lord Judge?'

'I believe nothing, sir,' Amerotke replied slowly, 'until I have the evidence.'

The Churat laughed, rocking backwards and forwards like a child listening to some funny story. He wagged a finger.

'My lord Amerotke, I have heard of you. They call you a hawk on the wing, ever ready to plunge, not at a lure but at some genuine morsel worthy of your notice.'

'You asked to see us,' Amerotke insisted. 'Why?'

'Because,' the Churat sighed, 'I decided to search for the Rekhet myself.' He glanced sly-eyed at Nadif. 'I have friends in the police, I have his description. I also possessed other information which I used. You do know we captured him?'

'You did what?' Amerotke exclaimed.

'Oh yes, Lord Judge, I know what happens in Thebes as much as Lord Senenmut does. Have you heard the most recent news?' The Churat, the Eater of Vile Things, cocked his head inquisitively, reminding Amerotke of some wise man in a temple.

'What news?' Nadif demanded harshly.

'You haven't heard it? Ah well.' The Churat smacked his lips. 'There was a great fire at the Temple of Ptah last night. The librarian was killed, part of the House of Books gutted by flame. You'll discover that soon enough. I'm sure that Lord Senenmut's men are already searching for you.'

'And what else?' Amerotke asked.

'There was also an attempt on the Divine One's life last night. Some poisoned food was left in the passageway of a temple palace; only a hungry servant saved an even greater tragedy from happening.'

'You said you'd captured the Rekhet?' Amerotke insisted. The Churat's news startled him but he couldn't comment – not now.

'So I did,' the Churat agreed, 'but unfortunately he escaped. I sent out two men yesterday morning. They captured him as he entered the Lion Gate but the fools made a mistake. He claimed he was thirsty. They went to a beer tent. He bought a jug, secretly poured in some poison and my two men were left writhing on the floor. They were dead within a few heartbeats and the Rekhet escaped.'

'Why do you want him?' Amerotke asked.

'For two reasons,' the Churat replied. 'First, Lord Judge, four years ago when the Rekhet manifested his power throughout Thebes, I became curious.'

'Why?' Amerotke asked.

'My friend, this is the Abode of Darkness at the heart of the City of the Dead; across the river lies eastern Thebes, housing the rich and powerful, who always want more. They wish to remove a rival or a troublesome wife, so they come to people like me, what they call the gang leaders. They enter into a contract, they hire an assassin, a knife, the noose, the poisoned cup. Accidents can be arranged. Death strikes often, so it comes as no surprise to anyone,' he laughed sharply, 'except the victim. The Rekhet was different. Here was a man who, by his own confession, was able to dispense his deadly powders and potions throughout Thebes and yet he apparently needed no one else. He must also have amassed a fortune, though only some of that was found.' The Churat held up a hand, index finger raised. 'Not one apothecary, physician or seller of powders was approached by this Rekhet, at least to my knowledge. I suppose if I was a merchant,' he sipped from his cup, 'I would call it a problem of distribution.

Yet as I have said, the Rekhet was able to dispense powders all over eastern Thebes without the apparent use of a middle man or a messenger. Can you answer that, Lord Judge?'

Amerotke shook his head.

'Fascinating,' the Churat commented, 'yet on the other hand, this man was easily captured and that just doesn't make sense.'

'What do you mean?' Nadif asked sharply.

'Well,' the Churat rolled the goblet between his hands like a master in the House of Light debating some academic problem, 'now and again assassins are caught, as well as those who hire them, usually because they make a mistake. This man never did, except on one occasion. He poisoned three of his comrades and when you, Standard-Bearer Nadif, searched his chamber, lo and behold you found all the evidence you needed. Quite frankly I don't believe that.' He leaned over and touched Nadif gently on the chest. 'And in your heart I don't think you do either. So you see, my lord Amerotke, Standard-Bearer Nadif,' he continued hurriedly, 'I have a great desire to meet this man. I want to know what really happened. If it hadn't been for those two fools yesterday morning, he'd now be in my care and protection.'

'And the second reason?' Amerotke asked. 'You said there were two reasons.'

'Ah, yes.' The Churat smiled. 'Unbeknown to the Divine One, Senenmut or you, my lord Amerotke, the Libyans want the Rekhet dead. They want his mouth silenced.' He laughed merrily at the look of surprise on Amerotke's face. 'The Libyans are no fools. They know as much about Thebes as you do: who to go to, what to buy when, where, how. Anyway, even before the poisonings took place at the Temple of Ptah, they sent a message into the Abode of Darkness: could I find the Rekhet? After the poisonings took place, they become even more insistent. They offered gold and silver not in pouches, but in sacks.'

'You accepted?' Amerotke asked.

'Of course!'

'So why are you telling us?'

'I hate Libyans,' the Churat replied. 'I take their gold dust, their silver, their precious jewels, but whether I would hand over the Rekhet alive, well, that's another matter.'

'And why do you think,' Nadif asked, 'the Libyans want the Rekhet?'

'I don't know.' The Churat laughed. 'But when I capture him again I'll certainly ask him that. An interesting problem! Why should Libyan war chiefs want to have anything to do with an escaped prisoner?'

'And why are you telling *us* all this?' Amerotke asked. 'What do you want in return?'

'Oh, a number of things, Lord Judge. First, I am very curious. Second, as I have said, I hate Libyans. Third, I know your reputation for honesty. When the

Rekhet is trapped, before he is sent to the wood, I would like to talk to him.'

Amerotke pulled a face but nodded.

'And finally,' the Churat put his head down, then glanced up, eyes glistening, 'no one lives for ever. One day I will die. I have wives, children. They are dear to me as yours are to you. I would like the Divine One's word that I will be allowed to build a tomb, a House of Eternity in the Valley of the West.'

Amerotke stared at this master criminal, a man whose fingers dabbled in every pot of iniquity in Thebes, be it prostitution, violence or sudden death.

'You don't believe me, Amerotke? We all have to go into the Far West. When I die, I want a proper tomb, the full ritual, a shrine where my wives and children can come and talk to me after I've journeyed on.'

Amerotke sensed this man was speaking with true voice. He leaned across the table, hand extended.

'You have my word, sir, your conditions will be met.'

The Churat smiled benignly and clasped Amerotke's hand.

'Don't worry, sirs, when you leave you will go safely out of the Abode of Darkness. If you ever return you will find no danger here, you have my word.'

'And if you capture the Rekhet before I do?'

'You have my solemn assurance,' the Churat replied. 'I will question him then hand him over, though others might capture him first!' He chuckled at Amerotke's puzzlement. 'Lord Judge,' he whispered, leaning forward, 'think! Reflect! Do you think the Libyans trust me completely? Nonsense! They have hired others for the task. They've made no pretence of it!' He turned, hawked and spat. 'That's what I hate about them: they show little trust and very little respect. They've hired the Amemets, that nasty guild of assassins, to find the Rekhet. Nobody,' the Churat continued mournfully, 'trusts anyone. Do you know,' he sighed, 'they've even taken to spying on us.' He pointed at Shufoy. 'Little man, you remember my messenger Skullface?'

The dwarf nodded.

'Gone!' The Churat shook his head, his face a mask of sadness. 'Disappeared! Taken up! Not by the Medjay; probably by the Amemets. They'll torture him, and Skullface will have no choice but to tell them the little he knows!' He spread his hands. 'Why couldn't the Libyans just leave the task to me?'

'How do you know all this?'

'Nadif,' the Churat grinned, 'even the sparrows who visit the Abode of Darkness do so at my bidding. I cannot say anything more except that the Amemets, hired and inspired by Libyan gold, are searching for the Rekhet.'

'Ipuye?' Nadif asked abruptly.

'Standard-Bearer, what do I know about a dead merchant found floating face down next to his wife in a lotus pool?'

'Do you think he was murdered?' Nadif demanded.

'Yes, I do.' The Churat, lower lip jutting out, moved backwards and forwards on his cushion, nodding wisely. 'Ipuye was a powerful merchant but he loved soft flesh. I would wager he was a man who made all sorts of promises to people, particularly women, and one day he was found out in his lying. However, who killed him and how he died . . .' He shook his head. 'I cannot say. Now, sirs,' the Churat smiled, 'unless you have further business, I will not detain you any longer.'

Amerotke rose to his feet. He nodded at the Churat and walked back to where the Medjay were waiting. Nadif followed. Shufoy stayed to share a few whispered words with their host, then scurried after them. Amerotke was just about to leave the chamber when the Churat called him back.

'Lord Judge, please?'

Amerotke turned. The Churat was standing tightening the coloured sash around his waist, tying the knot methodically.

'Shall I give you some advice, Lord Judge? I think you are hunting the wrong man.' He tapped the side of his head. 'I have no evidence, no proof to place before your court, just a feeling! Remember what I said.'

Amerotke, Nadif, Shufoy and the two Medjay left the Abode of Darkness, walking back through the needle-thin streets into the City of the Dead. Amerotke paused at a corner and glanced round. He glimpsed him moving swiftly back into the shadows, a one-eyed beggar with a crutch. He was sure he'd seen a similar beggar when they'd landed at the Resting Place of Osiris in the Necropolis.

'I told you,' Shufoy exulted, 'I told you the Churat wished to see you.'

'How do you know him?' Amerotke asked.

'Master,' the little man held up his hand, fingers splayed, 'I was five years amongst the Rhinoceri; it's wonderful whom you meet.'

They turned into the trade quarter of the Necropolis, along the widening streets, past embalming shops and booths where the corpses of the poor were hung out to dry. The heat, stench and flies were so intense that Amerotke traded grains of silver for perfume pomanders so they could obtain some relief as they made their way through the frenetic bustle and on to the paths leading to the western valleys. The buildings of the City of Dead petered out. On the outskirts stood the village compounds, housing those who worked permanently on the royal tombs. Patronised and favoured by the court, these skilled workers were provided with every comfort and amenity. Amerotke recalled that this was an inauspicious day when no work would be done, so the compounds were noisy with children playing, the laughter of men at the wine booths, clear indication that no quarrying was being carried out in the Valleys of the Dead.

Once they were out of the city, on the edge of the western Redlands, the terrain changed abruptly, turning gloomy, with brooding hills and narrow trackways which cut through shadow-filled gorges. They passed chariot patrols, and now and again were stopped by the Guardians of the West, crack Nubian and Syrian archers ever vigilant against tomb thieves. Eventually they reached the Mysterious Abode. Despite the sun, the pounding heat, the sandy, stifling air, Amerotke felt as if some malignant invisible mist had come swirling out of the rocks. To distract himself the judge opened his linen satchel and pulled out the maps he'd taken from Hutepa's chamber. He knew where he was going. The Valley of the Forgotten was a place he'd visited with his father and brother. They had regaled him with stories about how all sorts of monsters lurked hereabouts: sphinxes with human heads, griffins with jackals' bodies, eagle heads and wings, grotesques who, with one baleful glance, could turn a man to stone. He did not wish to recall these. He wiped the sweat from his face, refusing Shufoy's offer of the parasol, and studied the map, clearing his mind of the phantasms and stories of his childhood. They continued walking in silence, the enervating heat smothering them like a thick, uncomfortable blanket.

At last they reached the Valley of the Forgotten. The trackway into it was of fine sand, peppered with stones and boulders dislodged from the rocky sides by sun, wind and rain; an oppressive, silent place with narrow paths leading off here and there. In the shadows of the rocks caper bushes flourished, their violet flowers and fleshy leaves a welcoming relief from the black and grey of the rock. Amerotke stopped and stared up. Vultures circled. From somewhere up the valley slopes echoed the coughing roar of the great striped hyaenas, savage, predatory beasts, truly dangerous once darkness fell. He took a mouthful of water from the gazelle skin one of the Medjay carried and strode on, glancing at Hutepa's map. When he reached the place marked, he turned to his left and stared up.

The tombs hewn in the cliff face were old and forgotten. He could make out the entrances to seven, but the eighth was missing. He and his companions withdrew to consult in the shade of some rocks. After listening to Amerotke, one of the Medjay studied the map again, then went out and, shading his eyes, stared up at the rocky face. He grunted and swiftly climbed the loose shale, sending down a shower of pebbles and sand. When he reached a ledge, a lip of rock jutting sharply out, he turned and waved Amerotke up. The judge had no choice but to follow. The shale was loose and cutting; the heat was intense. Amerotke was only halfway up before his entire body was coated in sweat. Grunting and gasping, forgetting all sense of dignity, he reached the ledge and the grinning Medjay helped him up. The man explained how part of the cliff face had fallen to block the entrance. Amerotke, standing on tiptoe, could just see the top of the door peeping above the shale.

'But why this one?' he asked.

The Medjay grinned and pointed further up the rock face.

'Fire,' he explained. 'The shower of shale was deliberate. Someone climbed up there and thrust burning torches into the crevices, enough to make them crack open; the rest you know.'

'Can we clear it?' Amerotke asked.

The Medjay shrugged and began to scoop away at the pile of shale; Amerotke helped, shouting to his companions to wait where they were, as the ledge, for the time being, could only take two men. At first it seemed an impossible task. The shale cut at Amerotke's hands and nails, and bits and pieces scarred his legs, but at last, by concentrating on one spot at a time, they cleared the pile. Amerotke stood back and stared at the doorway once hidden by the shale.

'Someone, my lord,' the Medjay muttered, 'was here before you.'

Amerotke nodded. He shouted down at Nadif to light the torches they'd bought in the Necropolis and bring them up. With some difficulty the shale was climbed, Shufoy using the parasol, the other Medjay moving as nimbly as a monkey. He took one of the torches and, pushing Amerotke gently aside, clambered over the shale and in through the hole. Amerotke saw the light flare, then another as the Medjay found old cresset torches fixed into crevices.

'My lord,' the Medjay's face appeared through the hole, 'it is now safe for you to enter.'

Amerotke, taking off his robe and linen satchel and clad only in his loincloth, climbed over the shale and in through the narrow hole. The Medjay helped him down and held up the torch. The tomb was composed of two small chambers, one for the funeral goods, the other containing the sarcophagus. Looking round, Amerotke realised the corpse had been buried in some haste. It had certainly not been a costly funeral: the baskets, chests and coffers looked cheap and tawdry. All of these had been opened, their lids forced. The sarcophagus itself, a simple mummy case lying on a ledge, had not been tampered with. Amerotke searched amongst the meagre possessions, moving aside the canopic jars, the statues and household items the widow must have asked to be buried with her. At last he found a leather writing case made by some skilled worker. Its cover had been ripped off; fragments of hard seal still littered the floor. Inside there was nothing. Amerotke rose to his feet. The others were now idly looking round the tomb. Shufoy pointed out that there were no paintings or any trace of a funeral feast.

'They must have brought the poor woman here,' he declared, his voice echoing through the cavern, 'buried her and left as quickly as possible. Have you found what you came for, master?'

'Yes and no,' Amerotke replied. 'The tomb has certainly been entered and robbed. Whoever that was,' he picked up a small alabaster jar of perfumed oil, 'certainly wasn't after wealth; they would have rifled the mummy case. No, they came looking for something in particular.' He pointed at the leather writing satchel. 'And I suspect they found it: the Books of Doom, the Ari Sapu. They took these, left the tomb and created a rockfall to cover the entrance as well as their own handiwork.'

Nadif took a spluttering torch out of a crevice. Holding it at arm's length, he studied it carefully. Then he lifted it up and pointed to the other torches pushed into crevices and cracks.

'Whoever it was,' the standard-bearer declared, 'came well prepared. They brought torches to provide enough light for their search.' He took another of the torches down and lit it. 'The resin is dry and hard but still good. I would say, my lord . . .' he stared round, put the torch on the floor and went across to a small table which had been moved, rubbing his hand along this and staring at the dust, 'that Huaneka was buried probably some forty years gone. I'd suggest this tomb was violated probably five or six years ago, just before the Rekhet began his reign of terror in Thebes.'

'A wasted errand?' Shufoy asked. 'I mean, coming here.'

'I don't think so.' Amerotke squatted down, hands dangling between his knees, and clicked his tongue as he stared across at the leather writing case. 'First, I believe the Ari Sapu, the Books of Doom, were hidden when their author was arrested and executed. Second, his wife, for whatever reason, couldn't bring herself to destroy them so they were buried with her. People must have thought they were family papers. I suspect she became an outcast.' He waved around the tomb. 'This proves it: no one really bothered about her. Third, the heset Hutepa began to suspect the Ari Sapu were here; she searched the archives and discovered where Huaneka was buried.'

'But she never came here,' Nadif declared.

'Of course not. Hutepa was a heset; how could she come out to a lonely valley like this? Climb that rocky shale and force an entrance? No, no.' He paused. 'Perhaps she realised they'd been stolen without coming here. Perhaps she just wanted to prove that the Ari Sapu were not lost. We will never be able to answer that question. However, I believe she was murdered because of what she knew, though that is only one mystery amongst many waiting to be resolved.'

'Master!' Shufoy, who had been digging amongst some debris in the far corner, came forward holding a battered toy in his hand. Amerotke took it over to beneath one of the torches and carefully examined it. It was a small wooden giraffe with a piece of toughened twine attached to make the head move.

'A child's toy,' Nadif breathed. 'Did Huaneka have a child?'

'Did it survive?' Shufoy asked. 'Or did this belong

to Huaneka herself – a memento of her own childhood?'

'You've discovered no other evidence for a child?'

Shufoy and the Medjay shook their heads.

'Keep this.' Amerotke thrust the toy into Shufoy's hands, then turned and wandered into the funeral chamber. He stared down at the battered mummy case and wondered what sort of life this woman had led. She'd probably been a heset with high hopes and aspirations but her husband had proved to be a killer, a man responsible for the deaths of many innocents. Yet in that same temple, fifty years afterwards, another Rekhet had appeared. Someone had broken into this tomb, secured the Books of Doom and used them for their own evil purposes.

'Nadif,' Amerotke called over his shoulder.

'Yes, my lord.' Nadif came and stood by the tomb, running his hand over its painted, gessoed framework.

'I've asked you this before. The Rekhet, what was he like?'

Nadif pulled a face. 'My lord, I have nothing to add. He was quiet, a bachelor. He had lodgings in the temple, a priest physician, studious and learned.'

'Do you think he was the real Rekhet?'

'In my lifetime, I have met people, as you must have in yours, who looked like the Lords and Ladies of Light but in truth had dark hearts and evil ways. I'm of the Medjay. I arrest people. I don't probe their hearts and loins looking for secrets. I depend on evidence. The men murdered at that banquet suspected that the Rekhet was a member of their temple; one of them had actually named the guilty party. When we searched that priest's chamber, we found enough potions and philtres to cause murder and mayhem throughout the city, not to mention considerable wealth he could not explain. Moreover, you must not forget, he confessed to all his crimes and threw himself on Pharaoh's mercy. Because of this, he was punished with a living death, life imprisonment in a desert oasis.'

Amerotke turned and tapped the standard-bearer on the chest. 'But what do you feel here? Do you think he was guilty?'

Nadif narrowed his eyes and stared around the ghostly chamber. 'In a word, Lord Judge, yes, I do. The evidence proved that.'

'Very well.' Amerotke decided to try another path. 'Do you think there could have been two Rekhets in Thebes?'

'Possibly,' the policeman replied. 'He may have had an assistant, the heset Hutepa, so he returned to take his vengeance on her.'

'Hutepa,' Amerotke breathed. He felt tired, dirty and sweaty but he wanted to follow this through to its logical conclusion. 'Hutepa went to the library in the Temple of Ptah. It seems some sort of incident occurred there last night, a fire, though the gods only know what truly happened. Anyway, Hutepa visited the library. She must have searched the records to find this tomb. Surely she would have asked the librarian if anyone else had made similar searches? Such work would be recorded, people have to make their mark or sign for precious manuscripts; even if they didn't, that librarian would certainly remember. Hutepa, surely, must have asked such a question? Is that why she was killed? Why the library was burnt last night? Yet,' Amerotke turned and leaned against the funeral ledge, 'if Hutepa had discovered someone else was involved, surely she would have reported that to the authorities? It's a puzzle, a mystery, but come,' Amerotke pointed to the torches, 'douse those, let's leave.'

'And the doorway?'

Amerotke smiled. 'Nadif, I am sure you will file a report on your findings at this tomb. The Lords of the Dead will make it secure. We have other quarry to hunt.'

On their arrival back at the small naval station near the Great Mooring Place on the Nile, Amerotke hoped to return home to bathe, change and relax. An imperial chamberlain, flanked by Nakhtu-aa, soon changed that. Searches had been made, the official told him, and once he'd discovered that Amerotke had crossed to the Necropolis, he'd waited patiently for his return.

'Lord Judge,' the chamberlain trumpeted, 'you must accompany me to the Temple of Ptah.' He flourished the imperial cartouche, Hatusu's seal.

Amerotke immediately kissed it before asking him why.

'Because,' the chamberlain replied, 'it is the Divine One's will! A fire has destroyed part of the temple archives. The librarian himself has been killed whilst Lord Ani and his assistants are deeply perturbed.'

'Aren't we all!' Amerotke retorted.

Nadif immediately muttered that he had other duties to attend to, which Amerotke quietly suspected included a bath, a good meal and a restful nap under a shady tree. He told the standard-bearer to first visit the palace, seek out the Lord Senenmut and tell him everything they had learnt. He himself would go directly to the Temple of Ptah. Shufoy groaned dramatically, but the chamberlain was insistent and the captain of the Nakhtu-aa was impatient to escape the heat, flies, stench and furious din of the quayside. Amerotke made his farewells to Nadif and the Medjay and followed the chamberlain back into the city. They were hardly within the temple pylons, mixing with a stream of visitors and pilgrims, when Amerotke heard his name called and Maben came bustling through the crowds mopping his brow on the folds of his robe.

'My lord Amerotke,' he gasped, 'High Priest Ani waits, but first you must visit the destruction.' He almost dragged Amerotke out of the chamberlain's entourage, hurrying him down colonnaded walks, through arched porticoes, across gardens and into the precincts of the House of Life. Even before he reached the gateway, Amerotke smelt the acrid tang of oil and smoke. They passed down a line of lime trees, turned a corner and the devastation stretched before them. Half the library, including the long passageway and the adjoining chambers, had been gutted, reduced to ash, nothing more than flaking, charred timber and piles of cracked mud-brick stone: a tangle of black desolation above which sparks still fluttered and grimy plumes of smoke trailed up and spread out. Amerotke walked over to the sea of ash, noticing how the nearby walls had also been badly scorched. Already labourers were busy with scaffolds and planks, eager to repair the damage. Buckets, tubs and rakes used for fighting the fire lay strewn on the ground. A troop of monkeys chattered stridently from a clump of trees; birds swooped low, drawn in by the unusual sight, only to veer away.

'Manuscripts lost,' Maben moaned, 'the librarian dead.'

As Amerotke crouched down and sifted with a stick amongst the ash, the smell of cheap oil wafted up.

'The fire was deliberate!' He squinted up at Maben.

'Of course.' The priest's plump face creased in anguish. 'It was so swift, even as the guards fought the flames they could smell the oil. Of course it was deliberate! We think sacks of oil were thrown through one of the low windows, a torch or lamp hurled in afterwards.'

'And the reason?'

Maben just shrugged. 'Lord Ani awaits,' he murmured.

'And Hinqui?'

'Oh, he's much recovered. He had a violent fit of vomiting and after that his health improved.'

They walked away from the blackened ruins, but instead of taking Amerotke into the temple buildings, Maben led him across courtyards washed by the sun and cooled by fountains into the High Priest's private paradise, a walled enclosure which included all the ornamentation of a rich man's garden: flowerbeds, sandy pebbled paths, a small pool fed by a fountain, sun pavilions and a cluster of sycamore trees. Under the shade of these, Ani, Minnakht and Hinqui sat on cushioned stools with flared legs, or low wide chairs with a fine inlay of ebony and ivory. Small three-legged tables stood before them; on these were gilt-edged platters heaped with food and precious goblets brimming with wine. Hinqui looked distinctly pallid, but Ani and Minnakht had drunk deeply from the tall, flower-decorated wine jars standing further in the shade. Around the eating area were wooden stands in the form of papyrus columns, brilliant green with yellow three-peg tops; from these, lamps flared to drive away flies and other bothersome insects.

Amerotke was formally greeted; Shufoy was ignored until the judge made a show of refusing the proffered stool as well as the rosewater to wash his hands and face. The High Priest bowed imperceptibly.

'Bring another stool,' Minnakht ordered.

Amerotke and Shufoy quickly washed, drying their hands and faces on scented linen napkins, then sat down to goblets of chilled white wine and mouthfuls of soft raisin bread, pots of fresh vegetables and platters of deliciously cooked meats.

'Lord Judge, the poisoning of the envoys?'

Ani's voice and face were strained, so anxious he forgot the usual pleasantries.

'High Priest,' Amerotke shrugged, 'we have a number of possibilities. You handed the bowl—'

'And it was handed to me by Maben.'

'Ah yes, but you took it from the Libyans and gave it in turn to each of the three scribes. No, no,' Amerotke raised his goblet, 'I'm not accusing you. I have simply considered the remote possibility that the Libyans grasped the rim of the wine bowl with their hands and somehow or other smeared a deadly poison on it, but,' he shrugged, 'I have no proof of that. The deaths of those three scribes remain a mystery.' He sipped the chilled wine, closing his eyes, relishing the cool taste at the back of his throat. 'And the fire?' he asked, glancing up.

'It started after dark,' Minnakht declared. 'We smelt the smoke first; many in the temple did. The alarm gong sounded, trumpets shrilled and we hastened down but there was very little we could do. We tried to pull down burning walls and douse the flames with water. In the end all we could do was protect other buildings and let the fire burn itself out.'

'And the librarian?'

Minnakht shook his head mournfully. 'We found his remains, what was left of them, really nothing more than bone. We could only tell it was he from a charred amulet found nearby.'

'And he never tried to escape?' Amerotke asked.

'From what we gather,' Minnakht sighed, 'he died in the flames; perhaps he was even killed beforehand.'

'The fire definitely started in his chamber,' Ani snapped. 'We think he locked the door behind him. It was often his custom to sit there once the library was closed, to eat, drink and pore over manuscripts, even though,' the High Priest's voice turned petulant, 'that was strictly forbidden.'

'So,' Amerotke sipped from his goblet, 'we have those three scribes poisoned in the temple forecourt; the heset Hutepa killed in her own chamber, some deadly poison fed to her wine. Now we have the librarian burnt to death in his chamber and part of the library destroyed. I suspect you are correct,' he pointed his cup at Minnakht, 'he may have been poisoned, strangled, clubbed or stabbed before that fire ever started. What is interesting is why a fire? The killer wanted to hide something, but what?' He put his goblet down and leaned forward on the stool. Beside him, Shufoy was eating as if he hadn't been fed for days, ignoring Hinqui, who sat nursing his belly, a withering look on his plump, sweaty face.

'High Priest Ani, legend has it that the Books of Doom, the Ari Sapu, lie buried somewhere here with their author, but that is only a fable. I suspect they were buried with his wife Huaneka, whose tomb can be found in the Valley of the Forgotten.'

'Never!' Ani declared.

Minnakht and Maben shook their heads. Hinqui simply looked startled.

'Oh, it's true,' Amerotke continued evenly, watching these priests carefully. 'About forty years ago, Huaneka had the Ari Sapu buried with her. She was probably frightened to destroy them, terrified of her husband's *ka* and menaces from the other world. Hutepa, by studying the temple lists, managed to establish where Huaneka was buried. She never went out there, but today I did. I discovered the diagrams she had drawn. Huaneka's tomb can be found in the Valley of the Forgotten, its door hidden by a fall of shale; when I removed this, I discovered the door to the tomb had already been forced, its contents ransacked with no sign of the Ari Sapu.'

'You mean someone had been there fairly recently?' Minnakht asked.

'I do.' Amerotke nodded. 'The Rekhet also discovered where the Ari Sapu were, went to the Valley of the Forgotten, took the books, then began his hideous work here in Thebes.'

'But when the Rekhet was arrested,' Ani spoke up, 'the Ari Sapu were never found on him.'

Amerotke blinked and suppressed a curse; he hadn't thought of that. 'Perhaps,' he chose his words carefully, 'perhaps he hid them somewhere in the temple and they are still here?'

'Or in that library.' Shufoy spoke through a mouthful of meat.

'Perhaps.' Amerotke shook his head. 'I suspect the library was set on fire to destroy not only temple documents but also any record of anyone asking for certain temple manuscripts. Such a record would exist?'

Ani nodded. 'But Lord Judge, Hutepa was a heset, she had no right to demand such manuscripts. The librarian should have refused, and certainly reported the matter to me, but he never did,' he added wistfully.

'But why kill the librarian?' Minnakht asked quickly. 'Why not just burn the library?'

'Perhaps the librarian knew the names of all who had consulted those manuscripts,' Amerotke replied. 'That is why he had to die, be destroyed along with any records he kept.'

'But that is not strictly true,' Maben declared. 'Lord Judge, the temple lists that could provide the date of Huaneka's death and the location of her tomb are kept in the library, but those are only copies; the originals are kept in a chest in my chamber.'

Amerotke shook his head in puzzlement, then

picked up a goblet and rolled it in his hands. 'So the temple lists kept by the librarian that locate the widow's tomb,' he repeated slowly, 'were only copies; the originals are elsewhere and nothing has happened to them?'

'Nothing,' Maben replied. 'I can show you. They are kept locked in a special coffer to which only I have the keys.'

'So why,' Ani persisted, 'was our library burnt, our librarian murdered?'

'My only answer to that,' Amerotke declared, 'is that the librarian must have had information dangerous to the assassin, whilst his archives housed something else, evidence that could have helped me. Lord High Priest, do you have any idea what that could be?'

Ani and his companions all shook their heads, answering Amerotke's question in a chorus of denials. Amerotke absent-mindedly ate some fruit, followed by a slice of beef; the wine was making itself felt. He pushed the cup away. He did not want to become heavy-eyed, and the way the four priests were staring at him made him uneasy. He gently poked Shufoy in the ribs.

'My Lord Ani, I thank you for your hospitality. It is time we left. I have no further questions. What you have told me only deepens the mystery. Before I leave, perhaps I could look at this special coffer?'

Maben quickly agreed and rose to his feet. Shufoy finished his wine, snatched two juicy pieces of meat from a platter and hurried after his master without a farewell, a thank you or even a bow to the High Priest. The little man chuckled to himself. The Sacred Ones were always repelled by his disfigured face, but as long as he sat in the shadow of Amerotke, what could they do? His master was already striding ahead talking to Maben about the coffer, the priest assuring him that it was secured by three heavy wooden locks, the keys carried only by him. He never handed them over to anybody; well, not without High Priest Ani's permission, and only to high-ranking members of the temple hierarchy.

Maben's chamber lay at the end of a colonnaded walk. It was a pleasant, cool room, its walls painted a refreshing green; flower baskets stood in the corner, the small table was littered with papyrus and quill pens, brushes and ink pots, and coffers and chests stood around. Maben unlocked the door to what he called his 'holy of holies' and led Amerotke and Shufoy into a small whitewashed chamber with a window grille set high in the wall. All around the room were shelves bearing documents, small coffers or caskets. Against the facing wall was a huge wooden chest, its top and sides carefully sculpted to display the symbols and signs of the Scribe God Thoth. Maben opened the wallet tied to the sash on his belt, took out a set of keys and released all three heavy locks. Then, pulling the chest away from beneath a shelf, he pushed back the lid and gestured at Amerotke.

'My lord, you may search these to your heart's content. These are the originals; the library,' he added rather pompously, 'only held copies. We do that just in case of accidents or events like last night. I will close the door to my chamber. I would be grateful if you would inform me when you want to leave.'

Amerotke nodded his agreement. Once the priest had left, he and Shufoy pulled the chest out into the main room. Amerotke took cushions for himself and his servant and began to sift through the manuscripts. The chest was crammed with documents, each bearing a tag giving the date it had been drawn up. Some were freshly done; others were yellowing with age or preserved in copper cylinders. Amerotke discarded those he didn't need, placing to his right those which had been drawn up in the last five or six years. Even so, it was a ponderous task. Shufoy, who now felt sleepy, had to be roused awake. They searched through the rolls and lists covering a wide range of temple activities: visitors, offerings to shrines, funeral goods, as well as the location of tombs. Amerotke soon realised that this important chest contained the most valuable documents of the temple. Others were probably stored in the coffers and caskets in the adjoining chamber. Heavy eyed, he went through the pile he had set aside, reading comments, noting dates but discovering nothing to alert his suspicions.

'Master,' Shufoy rubbed his face, 'the day is drawing on. It is time we went. There is nothing here.'

Amerotke bit back his angry reply. He felt agitated, uneasy. He was making no progress with this investigation. He was blocked at every turn, like being lost in a maze in some nightmare, no entrances in or paths out, whilst all around him evil swirled.

'Lord Judge!'

Amerotke startled and glanced towards the door. Maben stood there, behind him Asural, captain of the temple guard in the Court of Two Truths at the Temple of Ma'at, and next to him Prenhoe, senior scribe in the same court. Asural brushed by Maben and walked forward as if he was on parade. He was dressed in a rich leather kilt, marching boots on his feet, a leather baldric across his chest, in the crook of one arm his helmet, in the other hand a short baton which he used to marshal his men.

'Lord Judge,' he boomed, standing to attention before glaring at Shufoy giggling behind his hand. 'Lord Judge, I have a report to deliver.'

'Asural, Asural,' Amerotke murmured, getting to his feet, 'for God's sake just tell me why you are here.'

Asural looked over his shoulder at Prenhoe, Amerotke's kinsman. The fresh-faced scribe was dressed in white gauffered robes, an embroidered sash around his waist, fingers stained with ink, and was looking back down the corridors as if overcome by the precincts of the great Temple of Ptah.

'And you, Prenhoe, don't look so frightened,' Amerotke declared. 'Both of you, come here.'

Prenhoe hurried to stand beside Asural, who now relaxed. 'Lord Judge, we have searched the grounds of the House of the Golden Vine. We have discovered the remains of a woman. I think you'd best come.'

KHENTI THEHENU: ancient Egyptian,
'chief in Libya'

CHAPTER 8

Naratousha, principal war chief of the Libyan tribes, scratched his sweaty back against the bark of the terebinth tree and peered around at his companions. The sun was still very strong, yet he needed them to be away from the Mansion of Ease where the Eyes and Ears of Pharaoh could watch and listen to their conversations. He gazed around the circle.

'Does the peace treaty hold, yes or no?' he repeated.

'I'm not sure,' replied the grey-bearded Libyan chieftain seated to Naratousha's right. 'Pharaoh might argue that the deaths of those scribes have nullified the peace treaty until the ceremony of sealing is carried through to her satisfaction.'

'Nullified, nullified?' Naratousha snapped, trying to control a surge of hot temper. He cradled the cup of beer in his hands and stared across the temple lawns, his gaze caught by the glinting light along the needle-thin canal that brought in river water to keep this paradise green and fresh. Sheep and ibex grazed peacefully. Doves from the temple cotes swooped low in flashes of white. Above the trees the glorious stonework of the temple blazed with light.

Egypt! Naratousha ground his teeth. To the west stretched the burning desert lands, hundreds of miles till they reached the fertile strips along the Great Green. His people had to cling there wedged between two deserts, one of sand, the other of salty water. If Naratousha had his way, the Libyan tribes would smash through the massed ranks of Pharaoh's chariotry, cross the Tuthmosis Line and reach the fertile banks of the Nile. They'd plunder its great cities, and swamp Egypt in a tide of warriors surging down the river. Who knew what the future might hold for a successful Libyan war chief? Could he wear the double crown and hold the flail and the rod? And Hatusu, the royal bitch? Naratousha closed his eyes and moaned in pleasure. He'd love to hold that imperial bitch in his arms and show her who the true master was.

He heard a sharp cough and opened his eyes. Themeu, Naratousha's kinsman and close ally, was staring across at him. The young man's beautiful face was strained and anxious, his eyes full of warning. Naratousha remembered himself. The chieftains seated in a circle around him were not his enemies but neither were they his friends, only allies in what Naratousha called his 'great venture against the might and power of Egypt'. Not all of these warriors trusted him. Some were bound by blood, others by common hatred of Pharaoh and a burning lust for Egypt's riches, but apart from that, by little else. Naratousha grinned, his heavy-lidded eyes glittering. He must remember to smile and smile again, not show his true feelings. He must impress these warriors, overawe them with his cunning.

'Who is responsible for the poisonings?' Themeu asked, eager to divert attention from Naratousha.

'Well, not us!' Greybeard scoffed, provoking laughter from those around him.

Naratousha kept his face impassive. The chiefs regarded such a comment as amusing, but Naratousha and Themeu had secretly discussed such a possibility. Not all the chiefs welcomed the peace. Some were openly jealous of Naratousha's assumption of power over them. Had one of these been responsible for the blasphemy that had occurred on the temple forecourt? An attempt to wreck his plans before they came to fruition?

'Are you sure?' Naratousha's voice, strident and harsh, cut the amusement short. He pointed at Greybeard. 'You drank last after Themeu. You handed the wine bowl back to their priest.'

The other chiefs tensed. Naratousha had voiced a suspicion that a few of them had also discussed in hushed tones and secret whispers. Greybeard fingered the coral necklace around his sweat-soaked neck. Eyes dark and wary in his high-cheekboned face, he forced himself to hold Naratousha's gaze.

'How could I,' he retorted quietly, 'have poisoned that wine?' He spread out his hands, the precious rings on his fingers glittering in the light pouring through the branches overhead. 'What poison could I have held?'

Naratousha nodded as if convinced.

'Were the wine dregs examined?' asked another chief, eager to break the tension.

'Yes.' Naratousha's abrupt reply silenced the whispers in the circle. He nodded his head, staring into the middle distance as if he could see something they couldn't. He knew what was coming next. He had to convince these men that his power was great and his reach long.

'How do you know that?' Greybeard asked.

Naratousha sucked on his teeth and narrowed his eyes. He was determined to show Greybeard, who regarded himself as wily as a jackal, that he was even better. 'I know,' he whispered, leaning forward, 'because I know.' He gazed round and smiled. 'We have a spy high in the councils of Egypt.'

'Never!' Greybeard countered.

'Themeu, do I lie?' Naratousha turned to his handsome kinsman.

'You speak with true voice,' Themeu assured him. He watched Naratousha's face, wondering where his cunning war chief was leading both him and his companions.

Themeu's declaration provoked surprise and consternation amongst the rest. The Libyans obtained information about Egypt from traders, merchants and prisoners. Sometimes they could buy petty traitors, minor officials, but to have a spy high in the councils of Egypt! The like had never been heard before! Naratousha, sitting cross-legged, fanned himself vigorously whilst he swiftly studied their faces. If there was a traitor, an enemy amongst them, he would now show his true colours, out of fear that the Egyptian spy might also have betrayed him. But Naratousha could detect no guilt, just surprise at his statement.

'Who is this spy?' Greybeard countered.

'A priest high in the Temple of Ptah,' Naratousha replied, 'who has sat at the feet of Pharaoh, the royal bitch, and listened to her pretty lips spout their secrets. Themeu,' he gestured, 'will corroborate what I say.' He held up both hands. 'I cannot give you a name; you must trust me on this. Themeu?'

'According to our spy, the wine was examined.' Themeu took up the thread. 'The dregs were fed to a dog. It suffered no ill effects.'

'So where did the poison come from?' one of the chieftains asked. 'Was it the royal bitch? Does she want to break the peace treaty? Does she know something of our plans?'

'No!' Naratousha scoffed. 'No!' He laughed aloud. 'She executed those sand-dwellers – now they could have told her! Perhaps they knew something, perhaps they didn't. If the royal bitch had really understood our plans, she would have saved their lives and questioned them.'

'So our secret is still safe?'

'Of course!' Naratousha retorted. 'Do you think I brought you here to act like Pharaoh's dogs, to kiss her painted feet and act all suppliant? We must,' he made a soothing gesture with his hand, 'convince the royal bitch that we wish peace whilst we plan secretly for war. Before we came here, I told you what would happen, and what I have said has come true. The merchant Ipuye claimed we would see the power of Egypt discomfited, and so we have. The poisoning of three of their senior scribes on the temple steps before the populace of Thebes? Do you really think Hatusu would want that? She must be furious!'

'Ipuye is now dead,' Greybeard declared. 'Was that Pharaoh's work, an act of revenge?'

'I do not know. I do not think so,' Naratousha replied bluntly. 'He died the very day those three scribes were poisoned. I doubt it. All I can say is that what Ipuye promised has happened.'

'Then if Pharaoh didn't kill Ipuye, did you, to silence his mouth?' Greybeard asked.

'Traders who sell one way can always sell another,' Naratousha replied blandly. It was best, he reflected, if his companions were left in some puzzlement over his deviousness. After all, that, together with his sword arm, was what had won him primacy on this council.

'The royal bitch,' one of the chieftains declared, 'could have arranged the poisonings.'

'Why?'

'To delay us here, to discover what is really happening out in the western desert.'

Naratousha nodded. He couldn't reject that; he'd wondered about it himself. Had Hatusu planned the killings so as to keep him and the other chieftains here, away from their tribesmen, their plotting? He was more than aware of the dangers they now faced. They could not leave; if they did so without Hatusu's permission, suspicion over the poisonings would fall on them. The peace treaty would truly collapse and then what would happen? Egyptian chariot squadrons dispatched deep into the desert lands? Yet if they were delayed, how could they find out how things were developing in their own homeland: Naratousha's scheme to destroy the great power of Egypt?

'We cannot leave without the royal bitch's approval.' Naratousha spoke slowly. 'She has her snoopers, her pryers into things. Amerotke the judge is searching for the cause of those poisonings. I believe the bitch is truly confused. She may not really want the treaty. Her brick-laying lover Senenmut is of the same mind, as are her generals, but they cannot resist our peace terms: safety and prosperity for their traders, soldiers and townspeople.' He paused, chewing the corner of his mouth. 'Our spy,' he announced, 'has also informed us that the royal bitch believes the poisonings could be the work of the Rekhet.'

His companions nodded and murmured amongst themselves.

'We know the Rekhet was discovered and imprisoned four years ago. Ipuye helped to free him. In the end, the Rekhet escaped. He eluded our patrols and was captured by sand-dwellers who'd also seized a merchant from Memphis.' Naratousha waved a hand. 'You know that story. What you don't know is what our spy has told us.' He now had their full attention. He'd given them sufficient proof that someone close to the royal circle of Egypt was passing on Pharaoh's secrets. 'Our spy in this Temple of Ptah has informed us that the Memphis merchant was one of Lord Senenmut's best searchers. In a word, he may have seen what he shouldn't have out in the western desert.' He raised a hand to stifle their protests and gasps of alarm. 'Themeu and I have taken steps. We have powerful friends in Thebes.' He smiled wolfishly, his sharpened teeth more like those of a hunting mastiff than a man.

Somewhere deep in the temple, conch horns, trumpets and booming gongs marked the passing of the hour.

'We must seize the Rekhet ourselves,' Naratousha continued, 'and kill him. By doing so we shall not only defend our own cause but show the royal bitch we have helped her bring such a wretch to justice.

She will have no choice but to confirm the treaty and we shall be gone.'

The chieftains clapped their hands softly, murmuring their agreement.

'There is only one problem.' Greybeard was insistent that Naratousha should not have the last word. 'If the royal bitch captures him first . . .'

'Oh, I hope she does,' Naratousha replied enigmatically. 'The Eyes and Ears of Pharaoh, not to mention the Medjay and imperial troops, are searching for the Rekhet, but,' he shrugged, 'we are also watching them.'

'And this spy?' Greybeard asked. 'How could you recruit a priest high in the temple, an Egyptian?' He lowered his head and glanced sideways at the handsome Themeu whilst secretly cursing his own rashness. Secretly he knew the answer to his question. Themeu was the pride and joy of his clan, a beautiful but ferocious warrior. Beloved by both men and women, as a seducer Themeu was unsurpassed. Had he suborned a high-ranking priest here in the Temple of Ptah? Greybeard had listened to the whispers of the others. The Egyptians regarded such illicit love as heinous, though not as repellent as consorting with a Libyan warrior! He glanced up. Naratousha was staring at him, deliberately allowing the tense silence to continue so as to cause the greatest possible embarrassment. Greybeard coughed and looked away: Naratousha would have the last word.

'Themeu,' Naratousha turned matter-of-factly to

his kinsman, 'it's best if you were gone. The hour has been marked. There's business to be done.'

Themeu nodded, took off his necklace, bracelets and rings and, stretching across, dropped them into Naratousha's hand. He then rose, strapping on a leather belt on which hung three sheaths for a stabbing knife and two smaller daggers. He picked up his striped robe, shook it out and put it on, then pulled up the hood, transforming himself into one of the many pilgrims who swarmed through the Temple of Ptah. He raised a hand in farewell and slipped like a shadow across the grass.

Themeu kept his head down, smiling quietly at Naratousha's discomfiture of Greybeard yet fully aware how dangerous this game had become. They had been in Egypt two weeks, and many of the chieftains were becoming restless, eager to leave. The matter had to be brought to an end, and swiftly. He slipped a hand through a gap in his robe and, for reassurance, touched the leatherbound handle of one of the daggers. He had played his part by suborning that priest. At first he had not believed what he'd seen, but he'd glimpsed the look of admiration, the lust burning in the priest's eyes, and after that? Well . . . Themeu paused at the top of some steps. It was so easy, like trapping some fat quail or plucking a bloated carp from a pond. The man had fallen ripe as an apple and Themeu had him in his net. He went down the steps, along the shadowed tunnel between two buildings and into a courtyard dazzling in the sun and adorned with statues of the Man God Ptah. Next to these, fountains spilled water over the sacred stelae, bathing the names, titles and honours of the god. Despite the sun's glare and the seething heat of the day, the square was busy. Pilgrims thronged around the fountains, eager to touch the stelae, dip their hands in, drink greedily, or fill bottles so as to take more of the sacred water to their homes.

Themeu stopped before one of the fountains as if admiring the beauty of a sculpture or the purity of the water. He gazed quickly around. The Eyes and Ears of Pharaoh were legion, yet he could detect no sign of being followed or watched. He recalled those trumpets and gongs marking the passing of the hour. His victim would be waiting, as well as a possible visitor from the Amemets, who had promised that if they had any news, one of their scouts would be at the Gate of Ivory, the beautiful postern door leading into the temple precincts, between the sixth and ninth hours. The Libyan looked round once more. He was satisfied. He hurried across the square and up some steps into the pink limestone Chapel of the Ear. Here penitents could confess their sins to a priest sitting in a recess behind a latticework screen. Such a ceremony would only be available after the ninth hour when the heat began to cool and the priests would not be so uncomfortable in their narrow stone closets. Now the chapel was deserted except for white-robed acolytes busy around a small altar under a square window at the far end. An eerie place,

Themeu reflected, with grim paintings on the wall reminding sinners of what might happen to them during their final journey through the Am-duat. Here the Devourer of Things, the Gobbler of Flesh, the Breaker of Bones, the Smasher of Skulls would await the damned sinners! Sobeck the Crocodile God also lurked waiting for any souls not purified, and thus unable to proceed into the Far West. Themeu did not believe any of this. He worshipped his own gods and had nothing but disdain for those of Egypt. Nevertheless, it was a chilling place.

He broke from his reverie and walked across the chapel. There were six 'Places of Penance' along the wall. Each recess was fronted by a thick latticework screen, polished and gleaming. On the floor was a cushion where the penitent could kneel to whisper his or her sins. The priests were never allowed into this part of the chapel, lest they saw someone they knew or be recognised themselves. Instead each recess had a small door in the far wall through which the priest could crawl to sit on a stool and listen to the penitents. Themeu walked along to the third recess and stood with his back to the wall; any curious acolyte would think he was admiring the chapel. He tapped at the wood of the latticework screen and waited.

'I am here.' The voice was a hushed whisper.

'So you are!' Themeu squatted down, turning his head slightly. 'Why are you afraid? Why can't you meet me?'

'You know why,' came the hoarse reply. 'We are watched. I have my own problems. Lord Amerotke snoops everywhere, searching out things, and there are others too. It is becoming too dangerous. Last night an attempt was made on Pharaoh's life. Here in this temple, part of our library, the House of Books, was burnt.'

Themeu stiffened. He and his companions had heard rumours but Naratousha had ordered them not to pry, not even to discuss the matter so as not to provoke the royal bitch's suspicions that any Libyan was involved in such incidents. Naratousha had dismissed the rumours of the attempted poisoning as possible hysteria, while the fire, surely, was an accident?

'Tell me,' Themeu turned, lowering his head, 'the fire?'

'Not an accident,' the voice replied. 'Not an accident at all. Amerotke had been there searching for certain manuscripts. They believe it was arson.'

'Why?'

'Perhaps to hide some evidence? I don't know.'

'What else?'

'Amerotke and the Medjay standard-bearer Nadif are becoming more inquisitive by the hour. It is, as I said, too dangerous.'

'The danger will pass,' Themeu whispered reassuringly. 'Then we will meet again. Yes? Stroll in the lonely gardens of the temple, lie in the shade where the grass is fertile and fresh . . .'

He heard a sound as the priest rose and fled through the small door. Themeu laughed softly. He got to his feet and leaned against the wall, squinting across at the paintings opposite. The priest had no choice but to come here and listen to him, tell him what he knew. Themeu breathed out noisily. It was time to go. He left the Chapel of the Ear and mingled with the crowds, following the path through the temple precincts. He glimpsed part of the blackened ruins of the House of Books; he didn't stop and stare but hurried on. At last he reached the Gate of Ivory, mingling with the crowds squeezing in and out, past temple guards lounging in the shade sharing a jug of beer. He forced himself through the gate on to the broad alleyway that would lead down into the city.

'Alms,' a voice whined. 'Alms, great lord!'

Themeu whirled round. The crouching man was dressed in beggars' rags and holding a staff, yet his face did not look pitiful, eyes glittering, lips bared. Themeu noticed how his teeth were stained blue.

'What alms?' Themeu replied in the patois. 'What alms shall I give you?'

'Great lord, I can show you wonders. I can show you the marvels of the city, born here I was.' The beggar glared at him. He'd given the password agreed between Naratousha and the Amemets.

Themeu nodded. The beggar sprang swiftly up and, grasping his staff, hurried ahead. Themeu had no choice but to follow. The beggar scurried down past temples and palaces glowing with gold, silver and lapis lazuli, along avenues fringed by snarling human-headed lions carved out of black granite; these glared across the avenue at other grotesque creatures sculpted from pink limestone. They reached the Great Mooring Place on the Nile with its porticoed quayside, its walls decorated with the exploits of previous pharaohs, their great victories over the Libyans, Kushites and other people of the Nine Bows. The beggar hired a craft and they climbed aboard. The Nile was sluggish but the bargemen were especially skilled. They recognised the beggar and swiftly took them across to the Place of Osiris, the great quayside of the City of the Dead dominated by towering statues of Egyptian gods. The beggar didn't pay. As soon as the barge landed them on the quayside, he hurried off along narrow trackways and wretched streets. The dirt was piled almost waist high; naked children searched the mounds for fuel. The acrid smells of rottenness and decay mingled with the foul odours of the embalming house. Casket-sellers, coffin-makers, tomb preparers and funeral managers bawled for trade. Garishly dressed scribes advertised to write letters for the Chapels of the Dead. Now and again the beggar would stop to make sure Themeu was following him, then hurry on past beer shops and drinking houses seething with prostitutes, pimps, tinkers, traders and scorpion and lizard men. Themeu could see that his guide, though dressed meanly, was treated with the greatest respect, people drawing aside as fearfully as they would before a squad of Medjay armed with club and sword.

At last they entered the Twilight Abode, a sinister, eerie place, and into a market square bounded on each side by houses. A few sycamore trees flourished, and in the far corner stood the House of the Evening Star, a tavern where Themeu had met the Amemets before. The inside was surprisingly clean, the walls limewashed, the floor covered with soft reed matting. It was furnished with comfortable stools and polished low tables. Various signs hung from the low rafters: 'Drink until you drop', 'Don't stop enjoying yourself, death will come'. Another sign boasted how the house had every type of wine from Avaris in the north to beyond the Fourth Cataract in the south.

Once the door behind him was closed fast, the beggar turned and came striding back, hand outstretched.

'I am Bluetooth,' he declared, 'leader of ten in the company of the Amemets.'

Themeu's own hand slipped beneath his robe to rest on a dagger. 'Where is everybody?' he asked. 'This place is deserted.'

'No it isn't,' a voice answered.

Themeu whirled round. The corner behind them was shadowed in dark. A man walked forward. He had the cruel face of a bird of prey.

'I am the Vulture.' He stretched out a hand like a claw. Themeu clasped it. 'Your master has hired us.' The Vulture tapped a foot, joining his hands as if in prayer as he studied the Libyan. 'You also hired the Churat.'

'We will hire anyone we want,' Themeu replied. 'All we ask is that we get what we pay for. Do you have it?'

'Not yet,' the Vulture replied, spreading his hands. 'But we have someone you might like to meet.' He led Themeu across the deserted room into the back of the house. The kitchens and storerooms were all eerily deserted, the ovens cold, the fleshing tables scrubbed clean; nothing but the buzz of flies above a pool of blood on the floor. The strident squeaking of some vermin echoed through the half-open door in the far corner of the kitchen. The Vulture led Themeu across to this, pulled it open and went down some steps into the hot, musty darkness. Torches flared in niches on the wall, dazzling the eyes and confusing the mind. Themeu carefully made his way down the steps, sweat starting on his skin. He did not like the foul smells that greeted him, the ominous, threatening darkness. He undid the clasp of his robe to draw the dagger strapped to his belt.

'No need for that,' whispered Bluetooth, standing behind him. 'You are safe.'

They reached the bottom of the steps. Themeu stood for a while shading his eyes against the torch-light. They were in a cellar, a cavernous chamber with a low ceiling. Torches spluttered fire and plumes of dark trailing smoke. The cellar was crowded.

Armed men dressed in loincloths, skin glistening with sweat, clustered around a figure stretched out on the floor, his arms and legs pegged into the dirt. They all turned as the Vulture and Themeu approached. Themeu was waved to one side of the fettered man. He crouched down and stared at the bony, unshaven face, the cavernous eyes and thin lips, the sweat that glazed the thin-ribbed body. The prisoner glared furiously back, eyes fluttering, torn between obstinacy and fear.

'This is Skullface,' the Vulture intoned gently. 'He serves the Churat, the Eater of Vile Things, who lurks in the Abode of Darkness. I suppose,' he tapped the prisoner's face, 'you could call him a business rival. He's been lurking in the Temple of Ptah. We think his master wishes to do business with the prying Judge, Amerotke. In which case,' he glanced across at Themeu, 'I hope you, my lord, were careful where you went and with whom you did business. Now we are trying to discover exactly what Skullface knows. He is proving difficult. He knows he is going to die.' He paused as his prisoner strained vainly at his bonds. 'If we don't kill him, the Churat certainly will.'

'I know nothing of my master's plans,' Skullface gasped. 'What can I tell you?'

'Skullface is also a liar,' the Vulture continued conversationally, then paused as if irritated by that ominous squeaking Themeu had heard earlier. 'So this is what we are going to do.' He lifted a hand and imperiously beckoned to one of the armed men, who shuffled forward carrying a wooden cage. Its narrow bars half concealed a long, furry creature which flipped and crashed against the wooden sides. He placed the cage on the ground next to Skullface, and the Vulture pressed the prisoner's head to one side, forcing him to stare at the gleaming eyes, quivering snout and sharp teeth of the great sewer rat glaring furiously through the bars. Themeu sensed a spasm of fear at the rodent seething at its imprisonment, teeth and claws pattering at its wooden prison. The rat screamed stridently, shattering the silence of that fetid cellar.

'Skullface.' The Vulture leaned down as he gestured another of the men forward. This one held a long, narrow copper pipe. 'Skullface,' the Vulture repeated, taking the cylinder and holding it before the prisoner's eyes, 'this is going to be strapped to your side and secured tight. The rat will be released into it and the opening will then be sealed by fire. Now the rat, already starving and furious, will have only one way forward.' He patted Skullface's stomach. 'By burrowing through your flesh. You are going to die, my friend,' he continued quietly. 'It's only a matter of deciding how. If you agree to answer our questions, it will be a swift death: a few goblets of wine, something to eat, then a quick slash across your throat.'

Skullface, soaked in sweat, chest heaving, lips dry, gazed wildly around. He closed his eyes, then opened them.

'And afterwards?' he croaked.

'Afterwards,' the Vulture intoned almost piously, 'your body will be taken to the House of Embalmers. We will pay for your proper journey into the Far West. Offerings will be made for you at a temple; the more honest you are, the greater the honour paid to you.'

'Offerings?' Skullface croaked. 'You'll ensure a Priest of the Stole prays for me?'

'At least for a month and a day after your death,' the Vulture replied. 'Now come, the rat waits, time is passing.'

Skullface stared up at the ceiling. 'A cup of wine, a deep-bowled cup, and some fresh quail meat?'

'Good.' The Vulture nodded. 'You know, Skullface, if our positions were reversed, you'd do exactly the same to me.' He snapped his fingers. The men holding the screaming rat and the copper funnel promptly disappeared.

The Vulture drew a dagger and deftly cut Skullface's bonds, pulling the prisoner up as if he was an old comrade. He severed the thongs at wrist and ankle, and Skullface sat breathing in deeply. Again the Vulture snapped his fingers. A man hurried up the cellar steps and returned a short while later, in one hand a platter of cold quail meat, in the other a deep bowl of wine. He placed these down before Skullface. The prisoner, pulling back the linen cloth, ate the meat hungrily, slurping at the wine. He belched and grinned at the Vulture.

'Your questions?' His gaze shifted to Themeu. 'The Libyans?' He gestured with his hand. 'He also hired us.'

'Whom he hired and what he wants,' the Vulture whispered, 'is now no longer important. Skullface, we have made a pact, you will answer our questions.'

Skullface nodded in agreement. Themeu sat fascinated as the interrogation began. At first Skullface told him nothing he didn't know already, though he quickly realised the importance of the prisoner. He'd been recently captured. He knew all about the fire at the library and the possibility that arson had been committed to conceal some secret knowledge. More fascinating, however, were the Churat's thoughts about the Rekhet. How he believed the Rekhet may have had more than one accomplice in Thebes responsible for the distribution of his poisons. Skullface even hinted that the Churat suspected that four years earlier the Medjay had arrested the wrong man. As Themeu listened, his unease deepened. The Libyans had come to Thebes because they believed the time was right and that Pharaoh was discomfited, but the more he listened to Skullface's chatter, the more concerned he grew. The Rekhet was the one who controlled this game, and now Themeu understood why Naratousha was so eager to seize him. One item caught his attention as Skullface chattered about what his master knew.

'Say that again,' he intervened, speaking in the patois of the Theban slums. 'What did you say?'

'We've heard news,' Skullface declared, grinning at him, 'that Lord Senenmut is deeply concerned. A chariot squadron sent out into the western desert has not returned. I learnt that from a servant at the temple.'

'And?' Themeu asked.

'The Lord Senenmut is sending out more chariot squadrons to discover what might have happened to it.'

Themeu ground his teeth. The priest had not mentioned this; perhaps he was becoming too frightened. Skullface chattered on, telling his captors the gossip from the Abode of Darkness and how the Churat had deployed his spies in and around the Temple of Ptah. Now and again he paused to pick up a piece of meat or slurp from the wine bowl, which he drained and asked to be refilled. The Vulture agreed. Skullface became drunk. He'd wander off into some memory from childhood or from when he fought the Libyans as a foot soldier in one of the imperial regiments, and the Vulture would gently bring him back to the matter in hand. Skullface gossiped on, repeating himself about events at the Temple of Ptah, the fire at the library, the murder of the heset and the mysterious sickness of Lord Hinqui, the assistant high priest. At this Themeu startled and gasped. He leaned forward and asked Skullface to repeat what he had said. The prisoner did so, before wandering back to his memories of life as a soldier. The air in the cellar grew hot and close. A voice in the shadows urged the Vulture to finish the matter, and the Amemet leaned forward and, picking up the wine bowl, forced Skullface to drink its dregs.

'One more thing.' Skullface pointed drunkenly at Themeu. 'I now remember you and that priest, in the long grass near the temple's apple orchards.' He gestured crudely at his groin. 'Every man has his own way. At the time,' he mused, 'I never realised the importance of what I saw. I wish I'd told my master, but,' he grinned, 'we all die with a thousand regrets on our lips and a million in our hearts.'

'We have finished, have we not, my friend?' the Vulture asked.

Skullface grinned. 'You'll keep your promise?' he slurred.

'Even now,' the Vulture whispered and lifted a hand. One of the men behind Skullface stepped forward and grasped the prisoner's head, pulling it back even as the knife in his other hand sliced Skullface's throat. Themeu started back as the hot blood splattered out. Skullface gagged, eyes popping; he gurgled on his own blood and, eyes rolling, tipped gently to one side.

'My lord,' the Vulture smiled, 'what you paid us has been repaid. We have kept our contract and we shall continue to do so. We must also be honest with each other. This business about Lord Hinqui seemed to disturb you.'

Themeu stared into the darkness.

'You realise,' Bluetooth hissed, 'that we are only the lieutenants. The chiefs of our guild lurk in the shadows beyond.'

Themeu nodded.

'We must know the full truth if you want us to help you,' insisted the Vulture.

'Hinqui,' Themeu declared. 'I suborned him. He has told us much about what happens at the councils of Pharaoh.'

'Why would an Egyptian priest betray his masters?'

Themeu's eyes flickered back to the Vulture; he smiled and shrugged.

'What you must ask yourself, my lord,' the Amemet declared, 'is this. Could your priest be the Rekhet?'

KHA'T: ancient Egyptian, 'corpse'

CHAPTER 9

The harmony of the House of the Golden Vine had been truly shattered. The gardens of the splendid mansion now thronged with Asural's guards as well as a horde of labourers from the Temple of Ma'at. They had searched and ransacked the place, and now, as the late afternoon sun began to dip, they'd sheltered in the shade of holm oaks and sycamore, as well as in the apple, plum and pomegranate orchards of the dead merchant. A grief-stricken Meryet, her face tear-streaked, accompanied by the Kushite Captain Hotep, was now informing a bemused Maben about what had happened. All three sat in the cool columned porch in front of the mansion. They rose as Amerotke, who had paused to chat briefly to his men, came to the foot of the broad sloping approach to the main door.

'So we have found a corpse?' the judge asked.

Hotep pointed at Asural standing behind Amerotke.

'He's the one, he'll show you.'

'I scrutinised the grounds . . .' Asural coughed and spluttered as Prenhoe raised a hand to protest. '*We* scrutinised the grounds,' Asural corrected himself. 'I could see no break in the lawns, but, master, come and see for yourself.'

Meryet and the others made to join them, but Amerotke objected.

'I would prefer it if you stayed here,' he declared. 'My companions and I must first see what has been discovered; afterwards I shall speak to you. You have examined the remains?'

Maben muttered something about doing it immediately on his return; Hotep looked embarrassed, whilst Meryet simply broke into a fit of weeping. Amerotke left them and, accompanied by Asural, Prenhoe and Shufoy, crossed the grounds to the northern corner. Here the grandeur and lushness petered out; there were shrubs and bushes, stretches of wild grass, untended pruned trees and a large sun pavilion, its paint peeling, the wood deeply weathered by sun and rain. In the corner of the wall rose a huge mound of compost, the detritus of the garden: rotting leaves, some black soil, vegetation cut and sliced and mashed into a green paste by the rain, plants and weeds culled from the lakes and ponds, all mixed with the muddy soil and stinking dung from the animal pens and stables.

The mound was massive, still moist due to its location and the shade from the trees; it reeked of corruption. It had been sifted and a hole quarried deep into the centre. Amerotke brought out the pomander he'd bought earlier in the day, and held this against his nose as he walked around the edge of that pile of rottenness.

'A good place to hide a corpse,' Asural declared, 'easy to burrow through. Decay would have been swift, the stench cleverly hidden.'

'And of course,' Amerotke declared, 'no one would think of looking here for poor Patuna, who was supposed to have run away.'

'She may have done,' Shufoy piped up.

Amerotke glanced down at the little man. 'What do you mean?' he asked. 'Explain yourself.'

Shufoy grinned. 'She may have run away, come back and been killed then. We just don't know the time and place.'

Amerotke patted him on the shoulder. 'Very sharp, my little man, very sharp indeed! However, I suspect she would have been seen by someone, somewhere. Yet from what I understand, since the morning Meryet found Patuna missing, no one has even glimpsed her. Until we establish otherwise, I think it is safe to presume that, on the evening before she disappeared, Patuna was hale and healthy. Sometime during that evening or night or early the following day, she met her killer and was murdered, her corpse buried deep beneath that dirt.'

Asural gestured at the shabby sun pavilion. 'The remains are in there.'

They climbed its steps and into the musty warmth. Linen sheets had been spread out on the ground, and the skeleton was almost hidden by gauzy veils. Amerotke knelt down and gently undid the folds. The weather, the compost and the passage of time had hastened corruption: hardly a trace of flesh remained, whilst the bones were beginning to yellow. Some bracelets and rings, as well as a necklace, all discoloured and caked with dirt, were still evident. Amerotke's attention was immediately caught by a heavy-looking wooden mallet with copper plates at each end.

'Found alongside the remains,' Asural whispered. 'Turn the skull.'

Amerotke picked this up and turned it round. The bone at the base had been so badly shattered that fragments had crumbled away. He tenderly placed the skull back into position, picked up the mallet and weighed it in his hands.

'Oh, the jewellery,' Asural intervened. 'Meryet recognised it as her sister's.'

Amerotke stared down at those pathetic remains. There had been no Osirian ritual for this woman's *ka*. No purification ceremony or cleansing. No procession, grave goods or funeral feast. He closed his eyes and quickly whispered the Prayer of Mercy to Osiris: 'May her heart be not found wanting. May you place tenderness in the scales. May your compassion outweigh her sins. May you look upon this daughter gently and lovely. May you recall her passing.' Then he opened his eyes, put down the mallet and got to his feet.

'Patuna never ran away,' he declared. 'She met her killer here in this lonely part of the garden, safe from prying eyes. I don't know what happened next: a quarrel, a fight? Anyway, she was brutally murdered. A swift, savage blow to the back of her head with that mallet. She must have died instantly, her corpse hidden under a pile of dirt.'

He walked to the entrance and stared across at the cool shade beneath the trees. 'Questions, eh, Shufoy – why did Patuna die? Who killed her? When?'

'Her wedding collarette and bracelet were found half burnt, not to mention the poetry,' Shufoy pointed out. 'Was all that the work of the assassin?'

'Questions, questions!' Amerotke snapped. 'Let's search for some answers.' He turned back into the pavilion, and went over to where Prenhoe sat on a bench just within the door. The scribe never liked what he called 'viewing the dead'. 'Kinsman,' Amerotke forced himself to hide his own tension and weariness, 'go with Asural, and tell the lady Meryet, Hotep and Lord Maben that I wish to meet them, here in the shade of those trees. Ask for a jug of fruit juice to be brought.'

A short while later Amerotke made himself comfortable on a cushion and eagerly drank the goblet of fruit juice a servant had poured. He waited until the man was out of earshot, then glanced across at Lady Meryet, Maben and Hotep. Meryet immediately confessed that she found it difficult even to look at the pathetic remains of her dead sister. Amerotke let her cry for a while before turning to Maben.

'You are sure it is the lady Patuna?'

'Yes.'

'Lady Meryet, on the morning you found Patuna's collarette burnt, the wedding bracelet lying beside it, you believed your sister was still alive. Why?'

'I saw her the previous evening.'

'And her mood?' Amerotke asked.

'Quiet and rather withdrawn,' Maben replied. 'She did not dine with us, I remember that. Just after dusk she said she felt unwell so she retired early; that was the last time Lady Meryet or I saw her alive.'

'What puzzles me,' Amerotke declared, 'is that if Lady Patuna was murdered here in this lonely part of the garden, why was the collarette half burnt, and the bracelet left with that scrap of poetry?'

'I wondered about that,' Meryet replied slowly. 'Perhaps she was going to run away, my lord Amerotke. Divorce Ipuye. Distance herself. Perhaps she met somebody here who could help her.'

'And who do you think that could be?' Amerotke asked.

Meryet closed her eyes, then opened them, staring full at the judge. 'I cannot say,' she whispered.

'You don't really believe that, do you?' Amerotke asked.

Meryet shook her head.

'You believe that Lord Ipuye, who indeed had not travelled to Memphis but simply to his pleasures in nearby Thebes, slipped back into this garden, met your sister and killed her.' Amerotke wetted his lips. 'There's one thing we have not fully discussed: the poem, yes?'

Meryet, between sobs, nodded quickly.

'It was in your sister's hand but could have been written at any time. The murderer left it with the half-burnt collarette and bracelet to deepen the impression that Patuna was unhappy and had decided to flee both her marriage and her home.' Amerotke recalled what Norfret had said, 'Though on reflection,' he continued, 'that was a harsh decision for a wealthy lady of Thebes, surely?'

His question was greeted with silence.

'Now tell me,' he insisted. 'Lord Maben, Lady Meryet, you never met your sister again after that evening before she disappeared?'

Both chorused their agreement.

'You, Lady Meryet, always claimed she had been murdered and you have been proved correct. You also believe the assassin was her now dead husband.' Amerotke stared down at the ground, conceding to himself that there was a certain logic to that. 'I've asked this before.' He lifted his head. 'Patuna was unhappy?'

'Of course she was!' Meryet replied. 'Ipuye's womanising, the whores, the courtesans – you've been to his pleasure chamber, Lord Amerotke – my sister had to live with that. When he went away on his so-called business journeys, we all knew he wasn't telling the truth.'

'If you suspected she was murdered,' Shufoy spoke up, 'why didn't you search these gardens yourself?'

'I did,' Meryet replied, 'but I never thought anyone would put my sister's corpse in a pile of dirt and rubbish! I did wonder whether Patuna might have gone into the city to reason with Ipuye and that that was where she was killed.'

'But of course Ipuye,' Amerotke countered, 'who cannot take part in this debate, thought differently. He believed his wife had been killed by the Rekhet. Why would he think that? Why should some lady in a mansion outside Thebes attract the attention of such a subtle assassin?'

'But we've told you,' Meryet replied. 'Ipuye's womanising. I'm sure it wasn't just whores and courtesans of the city, the Silken Ones, but others! Someone who really believed Ipuye had promised her marriage once Patuna was dead.'

'So,' Amerotke placed his cup down on the acacia-wood table and spread his hands, 'Patuna disappeared. Ipuye believed she might have been removed by a rival, the half-burnt collarette and bracelet, the poetry simply a device to mislead. Did he ever make accusations against anyone?'

Both Meryet and Maben shook their heads.

'Are you sure?' Amerotke persisted.

'I believe Ipuye,' Meryet replied slowly, 'was embarrassed about Patuna's disappearance, or pretended to be, hence the great drama about the Rekhet being involved and the reward being posted. It was to cover his own filthy deeds.'

'Why do you say embarrassed?' Shufoy asked.

'Embarrassed because his wife knew about his womanising. Someone else, like me, may have wondered what truly happened to Patuna, whether Ipuye had a hand in her disappearance.'

'When he went to his Place of Pleasure in Thebes,' Amerotke asked, 'did anyone ever accompany him?'

'No,' Maben replied, 'he went alone.'

Amerotke gestured at Hotep. 'So you were hired after Patuna's disappearance?'

'No, Lord Judge, before. The rest of the bodyguards were hired because Lord Ipuye considered himself vulnerable.'

'Was Ipuye frightened of the Rekhet striking at him as, he alleged, the criminal had at Patuna?'

'Correct, Lord Judge.' The Kushite's face remained impassive.

'And he issued special instructions, didn't he?' Amerotke pointed at Meryet. 'He'd only eat and drink what you prepared?'

'Yes, that's true, though he allowed Maben and Hotep to handle his food and drink as well. He trusted all three of us.'

'And on the day Ipuye died, what happened then?'

'Well, I was in the temple,' Maben replied. 'Lady Meryet was my guest. We left shortly before noon.'

'And Ipuye?' Amerotke asked.

'He and the lady Khiat,' Maben replied, 'remained in their chambers. Ipuye had declared the night before that he would enjoy what he called a day of ease—'

'Oh by the way,' Amerotke intervened, 'even though he was married to Khiat, he still went back to his Place of Pleasure?'

'Yes, yes, I think he did,' Maben replied.

'And did he eat or drink that day, Lady Meryet?'

'No,' Maben replied quickly. 'In fact, although Ipuye insisted that only Meryet prepare his food and drink, on that particular day he said he would tend to himself.'

'So you left for the Temple of Ptah,' Amerotke declared, 'and you didn't return until the early evening, after the tragedy had occurred?'

'Yes, that's right.'

'And you, Hotep, what happened then? You were captain of your master's guard.'

'He rose late in the day,' Hotep replied slowly. 'I was waiting in the coolness of the portico. I heard him call my name so I went into the house. He and the lady Khiat had brought down napkins and towels; they were clothed in light robes, reed sandals on their feet.'

'And then what?' Amerotke asked. 'Did they eat or drink?'

'No. My master and the lady Khiat had stayed in their chambers during the morning; they said it was cooler. The lady Khiat took in bread, fruit and a little wine, but that was early in the day. I asked Lord Ipuye if he wanted to eat or drink. He replied no. The lady Khiat would take across a jug of wine and two cups to the enclosure.'

'Then what?'

Hotep pulled a face. 'Lord Judge, they left the house. I followed them. As soon as Lord Ipuye and Lady Khiat entered the enclosure, my men took up their positions amongst the trees. It wasn't an onerous duty.' Hotep smiled thinly.

'And did you hear or see anything untoward?' Amerotke asked.

'No, my lord. One of the guards, Saneb, who was on duty near the gate, heard some splashing later on, that's all.'

'Fetch Saneb.'

'You've met him already,' Hotep declared.

'I'd like to speak to him again.' Amerotke sipped at his juice and bit into some soft bread. The day was now fading. He had done enough watching and listening; now he needed time to reflect as well as relax.

Hotep returned with Saneb. Amerotke filled a goblet with fruit juice and offered it to the Kushite, who bowed in thanksgiving, took it and drank greedily.

'Saṇeb, on the day your master died, you were on guard in the trees near the enclosure gate.'

The young Kushite nodded vigorously.

'You were distant from your companions?'

'Yes.' The Kushite swallowed hard. 'It was hot, Lord Judge. We knew our master was enjoying himself; so did we. I sat in the shade of a tree, dozed and listened, but I saw or heard nothing untoward except some splashing.'

'Tell me,' Amerotke thumbed the side of his face, 'if the Rekhet was caught and sentenced, why did Lord Ipuye still need a Kushite guard?'

Maben looked swiftly at Hotep, who gestured at him to reply.

'Lord Ipuye had business rivals,' Maben declared slowly.

'Oh, tell the truth,' Meryet snapped.

'Ipuye pretended that he'd been frightened by the Rekhet,' Maben replied, 'by his wife's disappearance. But I'll be blunt. He had business rivals, men who did not like the way he seduced their women-folk. I suspect that was the real reason. He was frightened they might retaliate, hence he increased his guard.'

Amerotke nodded understandingly. 'Now, going back to the day Ipuye died: Saneb, you entered the gate and saw the bodies floating face down in the pool?'

'Yes, yes, I did.'

'And you sent for Hotep?'

'Yes, my lord.'

'And what happened then?'

'I jumped into the pool,' Hotep replied.

'And Saneb, did you help?'

'Yes, I did. We carried both bodies out of the water into the sun pavilion.'

'Tell me now, Saneb,' Amerotke lifted a hand, 'and I want you to think very carefully. When you lifted the corpses out, were they warm or were they cold? I know they'd been in cool water, but did you think they had just died, or been dead for some time?'

Saneb screwed up his face in concentration. 'I have handled corpses before,' he declared. 'I've seen several out in the Redlands.'

'Of course you have,' Amerotke replied.

'The bodies were supple. I remember the water was cold, as was the flesh of both Lord Ipuye and his wife. Yes, they were definitely cold.'

Amerotke nodded. 'Thank you.' He pushed away the table and rose to his feet. 'I thank you for your answers,' he gestured at the table, 'and for the refreshments. Now we must leave.'

The Amemet called Bluetooth, a leading member of a guild of assassins in Thebes, sat in the shadow of the beer tent awning. He clutched his chipped cup as he watched the postern gate commonly called the Door of Chariotry in the imperial Palace of the Eternal Sun. His masters had given him this task because he had once been a member of the Nakhtu-aa, a veteran adorned with the Golden Bees of bravery and the Silver Collar of courage. However, that had been before the unfortunate incident over the Tedjen's daughter, not to mention the mysterious disappearance of the contents of the regimental strong box, as well as those missing cups from the squadron's refectory.

Ah well, Bluetooth reflected, I still have life, unlike poor Skullface. More importantly, Bluetooth possessed detailed knowledge about imperial garrisons, the reason why he had been chosen to watch, observe and report on any military activity out of the ordinary. His masters had told him that the Divine One and her lover, Chief Minister Senenmut, were residing at the Palace of the Sun. If they decided on any such military action, this was where it would begin. To be certain, other Amemets were spying on various houses throughout the city. Kennut, or the Ape, watched the House of the Golden Vine; Thesti, or Beak, the comfortable house of his former colleague Standard-Bearer Nadif; Tebb, or Scratches, because of his nasty but constant habit of scratching between his legs, the stately mansion of Amerotke the Judge; whilst Girt, the Mole, lurked outside the Temple of Ma'at. They all had their orders, 'to observe and act on anything untoward'.

Bluetooth chewed on his tongue and sipped more of the beer. He was about to order a fresh cup when the Door of Chariotry was flung open and a corps of imperial Maryannou, Braves of the King, came hurrying out. The men were armed for a fight. They carried long, rectangular ochre-coloured shields with the head of Amun emblazoned in blue on their front. Each man also carried a short stabbing spear, with a curved sword and a club hanging from the embroidered war belt around his waist. The soldiers' heads were protected by the imperial blue and gold striped headdresses, their groins and upper thighs by thick, embroidered leather kilts, whilst their stout marching boots showed they intended to cross rough terrain. About forty in number, they moved purposefully, scattering the crowd before them.

Bluetooth made his decision. He dropped his beer cup and trotted after them. The unit moved down streets past booths laden with all kinds of goods in their multicoloured variety. Confectioners, trying to take advantage of the afternoon crowds, held out their sweets. Cooks offered spiced strips of goose. Oil traders shouted for custom as they stood behind their range of sandstone jars. The drinkers outside the beer shops and wine tents sampling cups such as 'The Star of the Morning' and 'The Glory of Kush' forgot their thirst and scattered. A dog collector straining at the leashes of bassets, salukis and jackal dogs scampered hastily out of the soldiers' path. Bluetooth, gasping for breath, followed the unit down alleyways so narrow, the walls so high, they were no more than darkened tunnels. The house fronts on either side were like secret faces with only a few windows set high in the wall. Mounds of refuse, carts, donkeys, barrows, yapping dogs, naked children and screaming women proved no obstacle to the Maryannou. Bluetooth paused for breath then hurried on, knocking away a whining pie-dog and scattering a gang of hunchbacked dwarfs. He was certain the imperial troops were on a special mission. He turned a corner and abruptly stopped. The soldiers had dived through a low darkened doorway. Bluetooth, standing in the shadows, heard screams, yells, crashing and clattering, then the Maryannou emerged dragging a black-haired man, his face, darkened by the sun, half hidden by a shaggy beard and moustache.

'I am not he!' the man screamed. 'I'm no Rekhet!' He shouted at the crowd for help but these turned away. The prisoner continued to struggle and yell until a soldier hit him, whilst another member of the troop emerged from the doorway holding a sack. He handed this to the unit's officer, who opened it, searched through its contents and brought out a small stoppered jar. He opened the jar, sniffed at it, then smashed it on the ground, yelling at the prisoner that his guilt was already proven. Bluetooth watched fascinated. The Maryannou broke up the gathering crowd, manacled their prisoner, and pushing him before them made their back to the Palace of the Sun. Bluetooth followed, and watched them march through the Door of Chariotry before slipping away to report to his masters.

So immersed was Bluetooth in what he had seen and heard that he'd been totally unaware that he, in turn, had been watched and followed. The Listener, the Eyes and Ears of Pharaoh, one of the many imperial spies who swarmed through the city, had taken careful note of Bluetooth's actions. Once he was sure the Amemet had disappeared into the crowd, he made his own way towards the imperial palace.

Amerotke sat in his *kha*, his private writing chamber, which jutted out from the back of his house. The lintels and shutters of the windows on all three walls had been removed to allow in the cool, scented night air from the gardens beyond. Lamp jars, carved in the shapes of ducks, quails and geese, presents from Amerotke's sons, glowed brightly. On his left Amerotke had placed his writing box, and on his right a beaker and jug of cold beer; on a slightly sloping desk before him a piece of papyrus had been stretched out, kept in place by coppery clasps. The parchment gazed blankly back at him. The judge was puzzled and confused; he'd seen and heard so much that day. He wanted to concentrate on one problem, but others came as distractions. He picked up a cobalt-blue ivory-handled fan and wafted his sweaty face. The house lay quiet. He'd kissed the boys good night in their bedchamber. Norfret was probably sitting at her own writing desk studying accounts. Amerotke smiled. His wife was very keen to show the stewards and servants that everything was scrutinised. Outside the noises of the night rose and fell: the constant whirring of insects which came floating through windows, drawn in by the lamplight.

Amerotke could not decide which was more irritating, that or the monotonous croaking of the bullfrogs from the ponds, canals and gardens.

Amerotke sighed. He was irritable because he was tired, because he could not make any sense of the knotted, twisted problems confronting him. How had those three scribes been murdered? Surely they had not broken their fast? One perhaps, but not all three, and despite what had been said about the way the Libyans had handled the bowl, no such sleight of hand could transform a sacred vessel of wine into a poisoned one. So how had they been killed? Why? By whom? And Hutepa, lying twisted, poisoned in her chamber. Why had that temple girl worked so hard to discover the location of Huaneka's grave and the possible hiding place of the Ari Sapu, yet not attempted to go out there? Amerotke paused. Was it because she knew the Rekhet had already been there? Indeed, were these maps recent? Had they been drawn up after the Rekhet had been arrested or during his imprisonment? If so, why? Some evidence existed that Hutepa might have been the Rekhet's lover, but if that was the case, why betray him to Standard-Bearer Nadif only to shelter him four years later, even make love to him? Hutepa would have been very wary, surely, of the man she'd betrayed? She knew the Rekhet was a killer so why risk her own neck? In the end she'd suffered a swift, brutal death, but was the Rekhet responsible for that?

And the Rekhet himself? According to Nadif, he'd been a priest physician at the Temple of Ptah, but no explanation had been given for why he'd transformed himself into a murderer, or how he'd been able to deal out death to so many. The Churat was perceptive. How were all those potions and powders distributed across Thebes? How were the Rekhet's many victims chosen? And in the last resort, surely such a man, demonstrating all the cunning of a jackal, would not allow himself to be caught so easily: powders and potions found in his chamber; the suspicions of Userbati alerted. Moreover, few men ever successfully escaped alive from a prison oasis as the Rekhet had! Had he been helped, by Hutepa or someone else? Why were the Libyans so interested in him? Had they assisted him in his escape, but for what? Did the Rekhet have his own devious motives for disrupting the peace treaty?

Amerotke continued to write. If the escaped convict, understandably, wanted to remain hidden, why approach him, Chief Judge in the Hall of Two Truths? On reflection, apart from the knife to Amerotke's neck, more as a precaution than a threat, the Rekhet had not menaced, but simply asked Amerotke to watch and reflect. On the other hand, he'd dealt ruthlessly with two of the Churat's killers: they had posed a threat; Amerotke hadn't. The judge paused, pen raised. Indeed, he'd forgotten about that, the warning whistle at which the Rekhet had disappeared. Did he have an accomplice? The temple girl?

Was there one Rekhet or two, or even a group like the Amemets, the guild of assassins in the city? Had only one of this gang been arrested? Amerotke shook his head. Was the poisoning of the three scribes simply an act of revenge, nothing to do with Pharaoh's policies? Yet if so, why were the Libyans involved? Indeed, the Libyans seemed to be very knowledgeable and active in all these matters. Were they being given privileged information?

Amerotke felt he was going round in circles. He rose and watched the moths dancing frenetically above the lamp flame. Outside a night bird shrieked, to be answered by the dull roar of hippopotami along the river. Amerotke smiled. He felt like one of the moths, involved in a dance that made no sense. He returned to his writing. One mystery followed another. The librarian's death, the burning of those records. Why was the librarian killed and the manuscripts destroyed when the originals were held by Maben in those heavy carved chests? Who else had discovered the location of Huaneka's tomb, the hidden place of the Ari Sapu? Maben controlled that chest, yet he'd cooperated fully as if he had nothing to hide.

Amerotke walked to the window and stared out at the small garden pool glistening in the light of the full moon. He beat a fist against his thigh. Ipuye . . . How had that rich, lecherous merchant died? Everyone was certain that no one had entered the enclosure around the lotus pool, whilst Nadif had established that the wine taken in wasn't tainted. But how could two vigorous human beings be drowned without the alarm being raised? Was it, in fact, a most unfortunate coincidence? However, the murder of Ipuye's first wife Patuna certainly was not an accident. That poor woman had been lured to a desolate part of her garden and had her head staved in. Had Ipuye slipped back to his own house and burnt that wedding collarette and bracelet either before or after he killed his wife? Why would a wealthy merchant do that? Surely he would not bloody his hands but hire someone else to do it?

Amerotke slumped down on to the high-backed chair. If he could make no progress here, perhaps he should concentrate on the items on the edge of all these mysteries: like Assistant High Priest Hinqui. What was the cause of his illness? Was it a contagion, or had he been poisoned? Amerotke put his face in his hands. Other small things had, during the day, pricked his suspicions, but like the fireflies out in the garden, they flared bright yet proved illusive. The judge yawned, his eyes grew heavy and he slipped into a deep sleep.

He was woken just before dawn by an anxious-looking Shufoy, swathed in a heavy robe, the hood pulled over his head.

'Master, master?' Shufoy pushed his disfigured face close. 'Master, you should have gone to bed!'

Amerotke shook himself awake. Shufoy hastened across the chamber and brought over a quilted linen robe. Amerotke rose and put this round his shoulders whilst Shufoy busied himself extinguishing those oil lamps which had not gone out during the night.

'What is the matter?' Amerotke asked.

'You have visitors, master, you'd best see for yourself.'

Outside, the eerie, grey-tinged light that separates the night from daybreak persisted. A mist curled between the trees. Amerotke gazed up at the sky, which was dark except for the first few flashes and ribbons of light. Shufoy ran before him like a conspirator, urging him on, fluttering his hand and pointing down the pathway towards the porter's lodge. Amerotke hurried after him, then paused. A war chariot pulled by two sleek horses stood at the side of the path. This was no ornamental carriage: its harness was gleaming black leather whilst the chariot itself boasted no embossed decoration of electrum or gold. A group of Nubians squatted on the grassy lawn sharing a wine skin; nearby were two figures in the long open robes of charioteers, hoods pulled over their heads.

'What is this?' Amerotke exclaimed. 'Who are you?' He followed Shufoy down the path, but instead of coming to meet him, the two figures withdrew into the trees. Amerotke paused. Should he go back to the house, rouse his servants, fetch a sword or club?

'Come, master,' Shufoy called. 'You must come.'

HEMHEM-I: ancient Egyptian, 'battle cry'

CHAPTER 10

As Amerotke stepped in amongst the trees, the two charioteers pulled back their hoods. Amerotke stopped in amazement. Lord Senenmut and the Divine One Hatusu stood there smiling at him. He went to kneel, but Hatusu snapped her fingers and beckoned him closer. He had never seen her like this before, face unpainted, cropped hair combed back, yet she was no less beautiful. Her skin was translucent, unblemished, her blue eyes fierce and hard in their stare, lips compressed in a tight line as if anxious or angry about something.

'Your Excellencies,' Amerotke's voice was tinged with sarcasm, 'you are truly unexpected, but come, come into my house.'

He led them back up into his writing chamber. Shufoy brought stools and asked if they wished to eat or drink. Both Senenmut and Hatusu shook their heads. Amerotke told Shufoy to close the doors and, helped by Senenmut, they put back the lattice window covers, closing the shutters. Hatusu, seated in Amerotke's chair, watched and nodded.

'It's best,' she murmured. 'We came in secret and what we have to say,' she glanced warningly at Shufoy, 'must remain secret.' She nodded at Senenmut.

'Lord Judge, do you know the house called the Mansion of Horus the Red-Eye?'

'Of course I do.' Amerotke sat down on a stool. 'A lonely place not far from here. It stands in its own grounds protected by a high curtain wall. It gets its name from a statue of the god on a pillar on either side of the gateway. I often pass it. It once belonged, so I believe, to the royal house.'

'It still does,' Hatusu replied, 'and we use it for this secret purpose or that. Lord Judge, last night a unit of the Maryannou arrested the Rekhet in Thebes and now have him imprisoned there.' She laughed at Amerotke's astonishment. 'I am telling you stories, Lord Judge. Let me start at the beginning. We received the message you sent us through Standard-Bearer Nadif, how the Libyans have approached the Churat and hired the services of the Amemets. Oh, by the way,' Hatusu smiled, 'I have accepted the Churat's terms in return for the help he gave. Well, the Libyans came to Thebes to seal a peace treaty, but they also seem very eager to capture the Rekhet. Now everyone in the royal circle, each member of my council, distrusts the Libyans. They have insisted on this peace treaty and appear scrupulously intent on preserving its terms: no attacks upon our merchants or traders, on our garrisons in various oases, no raiding the villages along the Nile. That is all pleasing to us. At the same time the Libyans seem keen to develop their trade with the mines along the Horus Road in Sinai. We believe there is something else. They have constantly reiterated that they had no hand in those poisonings on the temple forecourt. They seem eager to prove themselves innocent of any deviousness or trickery, but, in a word, I don't trust them. Why, I ask, do Naratousha and his colleagues seem so intent on capturing the Rekhet? What is he to them? Did he escape from that prison oasis with their help? Is that how he so safely reached Thebes?'

'There is something else,' Senenmut added. 'The Divine One said that there have been no raids, no murderous activity by the Libyans, except in one matter. The day before yesterday a chariot squadron was sent out to patrol the western Redlands. It was led by a hot-headed officer eager to prove himself. He may have gone further than he should, but to cut a long story short, Amerotke, his squadron has not returned. We have sent out scouts and spies but they've found no trace of it, no remains, be it chariot or horse or human, whilst sand-dwellers and desert wanderers report nothing amiss. I simply do not believe that a chariot squadron can disappear into the desert haze as if it has gone across the Far

Horizon. Now, for sake of argument, let us say that squadron was wiped out. Only the Libyans have the military might to achieve that. Only they have the means to completely hide corpses, chariots, horses . . .'

'You believe our troops discovered something startling and were massacred?'

'Yes,' replied Senenmut. 'They must have been ambushed, either out in the open desert or at an oasis, but so far we've discovered nothing.'

'And have you really captured the Rekhet?' Amerotke asked.

'Well,' Senenmut continued, 'according to our own spies, those who work for the House of Secrets, the Eyes and Ears of Pharaoh, well-known Amemets have been seen in the city. I suspect, Lord Judge, that your house is under their close inspection; the royal palace certainly is. One of our spies reported that the postern gate, the Door of Chariotry, was being watched by Bluetooth, an Amemet well known to the House of Secrets. We then devised our plan. We decided to act as if we had captured the Rekhet. One of our mercenaries, a Syrian, was sent into the city to lodge in some shabby house and to act when he was arrested as if he were the Rekhet. He was supplied with a sack of small jars containing innocent powder and water. A detachment of the Maryannou was dispatched to arrest him. Our mercenary acted the part and was brought back to the palace.'

'And of course the Amemets now know all about it?'

'Yes,' Hatusu declared, her voice loud and carrying. 'Bluetooth saw the Rekhet, as he thinks, being hustled into the palace. Later on today he will see him escorted by a small cohort of soldiers to the House of Horus the Red-Eye. He will also see you enter that house.' Hatusu's glance fell away and her voice became more uncertain. 'Lord Judge, I ask a great deal of you. The Amemets will soon realise that the Rekhet is in the House of Horus the Red-Eye, guarded only by a small escort, being questioned by Lord Amerotke.'

The judge closed his eyes. He knew what Hatusu was going to ask.

'The Amemets never attack by day.' Senenmut picked up the narrative. 'They are too prudent and cautious. Tonight, however, I believe they will attack the House of Horus the Red-Eye in force. They are determined to lay their hands on the Rekhet and snatch him away, for which the Libyans will pay them a very high price.'

'But that's extremely dangerous!' Shufoy's voice was almost a squeak. 'The Amemets will kill my master.'

'There are two reasons we ask this,' Senenmut continued evenly. 'First, the Amemets are a pestilence; this will be a unique opportunity to wipe them out!'

'How?' Amerotke asked.

Senenmut shook a hand. 'No, listen. Second, if the Amemets do attack, that's the final proof that the Rekhet knows something very important. It will confirm our deep suspicions that something startling, dangerous to Egypt, is happening out in the western desert.'

'And then what?' Amerotke asked.

'If necessary,' Hatusu replied, 'I shall offer full amnesty and pardon to the Rekhet, provided he surrenders himself to Pharaoh's justice so we can discover what he knows.'

'You referred to the Amemets being massacred,' Amerotke declared, 'and yet on the other hand you talk of a small escort of soldiers . . .'

'Ah,' Hatusu grinned, 'what the Amemets do not know is that much earlier today I sent out couriers, secret messengers to the garrisons around Thebes. Since the early hours of this morning, long before the moon began to set, crack troops, Maryannou, Nakhtu-aa, Syrian archers, Kushites, men we can really trust, have been filtered out to make their way stealthily to the House of Horus the Red-Eye. They are under the command of General Omendap. When the Amemets attack tonight, and I suspect they will, they will be ambushed and killed.'

'And so will my master,' Shufoy repeated, 'and me!'

'There's something else, isn't there?' Amerotke asked.

Senenmut's face remained the same, stony and impassive; Hatusu, though, was slightly nervous.

'To be honest, Lord Judge, this Rekhet troubles me. I am beginning to doubt whether we know the truth at all about this man. The night before last he struck at us in the very heart of the temple.' Hatusu briefly described the poisoning of a servant outside her chamber.

'Amerotke,' Senenmut spoke up once Hatusu had finished, 'we are uncertain about the Libyans. Were they responsible for the temple poisonings? Are they responsible for the attempt on us? Who is behind this wickedness? Moreover, why didn't the Rekhet flee to Memphis or somewhere else? Why come back to Thebes and resume the same evil trail that led to his capture and imprisonment in the first place?'

'And you, Lord Judge,' Hatusu's voice was harsh, 'have you discovered anything to resolve these mysteries?'

Amerotke shook his head.

'And will you do what I ask?'

Amerotke stared at the floor. 'I will,' he replied, 'on two conditions. First, that my wife is not told about what is going to happen.' He turned and winked at Shufoy. 'Second, little friend, you cannot come. You must stay here and look after the Lady Norfret and my sons. Don't worry, I will be well protected. If the Amemets attack, perhaps we might learn something we don't know.'

'Finally,' Senenmut gestured around, 'we are here for a purpose. We came in disguise to deceive not only the Amemets but also the traitor who is sitting close to our councils. You do realise we nurture one, Amerotke?'

'I have my suspicions. The Libyans seem well versed on the importance of the Rekhet.'

'I believe,' Senenmut replied, 'they have now learnt how the Rekhet assumed the identity of that Memphis merchant who also worked for me, one of my best spies in the western desert—'

'These matters have been discussed at meetings of the Royal Circle,' Hatusu intervened, 'but the only other place we mentioned them was when we met the high priests of Ptah on the very evening the three scribes were poisoned!' She smiled. 'Either you, Amerotke, or one of them is a traitor. The room in which we chose to discuss such important issues was safe and sealed against any eavesdropper. It can only mean one or all of three things. Either one of those priests is the Rekhet – I doubt it. Or an associate – a possibility. Or, for his own nefarious reasons, a traitor to Egypt.' Hatusu rose to her feet. 'We shall have no more discussions with the priests of Ptah or lodge at their temple till you, Amerotke, solve these mysteries.'

After Hatusu and Senenmut had left, Amerotke prepared himself. The first hours passed like a dream. He joined his family out in the glorious coolness of the garden, acting absent-minded as the day slipped away, playing *senet* with his sons whilst Norfret talked about the new wig she had bought.

Shufoy was sent into the city with a letter for Hinqui. Amerotke instructed him to wait for any reply and say nothing about what he knew. Amerotke then returned to his chamber to pack panniers and bags. He informed Norfret that he was to meet Lord Senenmut on business connected with the House of Secrets. Norfret wasn't fooled. She recognised something was wrong and watched her husband intently, large dark eyes sorrowful in her beautiful face. During the late afternoon Amerotke collected his possessions, kissed Norfret and told her it was time for him to leave. She simply stared back then accompanied him down to the gate. As he made to go through, she clutched his wrist.

'My heart', she whispered the words of a poem, 'lies heavy, my desire is to be with you in all things.'

'As you are,' Amerotke replied fiercely. He kissed her on the lips and slipped between the half-opened gates.

For some strange reason Amerotke felt that once he was free of his house he was vulnerable to all forms of secret violence, deceit and sudden attack, yet his journey to the House of Horus the Red-Eye was no more dangerous than a stroll in the evening air. When he arrived there he found it quiet. He knocked on the main gate and looked around. The pathway behind him was deserted except for a beggar scratching vigorously between his legs. When Amerotke caught his eye, the man stopped and stretched out a claw-like hand, voice wheedling for money. Amerotke turned away. The man was a counterfeit, a scorpion man, quite capable of honest labour and earning a wage. Amerotke heard the bolts being drawn and the gates swung open, admitting him into a world of secrets.

The House of Horus the Red-Eye was supposed to be deserted, but the overgrown garden teemed with fighting men, warriors from the crack regiments, sitting in groups, eating spiced meat and drinking from jugs of sugared beer. Amerotke almost had to pinch himself. Was he dreaming? The soldiers were all dressed for war in leather kilts and baldrics, their weapons close at hand, yet an oppressive silence reigned. No hum of conversation betrayed their presence. Amerotke walked past them and up the sloping entrance to the house. Inside, the shabby hall of columns housed the officers, also attired for battle. Amerotke recognised Omendap, Hatusu's commander-in-chief, a burly, strapping individual, his shaven face and head gleaming with oil. He too was dressed for war, in leather marching boots, stiffened kilt and a breastplate of chain mail, the bronze discs sewn together on the thick linen undergarment beneath. Omendap greeted Amerotke and waved him over to a corner.

'Lord Judge, the Divine One said you would come. What do you think of our preparations?'

Amerotke gazed round. 'And the prisoner?'

Omendap walked to the door, put his fingers to his lips and blew a shrill whistle. A short while later four Maryannou, armed to the teeth, brought in a man with black hair and tousled moustache and beard. The judge ordered him to sit on a stool.

'The Divine One has chosen you,' Amerotke began, aware of Omendap standing behind him. 'Tonight the Amemets will come. They will be searching for you. The enemy will be men like yourself, former soldiers. Now whatever happens,' he looked quickly over his shoulder at Omendap, 'you must not be taken alive. We shall do our best to protect you.' He stretched out a hand. The mercenary grasped it and, lifting it, kissed Amerotke's wrist.

'Lord Judge,' the man replied softly, 'the Divine One has showed her face and smiled at me.' He grinned up at General Omendap. 'I do not think the Amemets will reach me.'

Amerotke spent the rest of that day in a small chamber at the back of the shabby, dilapidated mansion. Shufoy, to keep up pretences, arrived with a parcel of food wrapped tenderly in linen by Norfret. The dwarf squatted before the judge, who sat on a cushion with his back to the crumbling wall, biting into the soft bread and olives.

'A ghost house!' Shufoy murmured. 'Outside, master, you'd think this place was deserted, but once you are through the gates and into the trees . . .'

Amerotke laughed. 'Omendap is afraid an Amemet spy may scale the wall,' he declared, 'to search for a possible ambush. He has ordered all his troops deeper into the trees with strict instructions to remain hidden.' He shook his head. 'I feel sorry for them. They have to relieve themselves where they are, eat what provisions are available and bear the heat of the day.'

'Harsh but sound advice.' Shufoy helped himself to a slice of fruit. 'As I came in I noticed two beggars . . .'

'Amemets?'

'Undoubtedly. One looks like an ape; the other is constantly scratching his crotch! Beggars have a certain look and posture; those two are undoubtedly Amemet scouts.'

'Good,' Amerotke declared. 'Let them stay there and see what they are supposed to see, like a mirage in the desert: a poorly defended house which can be easily attacked once darkness falls.'

'You will be safe, master?'

'Shufoy, Shufoy,' Amerotke leaned forward, 'you and I both know that every time we investigate a sudden mysterious death, or walk through the streets of the Necropolis, Death, like a shadow, lurks not far behind. This is no different. However, as you said, the gardens of this house are thronged with soldiers. The Amemets, not I, will be ambushed tonight. Shufoy, we have done business with those assassins before. Lord Senenmut is correct. Tonight we might inflict such a blow, it will take them a long, long time to recover.'

'And the poisonings, the mysterious deaths?'

'I have gone down one path and then another only

to find them all blocked. There must be another way.' He leaned over and clasped Shufoy's hand. 'Keep your counsel. Do not make Norfret anxious. Give my love to my lady wife and my sons. Oh, and by the way . . .' Amerotke felt in the folds of his robe and brought out a small scroll. 'Before you return home, go to the Temple of Ptah, seek out the priest Hinqui again and give him this. Ask him to study it most carefully, and when he is ready to send a reply, he must do so directly to me.'

Once again Shufoy grasped his master's hand. When he had left, Amerotke slept for a while, then returned to reflecting on the mysteries that confronted him, but he was restless, unable to make any headway, and was relieved when the sun began to set. He had been under instruction from Omendap not to leave his chamber, but once darkness had fallen, he joined the mercenary on the roof terrace to eat and talk in the glow of lamplight which he knew could be seen from beyond the walls. A military cook served food: hard bread, dried meat, fruit and bitter-tasting wine. Nevertheless, the mercenary proved to be a most congenial companion. He claimed the food was better than that served in the barracks, and under Amerotke's gentle questioning he described how he originally came from a family that owned a small farm in the delta. He regaled Amerotke with stories of the Sea People, their customs, and their hunger for gold, silver and precious stones.

'Our farm couldn't support more than one,' he joked, 'so I joined the army and saw service out along the Horus Road. Afterwards I took my pay and left. I married but my wife died in childbirth. I decided to sell my plot . . .' He then went on to describe how he'd even seen military service in warships on the Great Green, and his involvement in the furious pursuit of a raiding galley to an island far across the waters.

'The Sea People beached their ship and retreated inland,' he related. 'Our captain ordered us marines to follow. It was a living nightmare! I thought I'd entered the Underworld. The dense vegetation was truly dangerous due to the traps the Sea People had left for us: rockfalls which would be started off with a pebble, pits dug deep, their bottoms lined with sharpened stakes. The worst was the beach itself. They'd hidden a myriad of small thorns under a coating of loose sand.'

'So you scarred your feet?' Amerotke asked.

'Yes, but the real danger was that the tips of these thorns were thickly coated in human dung. A physician later described how deadly these things were. Those of our men who were scratched simply thought it was a nuisance, nothing much compared to a blow from a club or a thrust from a dagger. Only later did deep infection set in, and by then it was too late.'

Amerotke nodded understandingly. He'd heard of similar traps being used, simple, primitive but very lethal. An army physician had once informed him that human dung was probably one of the greatest poisons you could infect a man with.

'You see,' the mercenary continued, 'the tip went deep, the cut was made, the blood flowed. The injured man would go to a physician, who'd probably rinse it and then bandage it, but the infection was already working. Only later, perhaps two or three days on, would the victim realise that something was wrong. Sometimes the cut could be opened and cleaned, but on many occasion I saw men die raging, feverish, from a simple cut to their foot . . .'

He was about to launch into another tale when the night sky above them was scored by a fire arrow streaking up through the darkness.

'It's begun,' Amerotke murmured. 'Let's go down.'

Bluetooth the Amemet watched the fire arrow streak through the night. He was leading his unit of ten men, veterans, former members of the imperial army. Twenty such groups now circled the House of Horus the Red-Eye. They were the Restu, the Night Watchers. The Amemet chiefs had summoned up two hundred of their men to ring and scale the wall, brush aside any resistance, capture the prisoner and even take Judge Amerotke hostage. Such a prospect appealed to the leaders of these assassins. It would be a public boast of their power, a clear sign to all the other creatures who lurked in the Am-duat of Thebes that the Amemets were its true rulers, able to mock even the power of Pharaoh. Bluetooth secretly comforted himself that this would be an easy task. Amemet scouts had reported little or no activity in or around the house. The only visitor had been that little man Shufoy, Amerotke's assistant, who had now left. Bluetooth had been disappointed at that. If they captured Amerotke, they could have taken Shufoy as well and possibly sold him to merchants along the Nile; these were always on the lookout for some grotesque whom they could sell in the delta or beyond the Fourth Cataract.

Ah well! Bluetooth turned, peering through the darkness. His men were prepared, faces and bodies gleaming with cheap oil ready for close hand-to-hand combat, shields slung on their backs, curved swords and thrusting daggers in their hands. As Bluetooth rose to a half-crouch, a second fire arrow seared the night.

'Now!' he hissed. They ran through the trees to where makeshift ladders, poles with pegs on either side, were leaning against the wall. Bluetooth was aware of other dark shadows to his right and left. The wall was scaled, the men dropping down into the shadows beyond. They would not need ladders to leave. Soon this house would be theirs and they'd take full possession of its gates. Bluetooth gathered his men and ran to join the rest streaming along the path leading up to the main door and its colonnaded portico. They were spreading out, eager to surround the house, when a conch horn's wailing blast shattered the stillness. Above them windows were flung open, arrows whipped through the darkness. Bluetooth heard a second horn blast from behind him. He whirled round and stared in horror. A phalanx of soldiers was moving towards them in a curving line. All about him his men were dropping, hit by arrows that slammed into neck and chest. Torches were being thrown from the windows to provide better light. An ambush! Their only chance was to fight their way out. Any plan to seize the prisoner was quickly forgotten. Bluetooth realised that these imperial troops would show no mercy. The Amemet captain led a charge but it was futile: his men were broken up and surrounded. Bluetooth was lashing out with his sword when a crack to the side of his head hurled him unconscious to the ground.

Amerotke heard the horrible clatter of weapons, and screams and yells piercing the darkness. He and the mercenary were sheltering in a room at the back of the house, its windows firmly barred and shuttered, protected by hand-picked troops who guarded the door outside. Amerotke sat back against the wall, eyes closed. The horrid din of battle echoed through the house. A scream higher than the rest made him start; it was abruptly silenced as the clatter of combat faded. He heard footsteps, men's voices. The door was unbarred and thrust open and the glare of torchlight dazzled him. Omendap strode towards him, in his right hand a curved *khopesh* bloodied to the hilt. He threw this at Amerotke's feet.

'It's finished. You'd best come.' He turned to the mercenary, who was about to scramble to his feet. 'No, not you. I do not want them to realise they've been tricked, just in case. Perhaps one of them has escaped and still lurks amongst the trees.'

The front of the house was now a blaze of torchlight; some of the brands still burnt where they'd been flung on the ground. Other torches, freshly flamed, had been lashed to poles thrust into the earth or held by perspiring mercenaries who stood watching the surviving Amemets being marshalled into a line in front of the colonnaded portico. Now and again a scream echoed from the trees as the Maryannou and Nakhtu-aa searched for survivors and killed them. The Egyptian dead and wounded were being lifted on stretchers to a makeshift mortuary and hospital set up at the rear of the house. Amemets too badly wounded to be questioned were dragged to their feet and led to a line of stakes hastily fashioned out of the ladders they had set against the wall. Amerotke felt his gorge rise as the impalements began. The Amemets, stripped naked, were lifted up by Nubian archers and thrust down on to the razor-edged points. Black shapes jerked frantically against the dark, their screams of agony piercing the night.

'Is that necessary?' Amerotke turned and retched. For a while he leaned against one of the pillars, trying to control his stomach. Then he wiped his mouth on the back of his hand. Another hideous scream rang out, drowning the more subdued groans of those impaled first and now lapsing into death.

'General Omendap!' Amerotke snapped.

The general, face sweat streaked, eyes still fierce with the blood-lust of battle, walked over, his staff officers crowding around.

'It is necessary.' Omendap gestured to the line of prisoners, hands and feet now being manacled. 'They have violated Pharaoh's peace. They would have inflicted much worse on us. Those prisoners able to stand are to be questioned.' He poked Amerotke in the chest. 'By you.'

The judge knocked his hand away angrily.

'By you!' Omendap repeated. Amerotke held his gaze even as another heart-wrenching scream echoed from the line of impalements.

'Enough!' Amerotke hissed. 'I am Pharaoh's friend.'

Omendap blinked and wiped away sweat.

'Moreover,' Amerotke continued, 'they should be properly tried, even if it's before a military tribunal.'

'They are too badly wounded to be of use,' Omendap retorted.

'Then by the Lords of Light,' Amerotke whispered, 'kill them quickly!'

Omendap looked as if he was about to refuse, but then nodded in agreement and shouted across, pushing a staff officer forward to enforce his command.

Amerotke walked down the ramp. The impaled men were now silent; only the occasional low groan carried and then the hideous gargling noise as Omendap's men began to cut the throats of the rest of the enemy wounded. He moved down the line of manacled Amemets. Despite cuts and bruises, the heavy chains around wrists and ankles, they still looked fierce. As he walked, he studied hardened, scarred faces, bodies reeking of sweat, blood and cheap oil. They were dressed in the most grotesque collection of animal skins: leopard mantles, wolf-skin jerkins, jackal capes, hyaena cloaks. Dead eyes in cruel faces stared back at him.

They were mercenaries, Amerotke reflected, soldiers, lavishly paid but they only carried out orders, not gave them. He paused. 'Which one of you,' he shouted in the patois of the slums, the lingua franca of the quayside, 'is the leader?'

He stopped before one Amemet nursing an open wound to the side of his head: an ugly face, the nose broken, the mouth chapped and scarred, but his eyes were bright; indeed, Amerotke considered, slightly humorous. A veteran he suspected, a man who bravely accepted the harshness of his ill luck.

'Your name?' Amerotke asked.

'Bluetooth,' the Amemet whispered.

The judge saw a flicker of hope in those shrewd eyes. He spoke quickly. 'A pardon?'

'A pardon for what?'

'To name your leader.'

'Master, I'm not that.'

'But you know who he is and you don't want to die.'

'No one does, master.'

'A full pardon,' Amerotke repeated, 'your weapons, some silver. You must leave Thebes and never return.' He gestured at the stakes. 'Or it will be immediate impalement.'

'Silence!' a voice shouted from further down the line. 'Do not break your oath.' The Amemets stirred restlessly in a clink of chains. Omendap and his officers came hurrying down. Amerotke, still holding Bluetooth's gaze, lifted his hand.

'Lord General, this man is going to save his life.'

'I don't—' Omendap protested.

'I do!' Amerotke turned and stared full at the general. 'The Divine One wants information. Bluetooth will give us that, won't you?'

'You'll keep your word?'

'By the scales of Ma'at, the Goddess of Truth whom I serve.'

Bluetooth held up his chained hands. Amerotke ordered the manacles to be removed. Once freed the Amemet, shadowed by Omendap and Amerotke, walked down the line of men massaging his wrists. He stopped before another prisoner with balding hair and the ugly features of a bird of prey and pointed to him, then stepped back as the man lunged forward only to be grabbed by the guards standing behind him.

Bluetooth pointed again. 'The Vulture! He is our leader.'

'Liar!' the man shouted.

'Take him!' Amerotke ordered. 'And him!' The judge smiled as alarm flared in Bluetooth's eyes and face. 'Don't worry, soldier, I keep my promises. I just want to make sure you have told us the truth.'

The Vulture was released, and both men, heavily guarded, were taken into the house and forced to kneel before the dais where Amerotke and Omendap squatted on cushions. Amerotke allowed each prisoner a cup of wine. They drank greedily, now and again peering up at Amerotke or over their shoulders at the line of Nakhtu-aa who guarded them.

'You are the leader?' Amerotke pointed at the Vulture. 'You're an Amemet chieftain, aren't you?'

The Vulture stared back, licking his lips. He had lost that hostile look, and Amerotke could see he was a man already assessing his future and which path to follow.

'I am not a chieftain,' the Vulture replied, 'but I am a captain,' he added hastily, 'of a hundred. I sit on the council of the Amemets.'

'Very good,' Amerotke said. 'You will not be impaled.'

The Vulture loosened the clasp of his worsted cape, dabbing the sweat forming there, his deep-set eyes slightly frightened.

'You'll still die,' Amerotke added casually. 'Won't he, General?'

'Buried alive out in the Redlands!' Omendap declared with relish. 'Yes, a fitting fate for a captain of a hundred.'

'Do you want to live?' Amerotke asked softly. 'They call you the Vulture; would you like to spread your wings and fly north to Memphis, or perhaps out to join your Libyan friends in the western desert?' He saw a quick shift in the man's eyes. 'What I want is information.'

'My life?' The Vulture gestured towards Bluetooth. 'Life, some silver, my weapons. I'll fly from Thebes, Master Judge, to wherever you want. I will tell you whatever you want on two conditions.'

'There'll be no conditions!' Omendap snapped. 'Just mercy.'

'Two things,' the Vulture replied. 'First, I will tell you all I know and I will receive my life as an act of mercy. Second, those men out there—'

'They are prisoners,' Omendap retorted.

'The quarries,' the Vulture said, 'not impalement, or buried alive, or public execution.'

Amerotke glanced quickly at Omendap, who nodded.

'Agreed,' the Judge declared. 'But it depends very much on the song you sing! Now,' he leaned forward, 'did you deal with Naratousha, the Libyan war chief?'

The Vulture shook his head. 'Not him, but Themeu, the young one. He has tattoos here on the left side of his face and along his right arm. A water plant on his arm, a snake on his face, done in light blue and red.'

Amerotke nodded. He recalled seeing Themeu both at the temple ceremony and later on when he and Minnakht had visited the Libyans.

'First,' Omendap placed a restraining hand on Amerotke's arm, 'how do I know some of your men didn't escape tonight over the walls?'

'I don't think any did,' the Vulture replied.

'No, neither do I,' Omendap retorted. 'And if they did, they would have to get through a second line. Oh yes, more troops are waiting. We knew all about your plans.'

The Vulture clicked his tongue in annoyance.

'You led us here.' Bluetooth poked the Vulture, who would have reacted angrily if one of the Nakhtu-aa hadn't intervened.

'Tell us what happened,' Omendap snapped.

'About two full moons ago,' the Vulture intoned in a singsong voice, 'my masters on the council received a message from the Libyans to arrange the escape of a prisoner known as the Rekhet from the Oasis of Bitter Bread. Now of course,' he gabbled on, 'we knew about the disgraced priest physician responsible for the deaths of so many in Thebes. Indeed,' his cruel face broke into a grin, 'the masters of the council were eager to speak to a man who could dispense death so freely throughout the city. Anyway, we received payment and accepted the contract; half the gold was delivered, the rest would be paid when the Rekhet escaped. We hired sand-dwellers who traded out in the distant Redlands to visit that prison settlement and deliver the necessary materials.'

'Which were?' Amerotke asked.

The Vulture pulled a face. 'A knife, water bottles, sandals, a robe against the sun, some coins, and a map describing the whereabouts of waterholes and oases.'

'And you did this?'

'Yes,' the Vulture continued proudly, 'we did.'

'Why didn't the Libyans do it themselves?' Amerotke asked. 'They have war patrols; their tribes wander the Redlands.'

'I suspect they didn't want their hand to be detected in such meddling.'

'Yes, yes,' Omendap agreed, 'that is their way. What happened then?'

'The Rekhet escaped. The Libyans were taken by surprise. He was audacious. He managed to evade Libyan patrols but was captured by sand-dwellers on the prowl for profit. These in turn were ambushed by an Egyptian chariot squadron, and that,' the Vulture shrugged, 'was the last we heard of him, at least for a while.'

'And?' Amerotke insisted.

'Well, the Libyans arrived in Thebes. After the poisoning during the temple ceremony we received a fresh offer to find the escaped prisoner; our reward would be lavish.' He shrugged. 'So we tried.'

'And failed,' Omendap intervened. 'The masters of the Amemet council must have wondered why so much gold, silver and precious stones was offered for an escaped prisoner.'

The Vulture shifted nervously. He licked his lips,

blinked and gazed fearfully at Amerotke. 'I have my life, I will have gold?'

'Silver,' Amerotke replied. 'The good general here will give it to you. Now . . .' He tensed. They had reached what he considered the crossroads to the path of truth. 'Lie,' his voice turned harsh, 'and you die on the stake!'

'We . . . I . . .' The Vulture had apparently decided on his path. 'We met Themeu, the Libyan envoy, out at the House of the Evening Star, a tavern in the Necropolis. He came disguised, as we did, and insisted that we search for the Rekhet. We bargained. He informed us that they had also hired others to do the same task. The Churat.' The Vulture spat the name out. 'We maintained such a task was arduous and highly dangerous. The Medjay, imperial troops, the Eyes and Ears of Pharaoh from the House of Secrets, not to mention the vile Churat, were also hunting him. The Libyan insisted they would pay whoever succeeded most lavishly. We asked why they wanted such a man. He replied that life changes like the direction of the wind. He described how they had accepted a bribe from one of the lords of Egypt to free the prisoner in the first place.'

'Did he say who?'

'Yes,' the Vulture retorted, 'the prosperous merchant found dead face down in his lotus pool.'

'Ipuye?'

'The same.'

'What proof do they have of this? I mean,'

Amerotke spread his hands, 'the Libyans could just be mischievous.'

'The bribe was accompanied by Ipuye's cartouche, his seal; Themeu showed us that.'

Amerotke stared in amazement at Omendap, who gazed speechlessly back.

'Do the Libyans know why Ipuye wanted the Rekhet?'

'No.' The Vulture grinned, enjoying his interrogators' surprise. 'Ipuye prophesied that if the Rekhet was freed from his prison oasis, the Libyans would not only be paid in precious stones but would witness an event that would publicly humiliate Egypt.'

'The poisoning of the three scribes?'

'And so it came to pass,' the Vulture replied sarcastically.

'But Ipuye died the same day as the three scribes were poisoned.' Amerotke leaned forward. 'Did you have a hand in that?'

'No.'

'But you met this Themeu at the House of the Evening Star after the poisoning of the three scribes and the death of Ipuye.'

'Of course, on a number of occasions.'

'But Ipuye,' Amerotke laughed, 'no longer needed the Rekhet.'

'True, but the Libyans certainly did.'

'Did they say why?'

'To hold,' the Vulture retorted. 'They were insistent on that. He must be captured alive; a corpse was no use to them, but they never said why. Lord Judge, that was not our business, why should they tell us?'

Amerotke leaned forward. 'The Libyans seem well informed about the Rekhet.'

'Perhaps Ipuye told them.'

Amerotke smiled at the sudden shift in the Vulture's eyes. 'You don't think that, do you? What do you know, Vulture? Think of freedom, of the courtesans of Memphis waiting for you, goblets of wine, fresh meat, an end to all this. Come, what does it really matter to you now?'

'Themeu,' the Vulture cleared his throat, 'seemed most knowledgeable. He is very handsome.' The Amemet smirked. 'If you are that way inclined. Perhaps he became friendly with one of the principal priests of Ptah.' He shrugged. 'But that is only conjecture. I swear I can tell you no more.'

Amerotke turned to Bluetooth, who was nursing his bruised head. 'Is there anything else?'

'No, Lord Judge, except . . .'

'Except what?'

'How did you know we were coming?'

Amerotke grinned. 'How do you know when a storm is due?' He answered his own question. 'When the heavens hang dark. We looked for the signs and found them.'

'The masters of the council will not forget this.' Bluetooth spoke up. 'They have unfinished business with you, Lord Judge.'

'Ah,' Amerotke whispered, 'and as the lady Ma'at knows, I certainly have unfinished business with them. Is there anything else?'

Both men shook their heads. Amerotke studied them closely. Years of interrogation in the courts had honed his instincts. He sensed both Amemets had told him what they could, though he could make little sense of it.

'General Omendap, furnish both men with passes, their weapons, clothing, some food and a little water, half an ounou of silver, half of gold. They are to be gone within the hour.' Amerotke raised his hand. 'And I swear, if they look upon my face again, it will be for the last time.'

HEKAI: ancient Egyptian, ‘sorcerer’

CHAPTER 11

Amerotke got to his feet and went deeper into the house. The mercenary who had pretended to be the Rekhet had left. The guards informed Amerotke that he was now celebrating, looking forward to his lavish reward from Pharaoh's own hands. Amerotke went into the Syrian's chamber and crouched in the corner. He felt tired and dirty. He needed to shave and wash, yet what the Amemets had said concerned him. It was useless discussing it with Omendap; the general had completed his task and would be eager to report to the Great House. Amerotke felt his own task was only beginning. Why? He beat his fist against the ground. Why should a merchant like Ipuye be conspiring with the Libyans to bring the Rekhet back into Egypt to humiliate Pharaoh? It didn't make sense. Ipuye had no history of plotting against Hatusu or Senenmut. In fact, the opposite: he had been a fervent supporter of both of them, as well as the Temple of Ptah. Yet the Libyans had had his seal!

As Amerotke half listened to the sounds of the house, his mind teemed with questions. He gazed across at the makeshift bed where the mercenary had slept. If only they could capture the Rekhet and question him. He knew what questions Hatusu and Senenmut would ask. Omendap would tell them what he'd heard from the Amemets, but that still didn't answer the vital question: why were Naratousha and his comrades so intent on this business, on the one hand sealing a peace treaty with Egypt but on the other dabbling in all sorts of treachery?

He startled at a knock on the door. This was promptly flung open and Shufoy, armed with his parasol, strode in accompanied by Nadif. The little man hastened over to Amerotke and crouched down, his eyes concerned.

'Are you safe, master? General Omendap told me what happened. Outside it is like a battle ground, a slaughter house, awash with blood. The impaled, the prisoners . . .'

Amerotke clasped the little man's hands, then shook Nadif's. 'What hour is it?'

'Just before dawn, master.'

Amerotke clambered uneasily to his feet. 'The Amemets must have attacked in the early hours when they thought we'd all be asleep. Standard-Bearer Nadif, why are you here?'

'I received a message,' Nadif replied, 'from Maben at the House of the Golden Vine. The Kushite Saneb, the one we questioned last night, has disappeared; there's no trace of him whatsoever. Maben wishes us to come.'

'Not now,' Amerotke replied. 'I am tired and hungry. I need to wash and eat. Let's go, and I'll tell you what happened here.'

They left the House of Horus the Red-Eye and made their way along the narrow trackway down to the broad thoroughfare that skirted the Nile and thence back to Amerotke's house. The judge was so tired he was hardly aware of the journey: the merchants and traders, their cattle, oxen, donkeys and asses all processing through a cloud of dust towards the city, eager to be through the gates before the markets opened. He told Nadif and Shufoy about the attack but swore them to silence, especially in the presence of Norfret. Nevertheless, the judge was hardly in the house, washing his hands in a bowl of water, before his wife began to ask about what had truly happened. Amerotke realised that rumours of the attack must have seeped out, possibly fed by messengers or troops returning into the city. He gathered Norfret in his arms and kissed her gently on the brow.

'I swear,' he whispered, pressing his lips against her ear, 'when this is all over I shall tell you.'

She held him by the arms and stood back. 'And I, Lord Judge, will be the first to remind you of that.'

Amerotke bathed, ate and rested. It was late in the afternoon before he, Nadif and Shufoy reached the House of the Golden Vine. He apologised for the hour, adding that they should all shelter from the heat. Lady Meryet, who seemed more composed, invited them into the central hall, where she opened windows to create whatever draught possible. She served fruit juices freshly crushed as well as *mamoul*, delicious pastry tasting of walnut, figs and cinnamon. Amerotke asked her to join them. When she told him that Minnakht was also in the house, he tactfully conceded that the Chief Scribe of the Temple of Ptah could not be excluded. For a while there was some confusion as servants arrived, arranging tables, stools, tables and cushions. Amerotke walked over to admire a particularly fine wall painting showing vivid ochre-coloured peasants weighing bushels of corn in a granary. Minnakht came to greet him and clasped his hand.

'Lord Judge,' he whispered, 'the news is all over Thebes about an attack on the House of—'

'Yes, yes.' Amerotke guided the genial-looking scribe by the elbow back to join the rest. 'Indeed,' he raised his voice, 'I have certain information. Well,' he smiled thinly, 'it certainly surprised me.' Sipping at his juice, he told them all he had learnt, though only giving them those details he felt necessary. As he glanced swiftly round, he realised they were all genuinely astonished.

'Impossible!' Maben and Meryet exclaimed together.

'Nonsense!' Minnakht shook his head.

'My master was no traitor,' Hotep protested. 'He had no dealings with the Libyans. His traders went out into the western desert, but for trade, nothing else.'

'Yet the Libyans had his seal,' Amerotke replied.

They had no answer for that. Maben muttered how it might have been forged. Someone else claimed it could be a mistake. Amerotke ignored this and pressed on with his own questions, though he failed to discover any further links between Ipuye and the Libyans.

'And Saneb the Kushite guard, what's happened to him?'

'Lord,' Hotep replied mournfully, 'Saneb was here the day before yesterday, then he just disappeared with all his belongings, no trace whatsoever.'

'And it was he who discovered Ipuye's corpse?'

'Yes,' Meryet replied. She stared long and hard at Amerotke. 'Lord Judge,' she chose her words carefully, 'could Saneb have been an Amemet? This business of Ipuye and the Libyans: perhaps my dead brother-in-law was involved in something none of us knew about?'

Amerotke just shrugged. 'And there is nothing else,' he asked, 'nothing to resolve the mystery?'

'Is there a mystery?' Meryet replied. 'Ipuye's death may have been the work of the gods; perhaps it was just an accident.'

Amerotke tactfully brought the conversation to

an end, saying he must once more go through Ipuye's accounts and papers. He, Nadif and Shufoy then adjourned to Ipuye's private quarters. Meryet and Maben were unable to protest, Amerotke insisting that the new information he'd brought needed to be examined most carefully. Once inside the merchant's quarters they closed the door, brought out the baskets and hampers and began to sift through Ipuye's papers. In the end it proved to be a fruitless task. Amerotke concluded that Ipuye had been a very busy man, but nothing in his manuscripts linked him with the Libyans or indeed any wrongdoing. Nadif dropped a collection of papyrus rolls back into a reed basket. The standard-bearer was in a more dour mood than usual and confessed that Baka, his pet baboon, whom he privately regarded as more intelligent than many of his colleagues in the Medjay, was sick and the cause of his deep disquiet.

'However,' he declared, collecting up another pile of papyri, 'the symptoms seem to be subsiding. I wish I could say the same about the mystery here.'

'Mystery?' Amerotke queried.

'Ipuye kept his Place of Pleasure very distant from his home. Did he also do the same with treasonable and criminal correspondence?'

Amerotke was about to reply when the door quietly opened and a Kushite slid into the room. He crouched just inside the doorway, his back to the wall, and raised a finger warningly to his lips, then shook his head as Nadif's hand fell to the thrusting knife on his belt. The man had a round, fat face and crinkly black hair, and by the scars on his upper torso, neck and face, Amerotke judged him to be a veteran. He wordlessly waved the man towards him, and the Kushite crept forward.

'What is it?' Amerotke whispered.

'It is strange,' the Kushite replied. 'Saneb was like a son to me. Why should he leave, take all his belongings, but never say goodbye to me, his friend, a man he called his father, especially at a time when he declared he was about to acquire great riches.'

'Riches?' Amerotke asked. 'What riches?'

'Perhaps his heart was wandering,' the Kushite murmured. He lifted his left hand to show his ring and bracelet, the sign that he had once been a member of the Medjay. Then he took them off and moved them to his right hand. 'Saneb did that. I would catch him – he'd just be crouching, moving both ring and bracelet from hand to hand – and ask him why. He would reply that he knew even stranger things. I asked him what he meant.' The Kushite got to his feet and tapped his carefully knotted loincloth. 'He'd do this and mutter, "*Shu* will bring *sepses*."'

'The loincloth will bring riches – what on earth does that nonsense mean?' Amerotke stared up at the man, who shook his head. Yet there was something about what the Kushite had said, the way he was now standing, that recalled a problem Amerotke had wondered about. 'Is there anything else?' Amerotke asked.

The man shook his head, then lifted a hand as Amerotke went to open the pouch on his belt.

'My lord, there is no need to reward me. Saneb was a friend.' The Kushite bowed and slipped out of the room.

'Nadif,' Amerotke asked, 'what do you make of that?'

The standard-bearer pulled a face. 'I don't know.' He held up his left hand. 'Sometimes veterans of the Medjay place the rings and bracelets back to rekindle memories, but,' he let his hand drop, 'Saneb was different. Apparently he was joking, making references to riches. Lord Judge, I cannot understand it, but what do we do now?'

Amerotke gazed at Shufoy, who was examining a scarab depicting the god Bes which he'd taken from one of the baskets.

'Are you praying for help from across the Far Horizon?' Amerotke joked.

'Gerh,' Shufoy declared.

'Gerh?' Amerotke queried. He recognised the name for Night, a black vaulting figure who lurked in the Fifth Chamber of the Underworld and often played a prominent role in terrifying ghost stories told to children.

'Gerh!' Shufoy repeated, getting to his feet. 'No, I'm not talking about nightmares, master, but the lady Gerh.'

'The Lady of the Dark.' Nadif whistled. 'Of course.'

'What is this?' Amerotke asked. He vaguely recalled coming across that sinister-sounding name in official records.

'She is a Mistress of the Powders and Potions,' Nadif explained. 'She lives in the Abode of Twilight in the Necropolis just across the river.'

'And?'

'Well,' Shufoy was jumping from foot to foot, 'master, we are surrounded by mystery: corpses floating in pools, scribes dying savagely and mysteriously in front of Pharaoh herself. The solution to all this surely must be poison. Gerh, the Lady of the Dark, is skilled in what she knows. We could visit her, ask her advice.'

'Would she receive us?'

'She would have no choice,' Nadif replied. 'Indeed she would be flattered and, I am sure, as curious as we are . . .'

A short while later, Amerotke and his two companions took their leave of the House of the Golden Vine and followed the sycamore-shaded path down to one of the small quaysides that lay outside the city walls. The searing heat of the Noonday Devil was beginning to lessen, and the refreshing river breezes, although full of the sour stench of dried mud, decaying fish and rotting vegetation, were a welcome relief. They hired a broad craft. Amerotke crouched in the stern; Nadif and Shufoy, sitting opposite, discussed the possible cause of Baka the baboon's mysterious ailment. The river was busy with dangerously overloaded barges going to and from the City of the Dead. Merchant craft, crammed with all kinds of goods – malachite, alum, fruit, wood, exotic birds, monkeys, spices, crates and baskets – sailed from quayside to quayside. Gorgeously ornate funeral barges made their way ponderously across, with singers pretending to be the twin goddesses Isis and Nepthys standing in the prow. These leaned forward singing hymns of praise to Osiris, Lord of the Western Gates, as well as to the memory of the dead person. Warships full of troops made their careful way around other boats, barge after barge carrying black-skinned Nubians armed with spears and shields, Kushite infantry and Syrian archers with their powerful bows, all sailing further north to the boom of gongs and the wail of conch horns.

They reached the western bank, left the quayside and went up the wretched, narrow streets of the Necropolis. They walked cautiously past the midden heaps, children screaming, dogs barking. A place of danger. The shadows lurking in doorways and on corners slid away at the sight of Standard-Bearer Nadif, who was greatly feared throughout the City of the Dead. They made their way gingerly up alleyways past shabby wine booths and beer shops; the customers recognised Nadif and shouted abuse, but slyly so that the officer could not trace the person responsible. There were no shops or stalls here; traders simply piled their goods high on reed mats before them or shouted from shadowy recesses what they had to sell, most of which Amerotke suspected was stolen from somewhere else. They entered the Abode of Twilight, which was slightly quieter and cleaner, though the walls of the houses were flaking, dirty and drab. At last they approached the mansion of the Lady of the Dark. It stood enclosed by a high curtain, entered through a narrow wooden gate. Nadif pounded on this; a shutter at the top was pushed back and a pair of eyes glared through.

'Go away!'

'Either open the gate,' Nadif replied, 'or I, Nadif, standard-bearer in the Medjay, will force it.'

Locks were hastily turned and the gate swung open. An evil-looking character, squint-eyed, unshaven and dressed in a dirty linen robe, waved them through. Once inside, Amerotke exclaimed in surprise, for instead of some shabby courtyard, he had entered a small garden beautifully laid out, with bushes, trees, herb plots and flowerbeds. A lawn circled a pure white alabaster fountain carved in the shape of a dolphin, water spouting in the air from its gaping mouth.

'She is not what you think,' Shufoy whispered. 'Honestly, master.'

They went under a flower arbour and along a path, the brickwork neatly laid. A woman was sitting in a small sun pavilion, just before some steps leading up to a smart-looking doorway. She rose and came down the path to greet them, still plaiting a flower chain. She was of medium height, her long white hair, parted in the middle, fell down to her shoulders, and her face was serene with strange blue eyes, her skin the colour of ivory. Amerotke realised that she must have once been a great beauty. She was graceful and elegant in all her gestures. She wore a lovely gauffered robe with a fringed shawl about her shoulders, her feet covered by silver-edged sandals, and smelt fragrantly of some herb mixture which, Amerotke was sure, was very similar to *kiphye*, the rare and very expensive juice of crushed poppies.

'My lord Amerotke.' She stretched out a hand.

Amerotke clasped it; her touch was cool.

'Standard-Bearer Nadif and you, Master Shufoy, I heard you were coming.'

'How?' Amerotke asked.

The woman smiled to herself. 'News carries on the breeze in the Abode of Twilight. You have your ways, and we have ours. You have come to talk to me about the poisonings, haven't you?' She waved them forward into the sun pavilion. The inside was ringed with a soft-cushioned bench and she gestured at them to sit. Amerotke felt as if he was back in a schoolroom. This serene-faced lady was dressed so chastely, yet she enjoyed the most sinister of reputations. As if she could read his thoughts, she laughed merrily. 'What did you expect, Lord Judge, some night-hag? Some witch in black robes, swirling in evil vapours? I do what I do. I am not Egyptian, hence the colour of my skin and eyes. My mother came from an island in the Great Green. I am a physician, my lord Amerotke. I know the power of powders and potions. I can tell you the effect of this herb or that.'

'And these poisonings,' Amerotke asked, 'in Thebes?'

'At one time,' she replied, 'people thought I was responsible.' She laughed behind her fingers. 'But I was not. There is no great secret, Lord Judge, about poisons. They work like many things. Let me give you an example. You can take the most poisonous snake in the desert. Did you know that if you drink its venom, you suffer no ill? Nevertheless, God help you if you drink it and there is a cut to your lips or your mouth, for then you are dead. Or there are seeds you can swallow and, provided you do not chew, no harm will be done. Chew them, break them up and you will be dead within a few heartbeats. Or honey – there is poisonous honey, Lord Judge, that would give you the most horrid death. Why? Because the bees themselves feed on poisonous flowers, then weave their honeycombs with a juice deadly to the taste. There are poisons that can kill within a few heartbeats, poisons that, taken in small amounts, can do you a great deal of good. Poisons exist that you administer little by little; those take months to kill. Poisons you could drink at noon and suffer no ill effect, but three hours later you are writhing in agony. You take the simplest flower and mix it with another and you have a deadly concoction.' She paused to admire her flower chain. 'Those three scribes poisoned on the temple forecourt: they drank wine?'

'It wasn't tainted!'

'No, but did it mix with something else? Those scribes had been fasting, yes? Well,' she continued, 'an empty stomach and wine never mix. Once those scribes tasted and swallowed that wine, the juices of the belly would become more active. Each poison is unique in its nature and effect: powders you might rub on the thick, hardened skin of your feet may do little. Apply the same powder to where the skin is much thinner, around your eyes or wrist, and the effects are devastating. The secret of poisons is to know their potency and their effect. Take the almond seed: in itself it is innocuous, yet it is the source of a poison most chilling in its effects. Arsenic is another. Across the Great Green there are mounds of it. Taken in small quantities, it can be very good for the stomach, and is even used as an aphrodisiac; in great quantities it can kill, yet it doesn't corrupt the body but preserves everything in a sort of waxen fashion.'

'And the Rekhet of Ptah?' Amerotke asked.

'Whoever it is,' she replied, 'is most skilled.'

'It is a man?'

'Yes, probably, one who owns the key to a source of great knowledge on which he draws.'

'And his heart?' Amerotke asked.

'The heart is a different matter, Lord Judge. We human beings kill for many reasons: love, lust, greed, envy and hatred. Now and again, well, there are people who kill just because they love it. It allows their pain to come out. I have carefully studied the doings of the Rekhet.' She paused. 'He just liked to watch other people die; it gave him a sense of unlimited power.'

'And why are you telling me this?' Amerotke asked.

'For the same reason.' She laughed sharply. 'Power. You are Amerotke, Chief Judge in the Hall of Two Truths – who knows when I'll need your protection or help? So, ask me any question you want, Lord Judge, though I suspect I have answered them already.' She leaned forward and laughed again. 'I would offer you something to eat or drink but I doubt whether you would be comfortable.' She did not wait for a reply but pushed away the hair from her face and leaned back. 'If you are dealing with poisons, Amerotke, rid yourself of illusions. Think of a poison as you would a wine. Reflect on how many stages you go through when you drink a goblet: a sense of happiness, exhilaration, the heart sings, yet a few hours later the belly is disturbed, the head thick, the throat dry. So it is with poisons. What you must look for is someone with the inclination, the skill and the means to cause such effects. Once you have established that, the actual potion or powder used is immaterial . . .'

Amerotke made his farewell to the Lady of the Dark. He returned home and busied himself talking to Norfret and playing a game of skittles with the boys, who screamed with delight when their father confessed he'd been trying to cheat all the time. Shufoy accompanied Nadif back to the standard-bearer's house. He had now brought all his learning to bear, informing the bemused standard-bearer that he was an expert, skilled in the treatment of all kinds of animal ailments. They both acted as if the visit to the Gerh had been merely interesting. In truth, Amerotke sensed that they, like him, were fascinated by what that strange-looking woman had told them, each quietly applying the information to the mysteries that clung around them as thick and blinding as sand in a desert storm. Shufoy left, solemnly promising to join Amerotke and Norfret for the evening meal.

Amerotke decided it was time to reflect on what he himself had learnt. While the boys decided to chase a mongoose they'd glimpsed in the orchard, he retired to his favourite place in the garden, a shady nook under stout holm oaks, their leafy branches a thick screen against the sun. He loved to sit on the bench specially fastened to the base of the trunk of one of these magnificent trees. He watched the boys race off, then relaxed, breathing in deeply as he tried to recall all the little pieces, what he called 'glimpses of unfinished pictures'. Norfret came over with some chilled wine and a basket of cut fruit. Amerotke thanked her absent-mindedly.

'Ah, I forget.' She came back and smiled down at her husband. 'You had a visitor early this afternoon.'

'Who?' Amerotke immediately tensed.

'A stranger, well at least to me. He said his name was Qennu, an old acquaintance of yours when you studied at the Houses of Life in the temples of Karnak.'

Amerotke shook his head. 'I cannot recall him. What was he like?'

'Pleasant faced, skin very dark, lithe bodied, soft spoken. I think he served as a soldier. I told him you were away. He replied, "Of course," but promised he'd return.'

'He left no gift?'

'Nothing!' Norfret smiled. 'Why should he? Oh, those boys!' She hurried across to quell the screaming from the orchard.

Amerotke wondered about the identity of his visitor before returning to his nagging doubts about the various little mysteries: Hinqui falling ill, Hutepa's soiled bed, her tidy chamber. Abruptly he sat up: that was what had been missing from the dead girl's belongings! There was very little silver, gold or precious stones. Hutepa must have been a wealthy woman, and yet he'd found little evidence of that. Had she been robbed as well as murdered? He went back to Hinqui. Where had he been when the poisonings had taken place? Amerotke wasn't sure, but he had a vague memory of Hinqui attending one of those scribes as he died. And the burning of the library? What was the killer trying to hide? Surely other records and libraries would hold similar information? He recalled what the Gerh had told him and felt a tingle of excitement. He sipped at his wine and thought of Ipuye and Khiat floating face down in that lotus pool whilst their guards lounged and dozed. Maben and Meryet had been absent at the Temple of Ptah. He thought about that palisade as well as the ladder the Amemets had used to scale the walls of the House of Horus the Red-Eye. What had happened at the House of the Golden Vine? Ipuye had risen late; he and Khiat had eaten and drunk before going across to the pool to meet their deaths. All the time Patuna's corpse was hidden in that midden heap with her skull staved in. Did Ipuye, whilst he was enjoying himself, know that only a short distance away the body of his first wife was rotting like a piece of rubbish? And the merchant's Place of Pleasure, that scroll giving his mysterious lady visitors their pet names as well as describing their lovemaking skills . . . Ipuye was certainly lecherous, yet Amerotke had discovered nothing amongst his records to depict him either as a murderer or a traitor. The judge chewed on a piece of fruit, his dry mouth relishing the juice. He smiled. He was not only very much aware of what he ate or drank, but firmly believed that food and drink held the key to these mysteries. The Gerh had told him the danger of poisons, as had the mercenary at the House of Horus the Red-Eye, with his story about pursuing the Sea People.

Amerotke watched a swallow dart from the trees, circle, then sweep away. I must look for the constant, he reflected; there must be something that links all these. Except, he sighed, for the Libyans! He sipped at his wine cup. That path remained truly blocked, so he went back to those mysterious deaths at the House of the Golden Vine. He was beginning to speculate, though it really amounted to nothing, empty theory with no hard evidence. The absence of lapis lazuli on the feet of Ipuye and Khiat was a case in point, significant but hardly proof, not yet. Or Saneb's strange behaviour before his abrupt disappearance. Why move that ring and bracelet back to his right hand or talk about his loincloth and riches? A sexual joke? He rose to his feet and moved behind the trees, where he took off his robe and undid the folds of his loincloth, then quickly retied them. He did this again, amused at how he rarely considered what he was doing. The same must be true of Saneb, so why jest about it?

Amerotke finished his wine and returned to his writing chamber. He busied himself making list after list of names and places before writing a series of short letters demanding information on this person or that. Shufoy returned, declaring confidently that Baka the baboon was now as bright as a sparrow and would remain so if Shufoy's advice was strictly followed. Amerotke grunted his agreement, so Shufoy hastened off to tell Norfret that her husband had returned to the land of Resei, the Realm of Dreams.

And so it proved. During the evening meal on the roof of the house, Amerotke sat like a sleepwalker, grunting and nodding, lost in his own world. At last he kissed Norfret and said he would retire. Shufoy jokingly remarked how Baka the baboon hoped to become a judge. Norfret laughed when Amerotke blinked and said that Baka had all the requirements for such a post before going absent-mindedly down the steps.

The next morning Amerotke rose long before the brilliant hour. He went on to the roof top to feel the Breath of Amunn on his face, and knelt for a while praying, face in his hands, before going back to his chamber, where he washed, shaved, donned fresh robes and returned to his writing office. Shufoy joined him, only to be immediately dispatched to Nadif with orders that the standard-bearer and three of his best Medjay must wait upon the judge at their earliest convenience.

When the four men arrived, Amerotke would not answer any questions but begged them to take letters to various people in the city and collect certain information. For the rest of the day Shufoy, Nadif and the Medjay scurried backwards and forwards to this part of the city and that, and even across to the Necropolis. The same thing happened for the next two days. Norfret became exasperated but resigned herself to her husband's strange moods, going in to talk, serve meals or just watch him walk over to the shade of the oak trees and sit, arms folded, on the bench, staring at the ground as if he'd lost something.

On the fourth day, an imperial messenger arrived at the house demanding that Amerotke send any information about what he had discovered to the Palace of the Eternal Sun. Amerotke crossly replied that he had nothing to send but that when he did, the Divine One would be the first to know. He went out into the garden and was cradling a cup of fruit juice and nibbling at a plate of glazed walnuts when he heard his name called. Norfret came across the grass leading a man carrying a parasol which shaded his face.

'Amerotke,' said Norfret, 'this is Qennu your visitor. He's returned and wishes to have words with you.'

Amerotke glanced up, shading his eyes. 'I would see you better,' he said, 'if you removed the parasol.'

The man did so immediately. He was of medium height, with sallow skin, his head completely shaven. A ring in the lobe of his left ear gave him a priestly air, though his lithe body and quick movements reminded Amerotke of a soldier. He was dressed in a white linen robe, reed sandals on his feet, and despite the heat, he looked cool and calm as if used to the rigours of the sun.

'Your name is Qennu?' Amerotke watched Norfret

walk away, then moved back to the bench and patted the seat beside him. 'Sit down. You say you were with me in the Houses of Life at Karnak, but I cannot recall your face or name.'

The man made himself comfortable, placing the parasol on the ground, folding his arms across his middle, one hand beneath the folds of his gown. Amerotke immediately felt suspicious. It was just the way the man sat, slightly turned to face him, eyes watchful. The more he studied that face, the more Amerotke's suspicions deepened.

'I do not know you,' he said.

'Lord Judge, you do. You know me very well, though you have never met me.'

Amerotke went to stand, but the man placed a hand on his arm.

'Please.' He leaned forward. 'I mean you and yours no harm. My name is Qennu. I was a priest physician at the Temple of Ptah until I was condemned as the Rekhet and sent to a prison oasis.'

METUT ENT MAAT: ancient Egyptian,
'for words of truth'

CHAPTER 12

Amerotke felt a cold prickle of fear. The way the man was sitting, his calm voice, his intent gaze caught his attention. Undoubtedly Qennu's right hand, hidden under the folds of his robe, was not far from the hilt of a dagger. Amerotke glanced at the parasol lying on the ground.

'Why are you here?' he said. 'I could fight. I could shout. I could protest!'

'What's the use, Lord Judge? Why do that? I mean you no harm, or the lady Norfret or your boys. I swear on Hutepa's soul.'

'You murdered her.'

'No I did not, Lord Judge. No one's blood is on my hands, I swear that, except for the lives of those two villains who tried to seize me.'

Amerotke felt the passion in Qennu's voice. This man was either one of the best liars he'd ever met, or he was telling the truth.

'You took gold, silver and precious jewels from Hutepa's chamber?'

'Of course, Lord Judge. The imperial troops, the Medjay, the Amemets, the Churat, they are all looking for an escaped criminal, a man with shaggy hair and unkempt beard, burnt dark by the sun, clothed in rags, slinking down the alleyways of the Necropolis. No one spares a second glance for a well-dressed priest physician whose head is shaven, his face oiled. Moreover,' Qennu shrugged, 'I did not take anything. Hutepa gave them to me.' He leaned forward. 'Amerotke, I have studied you very carefully.' He laughed. 'I am sorry about our meeting in the temple. I do trust you. I did then: Hutepa advised me to – she knew of your reputation, as I do now. My trust has deepened. I wish . . .' Qennu brought his hands together, 'I would like nothing more, Lord Judge, than to go in front of you in the Hall of Two Truths and prove my innocence. First I beg you to listen to what I say then allow me to go. If you do that, I swear by all that is holy that I shall return and face you in court, answer your questions and accept whatever verdict you reach. In the mean time I have information which those who live in the Great House would dearly treasure.'

Amerotke gazed across the garden. Norfret, as if alarmed, had stopped at the doorway to the house and was staring back. He raised a hand and waved. 'Do you wish anything to eat or drink?' He gestured at the platter.

'No, Lord Judge, perhaps later. I wish to confess. This is the chapel, you are the Priest of the Ear. Listen to what I have to say.'

'You chose your time well,' Amerotke declared. 'Nadif and Shufoy are across the river, searching out more information.'

'Lord Judge, will you listen?'

Amerotke straightened up. 'You pose no threat to me or mine?'

Qennu raised his hands as if taking a solemn oath.

'Very well,' Amerotke decided. 'Tell your story.'

'I was born in Thebes, the son of a merchant. I was the only child, and my mother died young. I proved myself to be an ardent scholar. My father doted on me and enrolled me at the Temple of Ptah to study to be a priest physician. I lived a calm, serene life. I excelled at my studies and eventually I was admitted to the House of Life at the Temple of Ptah. I made good friends; High Priest Ani, Hinqui, Maben, Minnakht and Userbati were all my comrades, and I consider them to be so now. I did not marry but formed a deep friendship with the heset Hutepa. She had a marvellous voice,' he added wistfully, 'clear and fluted like a nightingale. Oh, she could dance and tease me. I was like one of the birds in your garden. I lived happy and contented. This was about five years ago, when the stories about terrible poisonings in the city had just begun to surface. Now as you know, many people were killed in a variety of horrid ways in Thebes. Some of these poisonings were amongst the high ones; they all had one thing in common: they had recently visited the Temple of Ptah, and their names, or those of their relatives, could be founds in books of offerings or temple lists. The House of Ptah has a reputation for healing. We are not only priests; many of us are physicians. People flock to us with their ailments, and by oath we are obliged to treat even the very poor. We are knowledgeable about medicines. I specialised in ailments of the stomach and the anus. The scandal of the poisonings was a storm that, I thought, had no bearing on me. Eventually, however, suspicions emerged that the Rekhet, whoever he might be, must be a priest physician at the Temple of Ptah. One of our leading practitioners, Userbati, claimed that he suspected what was happening. On that infamous night, just at the beginning of the Inundation, he organised a banquet, inviting me and three others to attend. He wished to discuss his theories before formally approaching High Priest Ani.'

'And who knew about this?'

'Ani, and I suspect his two nephews Maben and Hinqui. Others may have known.' Qennu smiled. 'Gossip and rumour are rife amongst temple priests.'

'Did you have any suspicions?' Amerotke asked.

'Oh, names were bandied about. They even mentioned Ipuye; he was such a powerful patron of the temple, and of course his wife had disappeared.'

Qennu pulled a face. 'Though of course she hadn't, had she? The rumours are all over Thebes about her corpse being found under a mound of dirt in Ipuye's garden.'

'Go on,' Amerotke urged.

'On the night the banquet was held, I was on my way to it when I received a summons. A small boy came running up to me and told me how, in the House of Twilight, the temple hospital, an old priest was very ill and wished to see me. I never saw that boy again. I never learnt who sent him. When I went to the House of Twilight, I found no such patient. There were other delays. I paused to talk to friends. I went looking for Hutepa. I was about to join my friends at the banquet when I saw guards running. Distraught servants told me that Userbati and three of his comrades had been killed. I made a terrible mistake: I panicked!'

'Why?' Amerotke asked. 'If you were innocent?'

'I cannot answer that, Lord Judge: just a premonition of evil? No, no, it was more than that; I told Hutepa the same. It was as if I had been watched, as if someone had been in my lodgings, though at the time I put that down to brooding about the Rekhet and his hideous work. I made a decision. I told Hutepa I would not return to my own chambers but took refuge in the city, in a shabby room above a wine shop in the coppersmiths' quarter. Hutepa kept me informed. Horrified, I learnt what was happening. My premonitions had been proved right. All four of my comrades had been killed by a deadly poison. The Medjay had raided my chambers and found potions and powders, not to mention wealth I never kept there. Lord Judge, I knew something about poisons, so I was already damned. They also found the curse with Userbati's name on it, as well as documents in his chamber voicing his suspicions about me. Lord Judge, what could I do? The evidence depicted me as the Rekhet. I was also concerned about Hutepa. I told her that if I was arrested, she might be taken up as an accomplice. I knew a little about the law as well as the temple's fear of scandal. I decided to plead guilty, to accept life imprisonment in an oasis rather than face execution, because whilst there was life, there was hope. If my case had been tried before you, Lord Judge, what verdict would you have reached despite my protestations of innocence? I used those days to prepare. I slipped from my hiding place. I went to the libraries and studied the maps of the western desert, the location of the prison oases. I also told Hutepa that when I said so, she must inform the Medjay where I was. This would put her above any suspicion.' He shrugged. 'The rest you know.'

'No, you tell me.'

'Standard-Bearer Nadif arrested me, directed to my hiding place by Hutepa. I was taken to the temple authorities. I invoked my status as a priest physician and confessed my crime. From the moment those chains were on me, I was determined to escape!'

'Did you . . . do you,' Amerotke asked, 'have any suspicions about who the Rekhet might be?'

'Lord Judge, no, not then and not now, except,' he sighed, 'when I was in the prison oasis I met murderers. I heard one of them joke that he just killed for the sheer love of it. I believe the Rekhet was such a one.'

Amerotke nodded. The Gerh had said something very similar.

'Surely,' Amerotke measured his words, 'if Userbati was talking to Lord Ani, organising supper parties for his colleagues, voicing suspicions publicly, he, or others, must have had some firm evidence about the Rekhet?'

'As I've said, gossip and rumour. You know temple priests.' Qennu shrugged. 'Arrogant, opinionated. Userbati was much worse. A very proud man, a scribe in charge of the water supply to the temple, he was eager for advancement, very ambitious about his own career. Oh, I've reflected on him.' Qennu laughed sharply. 'He may have learnt something – or he may have simply been exploiting the crisis for his own ambitious ends, to appear important, to enhance his status – but no, he actually told me nothing, not even his suspicions about me. I knew nothing,' Qennu concluded. 'And for that I was sent to rot in a prison oasis.'

'Did you escape to clear your name?' Amerotke asked. 'Was it a desire for justice or vengeance?'

'Both, I suppose,' Qennu replied. 'Before I was arrested, I kissed Hutepa goodbye and told her to act as if she were my enemy. When I returned to Thebes, I discovered that she had been very busy on my behalf. She explained how she had searched the temple archives to discover the location of Huaneka's tomb and if it held, or once did, the Ari Sapu.'

'But she never went out to the Valley of the Forgotten?'

'She did but found it impassable. She believed the tomb had already been opened, that the Books of Doom had been removed, so what was the use? She certainly had her suspicions. She disliked Maben, found him arrogant and secretive, but apart from him, she voiced no names.'

'And what happened at the prison oasis?' Amerotke asked.

'A living hell, a fiery chamber from the Underworld. You don't believe in the gods there, only what you can see, hear, taste and touch. Perhaps if I'd known beforehand, I would have fought for my innocence in any court in Thebes, but by then it was too late. The other inmates did not like me. I'd scarcely arrived when there was an outbreak of dysentery. Of course, the prison authorities were only too pleased to point the finger of suspicion at me and my so-called hideous reputation. The true cause of the outbreak was brackish water and stale food. I truly believed I had been buried alive and forgotten.

The prison oasis was visited by sand-dwellers, desert wanderers, traders, merchants, tinkers; the keepers allowed them in. They'd bring goods for sale; sometimes the occasional whore. In my last year, there was a change. At first I thought it was a mistake, but when I crowded around the traders, small parcels were secretly pushed into my hands. On one occasion a battered knife, on others a water bottle, sandals, even a tattered map of the western Redlands. I concluded that someone was trying to help me.'

'Hutepa?' Amerotke asked.

'I thought it was, but when I came back to Thebes, she declared she hadn't the means. She could do things in Thebes, but not out in the western desert.'

'And your escape?'

'By then I'd collected a number of items. I waited for my opportunity. An escaped prisoner was brought back and executed. On such an occasion, the Guardian and the rest celebrated. I decided to leave that night. I scaled the palisade and made my way out into the Redlands. The Guardian was arrogant. He always proclaimed how the heat of the day, the freezing cold of the night, the wild animals and the desert wanderers were guard enough, but I had planned well. I had maps. I had studied the stars at the Temple of Ptah; I knew where I was going. I had a water bottle, sandals, a knife, a cloth to protect my head as well as other items. Moreover, I knew it was highly dangerous to move by day – the heat kills you – whilst to be lying in some rocky gulley at night was to attract the night prowlers. So, using the map, I journeyed from one waterhole to another. Of course, sometimes I got lost.'

'So you rested by day and travelled by night?'

'Precisely. I would sleep, eat what little food I had or the oasis could provide, roots, berries anything. If I kept travelling east, eventually I would cross the Tuthmosis Line and reach the outstretches of the Nile.' He paused. 'Years of captivity had made me cunning.'

'And?'

'A very simple accident. I reached a small oasis. The well had been dug by Egyptian troops; next to it was a stele boasting about the achievements of some long-forgotten pharaoh. I was exhausted and fell asleep beside it. I woke up to find that sand-dwellers had arrived. They'd pitched camp and simply waited for me to wake. Once I did, I was their prisoner. They were gentle enough, questioning me about where I came from. I told them lies about being a merchant who'd become lost. They nodded solemnly, then talked of how much profit they'd make when they sold me. They dragged me along with them. I was not their only prisoner. At first, I was so angry with myself that I ignored my comrade in distress. He introduced himself as a merchant from Memphis. I could see he was hiding something, and eventually he confessed to what he called his "great secret". He'd gone out into the western desert not only to trade but to collect information about the Libyan tribes. He was an imperial spy and claimed he'd seen something he would never forget.'

'And?' Amerotke asked, trying to control his excitement.

'Well, according to this merchant – or spy – he'd arrived at a large oasis far out in the western desert. The Libyans were there, leading chieftains playing host to captains of the Sea People. He recognised them by their feathered headdresses.'

Amerotke stared in astonishment. Qennu laughed.

'I know what you are thinking, Lord Judge: Sea People, so far south, actually in the desert! We don't think of them there, do we? According to this merchant, the Libyans were entertaining them lavishly, treating them like honoured guests. Anyway, that was all he saw. He fell under suspicion and was forced to flee. A day later he was captured by the sand-dwellers, nomads roaming the desert looking for any plunder they could find. The merchant proved to be a genial companion; his gossip about Thebes made me homesick. I told him little about myself. Two days later we were ambushed by an Egyptian chariot squadron, reinforced by Nubian archers. During the fight my companion was killed by an arrow straight to the throat. I decided to assume his identity. I took his amulet, scabbard, whatever possessions had been left on him. When the fight was over, I presented myself as a merchant who'd had the misfortune to be captured, hence my appearance.

'Of course, the officers of the chariot squadron were hospitable. They tended my light wounds, gave me bread and wine and brought me back to Thebes. They thought I would go with them to report to their garrison commander, but I slipped away and that was the end it. I was intent on discovering what had happened four years earlier. I returned to the Temple of Ptah; Hutepa was there. We met, we kissed. I was so pleased to see her. She told me the astonishing news that she had not sent anything out to that prison oasis, but had done nothing except search for the Books of Doom. She told me about Huaneka's grave out in the Valley of the Forgotten. Hutepa,' Qennu held up a hand to fend off Amerotke's question, 'simply wanted to make sense of what had happened, to remove her own doubt and, if she discovered something startling, to petition the Great House.' He sighed. 'I was only with her ten days before she was murdered. She sheltered and fed me, brought me fresh clothes, shaved, bathed and anointed me.' He blinked away the tears. 'I asked her if she suspected who the true Rekhet might be, but she did not. When I learnt what had happened on the temple forecourt, I realised how truly cunning the killer was. I had escaped and the poisonings had begun again. Lord Judge,' Qennu paused, as if half listening to the sounds of the two boys still playing in the orchard, 'you should be flattered. Hutepa advised me to trust you. She said I had to eventually surrender myself to someone in authority, declare my innocence, demand a full investigation. I made love to her the day I met you. She gave me most of her wealth, gold, silver and precious jewels. She had a kind heart. She realised I had to adopt a disguise; become a man of wealthy appearance. She also told me that you were at the temple. I followed you, spoke to you and then disappeared. The following morning I returned pretending to be a pilgrim. It was then I heard the news: Hutepa had been poisoned.'

'Did she suspect anyone?' Amerotke asked. 'Anyone at all?'

'No, Lord Judge.'

'Do you suspect anyone of poisoning her?'

'Undoubtedly she was murdered, but by whom . . . ?'

'And Ipuye?' Amerotke asked. 'The merchant and his wife found floating face down in their lotus pool?'

'I heard the news. I had few doings with Ipuye, though I did with his first wife. You see,' Qennu wetted his lips, 'I was a priest of the Chapel of the Ear. I heard the confessions of pilgrims, visitors to the temple. Lady Patuna was one of these. She claimed she suffered from an illness, some sort of possession.'

'What do you mean?' Amerotke asked.

'She panicked,' Qennu replied. 'If she left her house she felt as if she was going to faint; she sweated, she felt frightened. Now and again she forced herself to come to the Temple of Ptah. She confessed her sins and also her deep unhappiness about her husband's womanising.'

'Did she say with whom?'

'My lord Amerotke,' Qennu laughed, 'Ipuye took his pleasures whenever he could.'

'And the lord Hinqui?' Amerotke asked. 'You know he fell ill?'

A shake of the head.

'And the fire at the Temple of Ptah?'

'I tell you this. Before I was arrested, I knew something about poisons. During my years in the oasis, Hutepa, may the Lords of Light accept her *ka,* also studied poisons very carefully. She told me all sorts of wondrous tales: how different ingredients, powders and elements could mix to form a killing potion, but how to achieve that, you had to make certain purchases, buy the actual ingredients.'

Amerotke nodded in agreement. The Lady of the Dark had virtually told him the same. Qennu rose to his feet, tightening the sash around his robe.

'The Churat's men?' Amerotke asked. 'You poisoned them?'

'They threatened me. Hutepa had given me some poison; I insisted on that. I was determined not to be taken, and if I was and there was no hope of escape, I wanted to be able to end it all.'

Amerotke caught his steely determination; he knew that Qennu was resolute in his convictions.

'My lord Amerotke, you will not stop me going?'

The judge squinted up at this man who had come to him in confidence.

'This must end,' he declared. 'One day you must surrender yourself, even if it is for your own safety. You are in great danger, not just from the imperial troops or the Medjay; others search for you.'

'The Libyans?' Qennu asked. 'What are they plotting?'

'Oh, I think I now know.' Amerotke smiled. 'I see the deviousness of their plan. Is there anything else?' he asked.

Qennu stared up at the sky.

'What do you want?' Amerotke asked.

'Life,' Qennu replied. 'I want to be free of all this.' He smiled at Amerotke. 'I came freely . . .'

'And you go freely,' Amerotke replied. 'One thing: how many people at the Temple of Ptah knew you were friendly with Hutepa, that she was your woman?'

Qennu closed his eyes. 'Very few,' he replied. 'I made no show of it, and nor did she. You know how such relationships are frowned upon. Ah well.' He gazed up at the sky. 'You can find me in the Street of Lamps above the sign of the Lantern.' He stretched out his hand. 'My lord Amerotke, I have no more to say, but I swear this, I am not responsible for those hideous deaths in the temple or anywhere else. When you decree it, I shall come before you in the Hall of Two Truths and plead my case.'

Amerotke clasped his hand, then Qennu turned and walked away. Amerotke watched him go, certain that his mysterious visitor had spoken with true voice.

Amerotke spent the rest of day and the following one reflecting on what he had learnt, as well as piecing together the other information Nadif and Shufoy brought in from various parts of the city. On the third day after his mysterious visitor's appearance, an imperial courier arrived demanding news. Amerotke informed him that he would, if the Divine One decreed, come into the city, but there again, time was pressing, and in the end he had more useful things to do. He hoped to delay informing Hatusu, though he realised that he would have to act soon. Of course Hatusu did not wait. The following morning, just before dawn, Lord Senenmut, escorted by a squadron of imperial chariotry and a file of sweat-soaked Nubian spearmen, arrived outside Amerotke's house. He let the troops rest in the garden, much to the delight of Ahmase and Curfay, whilst he joined Amerotke on the roof terrace to worship the rising sun, intoning the glorious hymn of praise: 'All power to you, oh Glorious One, whose true splendour lies hidden beyond the Far Horizon, yet you send your rays to warm the earth and dispel our darkness . . .' The two men then broke the first bread of the day. For a while they sat like schoolboys, legs crossed, chewing carefully on honey bread and sipping appreciatively at freshly crushed fruit juice.

'Very good, Lord Judge.' At last Senenmut winked at Amerotke. 'Now the courtesies are over, what have you discovered?'

Amerotke told him about his mysterious visitor, and Senenmut's jaw dropped in surprise as the judge described in detail what had happened.

'So you think he is innocent?' Senenmut asked.

'Yes, I do, hence his presence here.'

'Never mind that, never mind that.' Senenmut waved a hand. 'I feel like a child,' he said, 'presented with an array of dishes. In the end it's the Libyans who interest me. Murder, Amerotke, is a matter for you. Treason and foreign policy are what concern us. I find it hard to think of the dead Ipuye as a traitor to the Divine House, but there again . . .'

'I don't think he was,' Amerotke replied. 'It's all part of a very subtle game. The Libyans are party to that, deeply involved in their own meddling mischief.' He swiftly described the conclusions he had reached, and the reasons for them.

'Very clever.' Senenmut grinned. 'Very clever indeed. According to you, the Libyans demanded peace for one simple reason: they wanted to open and develop trade links with the mines in Sinai to amass gold, silver and above all precious stones.

They would use these to form an alliance with the Sea People. The Sea People are pirates. They harbour at islands in the Great Green as well as ports further north in Canaan. Some of our enemies there, particularly the Hittites, allow them docking facilities. The Sea People roam the sea looking for land to settle in, and the most fertile is the delta. Because they have no crops, no fields, no cattle, they cannot barter, so they must live and die by the sword. However, once they have precious stones, gold and silver, they can buy supplies and bribe harbourmasters. In other words, they become stronger. The Libyans were plotting to build up their strength in alliance with the Sea People. They would trade with the mines along the Horus Road in Sinai and use the precious stones and metals to cement their friendship with the captains of the Sea People. After a year, maybe two years, a massive fleet would appear off the delta. We'd move troops to counter them. At the same time Naratousha would declare the peace treaty with Egypt broken and send his war parties east to harass towns and villages along the Nile. We would be fighting a war on two fronts, along the Nile and across the delta. What the Libyans are now doing in Thebes is simply sowing a harvest that may take years to flower, but it will be a bloody one!'

'And their plan was discovered?'

'Yes, by that merchant – my spy. He reached the oasis and recognised Sea People amongst the

Libyans, a rare event even in the ports, but deep in the desert . . . ? The Sea People were there to negotiate as well as to collect the first fruits of Naratousha's plan. The merchant saw this and escaped. He may have been pursued, but instead of being captured by the Libyans, he was seized by sand-dwellers: the same group who later captured Qennu. The merchant, realising Qennu was a fellow Egyptian, passed his information on. Our squadron chariot ambushed these sand-dwellers; the merchant was killed, Qennu assumed his identity and came back into the city. I suspect he was going to use this information to barter with the Divine One, but when the poisonings began again he watched and waited.'

'What will the Divine One do now?'

'As regards Qennu,' Senenmut spread his hands, 'you must do what you have to, Lord Judge. I shall instruct the Medjay, the imperial troops, not to mention the Eyes and Ears of Pharaoh, to cease their searching. As for the Libyans, the Divine One will invite them to a banquet. She will coax and flatter them. She'll say the treaty is improperly sealed because of the deaths of those three scribes. Anyway, she'll announce that she has been reflecting and that she now wants new clauses to be added to the treaty, the most important being that if the Libyans are to become friends of Pharaoh, her enemies must be their enemies.'

'The Sea People.' Amerotke smiled. 'She'll demand that there be no trade, pact or alliance, written or verbal, between the Libyans and the Sea People.'

'Precisely,' Senenmut agreed. 'She'll also demand that Naratousha inform her why they need so much gold, silver and precious stones; what are they using it for?'

'And the Libyan chiefs?' Amerotke asked.

'Oh, they'll be covered in consternation. They'll mutter their thanks for a splendid banquet and ask for time to reflect. Hatusu will reply that they are her guests. If they wish to stay forty days more in Thebes then they are most welcome. Naratousha will have to agree to that out of courtesy to his host. He'll then adjourn to his lodgings. He'll be furious. The Amemets never found the prisoner, and we now know what mischief the Libyans are plotting. Time will pass. Naratousha will claim there's a crisis at home and demand to leave. Hatusu will agree but will point out that the peace treaty is now suspended until it is sealed properly and includes the extra clauses. She will demand that Themeu be left as a hostage, either to fortune or until we discover the name of the traitor he's been conspiring with. Of course she will also insist that the Libyans cooperate with us in finding that chariot patrol lost in the western Redlands. I suspect that will keep Naratousha busy for the next two years. He'll return to the tribes covered in confusion and having lost face. So, the other business?' Senenmut added quickly. 'The poisonings?'

'I don't know,' Amerotke replied. 'So far I have theories, a little proof. In the end I think it will be deceit and cunning that traps the killers. I will summon everyone into my court in the Hall of Two Truths. If Ma'at is with me, the truth will be revealed and the guilty justly punished.'

HRU UTCHA METU: ancient Egyptian,
'the Day of Judgement'

CHAPTER 13

Three days later Amerotke moved to judgement in the Hall of Two Truths in the Temple of Ma'at, the heart of Thebes, the City of the Sceptre. The curious had gathered along the back of the hall wondering what this special session of the court intended. In the mean time they admired the hall's painted pillars and columns, a swirl of dark green and light blue with golden lotus leaves carved around the base and silver acanthi and purple grapes at the top. They stared across the marble floor, polished and shiny so it seemed people were walking on water; so clear was the reflection that it dazzled like a mirror and caught the flowers, butterflies and birds carved on the ceiling. The Hall of Two Truths was a place of beauty as well as justice. Ma'at, the Goddess of Truth, could be seen everywhere. The wall paintings paid tribute to the many poses and roles ascribed to her: a beautiful young woman, the Divine Princess, either standing alone or kneeling before her father Ra; a judge in the Hall of Weighing-of-the-Souls, alongside the jackal-faced Anubis and the green-skinned Osiris when she and the other Divine Beings assembled to determine a soul's final fate; a warrior princess smiting the destroyers, the creatures of the Underworld who exalted in such names as Devourer of Faeces, Gobbler of Flesh, Drinker of Blood and Smasher of Bones; holding the Scales of Justice or stretching out the Great Feather of Truth. The paintings had a purpose, not just to praise Ma'at but to remind all who came here that this was a place where Pharaoh dispensed her justice, where the truth was established and proclaimed for all to hear.

In those last few days of Shemshu, the hot season, Amerotke had been preparing to publish certain truths. He sat enthroned on the dark red quilted Chair of Judgement, its acacia-wood arms inlaid with silver and gold, its back rising high above him, a tasselled awning stretching out over his head. The gold fringe depicted a frieze of lunging green cobras, symbols of the defenders of Pharaoh and Egypt. The ends of the arms and the feet of the throne were carved to represent the snarling face of Sekhmet, the Destroyer Goddess.

Amerotke had readied himself very carefully for the occasion. Face and head shaved, he was dressed in his most brilliant gauffered robes with an embroidered sash around his middle. On his chest rested a pectoral of Ma'at made out of exquisite cornelian and other precious stones; on his wrists were the sacred bangles, whilst the jewelled rings on his fingers depicted the holy symbols of the goddess. On the stool next to him lay the flail and rod he would grasp when he dispensed judgement. On the table to his left was a cluster of small scrolls that Prenhoe had prepared, though Amerotke knew all he needed. Now he lifted his hand, a signal for the session to begin. Asural strode forward, lifted the bar to the court and gave it to an assistant, who hurried away. Then he marched on and paused just before Amerotke; knelt, bowed and rose. Walking to the judge's left, he proclaimed:

'Behold Chief Judge Amerotke, the Divine One's own voice in the Hall of Two Truths. What he does is blessed by the gods for the good fortune of the Divine House and the Kingdom of the Two Lands.' He lifted his right hand, and a trumpet blew a long piercing blast. Then he turned, bowed towards Amerotke and took his position at the back of the court.

On Amerotke's left, just beneath the large open window, sat a line of scribes on their cushions, small writing tables before them, parchments prepared, quill pens sharpened. Glimpsing Prenhoe's anxious face, Amerotke smiled, then turned to the right and the colonnaded waiting area where most of those he had summoned should be gathered. He raised his hand, and Asural walked forward.

'All those summoned here must wait outside.'

Ani, High Priest of Ptah, already furious at being so imperiously summoned, glared in anger at Amerotke.

'My lord,' Amerotke soothed, 'I ask you to wait outside, please.'

Asural was already walking forward with some of the temple guards. Ani gathered his robes about him, hitching the linen shawl around his shoulders, then, followed by Hinqui, Maben and Minnakht, left the court. Once they were gone, Amerotke raised his voice.

'Only those who seek justice from Pharaoh may stay. Is there anyone here who seeks justice?'

'I do.' Qennu, hidden in the shadows, walked forward and knelt on the cushion before Amerotke's throne.

'By what name are you called?' Amerotke asked.

'I am Qennu,' the man replied in a powerful voice. 'Once priest physician at the Temple of Ptah, wrongly accused of poisoning.' The rest of Qennu's statement was drowned out by cries and exclamations from the back of the court.

Amerotke had his excuse. He raised a hand.

'Captain Asural, the court must be cleared of everyone except the guard and scribes; once done, they cannot leave without my permission.'

Qennu remained kneeling on his cushion. Once the court was silent and empty, the captain of the guard brought out a small wooden table on which he placed two jars of kohl, pulling off the stoppers:

one green, the other black. Amerotke smiled at Qennu. He had spoken briefly to the former prisoner about what was to happen and warned him not to force matters. He now told him to withdraw deep into the shadowy colonnade. Once Amerotke was ready, he gestured at Asural.

'Bring in Lord Ani.'

The High Priest entered in a flurry of robes; glaring at Amerotke, he knelt on the cushions before the Chair of Judgement.

'Lord Ani,' Amerotke smiled, 'on the table before you are two pots of kohl, the same used by the three scribes before the ceremony at your temple. I beg you, decorate your eyes with them.'

Ani made to protest.

'Please,' Amerotke insisted, 'at least a little.'

The High Priest shrugged and, using his finger, lifted a generous portion of the perfumed oil and quickly dabbed beneath his eyes.

'Very good.' Amerotke indicated a pile of linen napkins. 'Please clean your hands.'

The ritual was repeated with Hinqui and Maben. Both looked surprised but obeyed. Amerotke tensed as Minnakht swaggered in and took his place. Again the request was made. Amerotke realised Minnakht was too quick witted and cunning not to anticipate a possible trap. The Chief Scribe glanced at his colleagues and stretched out his hand, but then peered at the jars. He appeared more confused than concerned.

'These are not the same jars; that's impossible!'

Amerotke closed his eyes. At last! One small lie, one scrap of confusion!

'Why is it impossible?' he asked quietly.

'Yes,' Lord Ani spoke up. 'Chief Scribe Minnakht, the kohl pots were not your concern, at least, not their laying out or their taking in.'

'Because I washed them afterwards.' Minnakht stumbled from one lie to another.

'But that wasn't your task,' Maben declared.

Minnakht swallowed hard to cover his confusion, then dipped a finger into one of the pots.

'I remember . . .' Hinqui spoke up; he still looked drawn and pale, clutching his stomach. Now he turned on his cushion so as to face Minnakht. 'On the morning of the ceremony we all came down to collect the three scribes from their waiting chamber in the Chapel of the Divine Infant. My lord Ani, do you remember? We left. Minnakht said he'd dropped something and returned to the chamber.' Hinqui fluttered his fingers. 'Something I would not even bother to recall, except that . . .' he leaned forward, peering at Minnakht, 'how can you say these are not the same kohl jars? And why do you claim to have washed them – a temple servant would do such a menial task!'

'I did not!' Minnakht now made a bad situation worse. 'I did not!' he shouted. 'I've made a mistake. I did not wash them.'

'Yet you said you did!' Lord Ani replied.

'Now,' Amerotke broke in, 'when I visited that

waiting chamber with you on that same day, those pots were still on the table. What did you do, my lord Minnakht? Did you remove them and wash them; if so, why? If a servant removed them, why were those pots still on that table later in the evening, on the same day those three scribes died?' Amerotke pressed his point. 'You assured me you never entered the chamber where the three scribes waited for the ceremony. Now you say you did. You dropped something there. You returned to find it. You remember what the jars of kohl looked like. You claim to have washed them.' He spread his hands. 'What is the truth of all this?'

Minnakht, now fully flustered, aware of his colleagues staring at him, swallowed hard and sat back on his heels, staring at this hawk-faced judge.

'What is this?' Amerotke repeated. 'Over a matter of small pots. How can you remember so precisely, Lord Minnakht?'

'Why were you involved with the kohl pots? You had no reason for that.' Ani, now sensing the turn of events, was openly hostile.

'Let us move to the heart of the matter,' Amerotke declared, 'those eye pots the three scribes used, the green and black kohl. Who was responsible for supplying them?'

'Minnakht,' Ani declared. 'He is Master of the Ritual. He is responsible for the kohl, but he would delegate such a task to the servants, who'd also see to them being later cleared away.'

'Minnakht,' Amerotke's voice was clear and carrying, 'you are in this court to be accused. I believe you are the Rekhet, and this man . . .' Amerotke gestured Qennu out of the shadows on his right. His arrival caused consternation. At first the priests of Ptah failed to recognise him, then Ani half rose but sat down again and bowed towards the judge.

'What is he doing here?' Maben shouted.

'He is the Rekhet!' Minnakht bawled. 'Lord Judge, how dare you bring me into this court and accuse me! He is responsible—'

'How dare I?' Amerotke shouted back. 'Because I will soon produce the proof. Now quiet!' He leaned forward. 'You are the constant, Minnakht. You, as everyone here knows, sent those pots of kohl for the three scribes to use. By your own admission you later removed them, ostensibly for washing. In truth you replaced them with innocent pots. You came down to collect those three scribes for the ceremony. As the procession gathered you claimed to have dropped something. You went back into that waiting chamber, scooped up those pots and replaced them with others which I myself saw. Hence your confusion today. You know full well the ones that contained the poison were destroyed.'

Ani had lost his arrogance; fingers to his face, the High Priest was lost in his own thoughts.

'Lord Judge!' Minnakht bleated.

'My lord Minnakht,' Amerotke echoed back

sarcastically. 'You are responsible by your own admission for these eyes paints, so concerned—'

'I'm not concerned, I'm confused.'

'No, Minnakht, you are worried. And so we come to the second death: that of Hutepa.' Amerotke turned. 'My lord Maben, you hold the keys to the muniment chest. Did Minnakht ever ask to borrow them?'

'Yes, yes, he did.' Maben, plump face all startled, nodded vigorously. 'On a few occasions.'

'You supplied Hutepa with the temple lists, didn't you, Minnakht? You allowed her to keep and study them. You were intrigued by her line of enquiry. She was following the same path you'd taken when you studied the life of the author of the Ari Sapu.'

'You had no right to do that!' Ani broke in, his face all aquiver. 'A temple girl allowed access to the sacred muniments. Why?'

'Oh, I think I understand why,' Amerotke declared. 'Hutepa was a beautiful young temple girl. You, my lord Minnakht, are a widower.'

'I'm a bachelor.'

'No, we'll come to that,' Amerotke smiled, 'in a little while. Hutepa sold her favours to you and in return borrowed certain manuscripts.'

'What proof do you have of that? This is all nonsense.'

'No, it's the truth,' Amerotke retorted. 'You allowed her access, she borrowed what she wanted and you watched and waited.'

'What are you implying?' Minnakht's question was tinged with anxiety.

'Listen!' Amerotke looked towards the back of the court. Only Asural and his guards remained there, but outside he could hear the clamour of people discussing the judge's strange actions. To his left, the lines of scribes under the open window overlooking the temple gardens were also astonished. Some had even stopped writing and were staring open-mouthed at the drama being played out before them. 'Everyone listen!'

The scribes' heads went down, pens clutched more tightly.

'My lord Minnakht, I will lay a formal indictment against you and then you can respond. Your reply will be carefully noted, but, I assure you of this, you will go on trial for your life. If you are found guilty you will suffer the most excruciating death.' Amerotke deliberately let his threat hang in the air. 'Fifty years ago,' he began, 'a priest physician at the Temple of Ptah, the author of the Ari Sapu, made a great study of poisons and perpetrated hideous killings throughout this city. He was caught and executed but he left a family. His widow probably became a lonely recluse, but they also had a son, a young boy. Minnakht, I suspect that boy was you. Your mother was a broken woman. She wanted to hide and, above all, protect you, so she gave you to some good family, a couple without a child. I am sure the temple records, if you haven't destroyed them, will prove that.'

Amerotke saw Ani nodding as if he too knew something.

'Your mother died and was buried out in the Valley of the Forgotten. One thing her husband had left, which the authorities failed to seize, was the Books of Doom, the Ari Sapu.' Amerotke paused. Minnakht made no attempt to reject what he said. Instead the Chief Scribe was listening intently, lips moving soundlessly. Amerotke wondered if some sickness of heart was masked by that amiable face. 'The years passed. The family who fostered you probably knew of your links with the Temple of Ptah, so you entered its service. You found out about your past, but of course the sweetness of youth can act as balm for many a pain. You told me you were a bachelor, Minnakht. According to the temple records I've studied, you once made a votive funeral offering for a wife and child. I suspect your young wife died soon after your marriage, probably before or during childbirth. Is that what tipped your heart into darkness? The death of your wife and baby child? I suspect you are no believer in any god. You are in deep pain over what happened to your father, your mother, your own wife and child. Middle age adds bitterness to all our grievances. You once told me you'd been assistant high priest. I wonder about your disappointment when Lord Ani here became high priest then appointed his own nephews as assistants. You felt disgraced and humiliated at being moved to a lesser post. Are you ambitious, Minnakht? Is that something else burning within you? Were you insulted at being removed from your post but hid it behind that smiling face? Did you come to hate the Temple of Ptah and all it stood for; the House of the Great Healer? For you it was the House of Deep Wounds. You went to the temple records; in fact you knew them well, for as assistant high priest you held the key to that muniments chest. You mentioned a legend about the author of the Ari Sapu being buried alive in the Temple of Ptah. You probably searched for any evidence of that. You found none so you scrutinised the records to find out about your mother and discovered her tomb in the Valley of the Forgotten. You visited that place, found the Books of Doom and removed them, but you also found certain artefacts, children's toys which she had asked to be buried with her as a memorial of you. You overlooked one.' Amerotke's voice became soft. 'A wooden giraffe with a piece of string so the head could be moved.'

Minnakht put his face in his hands, rocking himself backwards and forwards.

'You seized the Books of Doom, brought them back to the Temple of Ptah and planned your reign of terror. However, to have a book of recipes is one thing, but like any good cook, you needed the ingredients. You visited the herb markets and traded with the scorpion men. You were prudent. However, when Standard-Bearer Nadif took your description to the herb quarter of Thebes, people recognised it: "the smiling man". You were careful, but there again, what did you have to fear? There's no crime in buying certain plants, herbs, powders, but of course you used your father's knowledge to mix them. You became skilled in the use of poisons and began to test them. Everyone in Thebes wondered how you could dispense poisons here and there.' Amerotke shook his head. 'What need for that? In the temple precincts are stelae holy to the God Man Ptah over which holy water trickles. Visitors, many of them prosperous pilgrims, drink from that, collect it in their bottles and take it home. You poisoned it, though not all the time.' Amerotke paused at Ani's exclamation of disgust. He noticed how Hinqui and Maben had moved their cushions slightly away from Minnakht. All three were now staring in horror at their colleague. 'You enjoyed that, didn't you?' Amerokte continued. 'It was so easy: all you had to do was poison the water supply feeding the stelae. One day this small fountain, one day another; sometimes you'd leave it for a week and then return. You'd stand there and watch your victims drink or bottle their death. Did you ever follow your victims home to measure the time? You are fascinated by time, aren't you, Minnakht? When I visited your chamber I noticed the water clocks, the hour candles. You are an expert not only in poison but in the actual time those potions take to wreak havoc on their victims. No one suspected Minnakht, the genial-faced Chief of Scribes, friend to everyone, ally to each, until Userbati became suspicious. He was the scribe in charge of the water supply to the temple. He began to wonder whether that was the source of the poisonings. The secretive, ambitious Userbati kept that information to himself. After all, he would win great glory and recognition as the priest physician who trapped and caught the Rekhet.' Again Ani nodded. 'Of course, he would voice his concerns to Lord Ani but without telling him very much.'

The High Priest nodded again at this. Amerotke picked up the flail and pointed it at Minnakht.

'You decided to act. Userbati summoned guests, a few select friends to dinner. One of these was Qennu. You chose him as your catspaw and arranged for him not to attend that fatal dinner. You were responsible for the urgent message for him to visit the House of Twilight, where, of course, there was no one waiting. No one had sent for him. Meanwhile you entered the temple kitchens and poisoned the dishes prepared for Userbati and his friends. You also busied yourself in Qennu's chamber, hiding potions, powders and precious metals there. Later you visited Userbati's quarters and left that curse, a document pointing the finger of suspicion at Qennu. This unfortunate man was your next victim. He was accused and had no other choice but to throw himself on Pharaoh's mercy, confess to crimes he hadn't committed and be exiled to that prison oasis. Now that the Rekhet was ostensibly arrested and confined, the deaths had to stop, otherwise suspicions would have been raised that the wrong man had been arrested. However, Minnakht, this is where your evil heart becomes more obvious. You'd grown to love killing. You'd become so skilled in the use of powders and potions that you found it difficult to resist, and yet what could you do? If more deaths occurred, Qennu would be brought back and a proper investigation carried out. So, what happened?'

Amerotke paused, putting down the flail before continuing.

'First, you became aware that Hutepa was also interested in the very manuscripts you had studied. She had betrayed Qennu at his request so as to protect herself. She was convinced of her lover's innocence. She had a keen mind, and followed the same path as you had, Minnakht. Did you discover this and cultivate her friendship to establish how much she knew? You certainly obtained those manuscripts for her, in return for what, sexual favours?' Amerotke ignored Qennu's agitated stirring on the cushions. 'Of course you had already been out to the Valley of the Forgotten. What could a temple girl do by herself out in the rocky, searing hot Valley of the Forgotten? More importantly, the Ari Sapu were firmly in your possession. Second, Minnakht, you became hungry again; your appetite for death had only been whetted. Third, you wanted revenge, certainly against what you regarded as the House of Deep Wounds, the Temple of Ptah, the scene of so much sorrow for you and your family. What better time to indulge your deep vitriol than the peace negotiations with the Libyans and the preparations for the sealing of the great treaty at the Temple of Ptah? Finally, you had unfinished business with Ipuye, the prosperous merchant, the one who had posted a reward for your capture. How dare he do that? He too would feel your revenge. You'd already sent him poisoned wine, but then you decided on more subtle mischief. Once again you asked for the keys to the muniments room. Amongst those documents are grants by Ipuye of monies and other gifts to the Temple of Ptah. They would bear his seal. You simply removed one and sent it to the Libyans using Ipuye's name, promising they would see Egypt publicly humiliated. In return you asked them to help liberate the Rekhet from the prison oasis.'

'Why should I do that?' Minnakht burst out. He had been kneeling for most of Amerotke's speech with his face in his hands, lost in his own private thoughts. 'Why should I want him freed?'

'Because of what you were planning; because you needed him back so that you could continue dealing out death. Of course, nothing works out as you plan, does it, Minnakht? Qennu escaped and managed not only to reach Thebes, but also to acquire very valuable information about the Libyans. You couldn't care if he lived or died; the Rekhet had escaped so the poisonings could recommence. You arranged the deaths of those three scribes, and it was so easily done. I have spoken to Gerh, the Lady of the Dark, and she informed me that where the skin is thinner, around the eyes or the lips, poison can be more quickly absorbed. Those temple scribes were going to perform a public ceremony out in the open. They would need protection against the glare of the sun, the wind and the dust. Moreover, as part of the ritual they would have to dress appropriately, and that would mean deep kohl rings around their eyes. They would apply it generously, rub it deep into the skin. You knew exactly how long it would take for that poison to work. After all, you are Master of the Ritual, the one who planned the ceremony, yes?'

Ani and Hinqui were nodding vigorously at this. Maben still sat shocked.

'You replaced the harmless pots with others bearing a deadly poison, one that you had tested and measured. With all your skill in potions and calculating the time, you knew exactly how long it would take for the poison to be absorbed by the skin, enter the body and strike at the heart. Many poisons are like wine, aren't they, Minnakht? You drink two or three cups then you feel the effects: first the beneficial, followed by those not so beneficial, the sore head, the dry throat. Your poison did the same. Only Ma'at knows what concoction it was. At first those scribes would feel nothing, but then at the appointed time, the one who had anointed himself first would begin to feel the symptoms, followed by the others. I don't think you could specifically state when the poison would manifest itself. Nevertheless, you calculated that all three would die during a public part of the ceremony, and all three did.' Amerotke paused as Ani raised a hand.

'Did he plan it for the wine-drinking ceremony?'

'He hoped for that,' Amerotke replied. 'The Gerh pointed out that the three scribes had been fasting: a generous mouthful of wine would stir the stomach, make the lifeblood course more swiftly. Who knows?' he shrugged. 'Only the Ari Sapu will tell us – was it a poison that became virulent when mixed with wine? I cannot say, except that the wine-drinking appears to have been a catalyst for the poisoning of all three. And now,' he turned slightly, 'we come to Hinqui. Usually most priests, after they have anointed their eyes, wash their hands. I suspect that that morning one of them didn't. You, Hinqui, grasped that scribe's hands when he was jerking on the temple floor. I sent Shufoy to ask you that and you confirmed it. You picked up slight traces of a powerful poison, and later, either through raising your fingers to your lips or by touching food, you digested some of that malevolence. Even a faint trace would cause your sickness.'

Hinqui started to scream abuse at Minnakht. He would have sprung to his feet but Ani pressed him on the shoulders to stay still.

'You tried to protect yourself,' Amerotke shouted, 'by claiming to have been poisoned yourself by the Rekhet . . .'

'Not true!' Minnakht screamed back.

'It is true,' Maben declared, shaking himself from his reverie. 'This is all true! When we collected those three scribes you did go back, I remember that. You returned holding something in a napkin as if you didn't want to touch it. At the time I didn't think anything of it. You are correct, Lord Judge! On that evening when Lord Ani came to tell you about the death of Ipuye, those pots were still on the table, but why?' Maben shook his head. 'Why should the Chief Scribe of the Temple of Ptah be so concerned about kohl pots? Why do you keep contradicting yourself about leaving them or washing them?'

'And now we come to Hutepa,' Amerotke declared. 'That poor temple girl was delighted to find her lover was freed. He visited her, dirty and dishevelled, and they slept together, made love. Hutepa gave him silver, gold and precious stones so he could wash, change and disguise himself properly. She also told him what she had done about those manuscripts. Of course, she would not tell him the price she had paid. Nevertheless Hutepa, with her sharp wits, probably had suspicions about Minnakht; maybe you were too amiable, too ready to help; perhaps she'd seen something.' Amerotke's voice turned harsh. 'In your eyes Hutepa had to die. She knew too much. She was Qennu's lover, and her death, perhaps, might also explain how the Rekhet had crept into the temple to poison those scribes. You watched Hutepa. You may even have seen her with Qennu. You slipped into her chamber and poisoned her wine cup. She was agitated and, like anyone who'd been involved in something dangerous, grasped that cup and drank the deadly poison. When she realised her hideous mistake, she wanted to voice her suspicion. Who could have slipped into her chamber? If not her lover, perhaps Minnakht? In her death throes she picked up that wooden clapper found clenched so tightly in her dead hand. The inside of the clapper shows a dancer; closer inspection reveals it to be Min, the Goddess of Dance. In her dying seconds Hutepa was referring to you, Minnakht, by the first part of your name.'

'And the librarian?' Ani's voice grated harshly through the ominous silence of the hall. Amerotke shook his head sadly.

'I first thought that the person who had killed him had set fire to the records in order to hide the temple lists, but that's not true. If the fire hadn't started and the librarian not been murdered, he might be able to tell me how you, Minnakht, were deeply interested in any work on minerals, plants or herbs. In fact I sent Shufoy and Standard-Bearer Nadif to other temples and libraries in the city. My lord Minnakht, you are well known in all of them. Oh, nothing suspicious, just consulting certain books, but always the same books, the same works, the same treatises: the location of certain plants and minerals, the identity of certain snakes or insects. Yet when I questioned you, you told me you had little knowledge of poisons. No, the librarian had to die because he was garrulous; he may have reflected and become curious. You poisoned him, and when he was powerless, set fire to those archives. You have every right to go where you want. When the Divine One lodged at the temple, it was easy for you to slip into the kitchens and sprinkle a deadly potion on a certain dish. Pharaoh might have her tasters, but the chaos caused . . . What a scandal for the Temple of Ptah! You are, Minnakht, what I called the constant factor. You are free to wander the Temple of Ptah. You have access to manuscripts. You were friendly with Hutepa. And of course, you made one terrible mistake with those pots of eye paints and your deep concern about them. At first I am sure you laughed quietly behind your hand when everybody was suspicious about the wine. The poison was already in those poor scribes long before they were ever offered the sacred bowl.' Amerotke paused. 'This is the indictment against you, Minnakht, or at least part of it. Lord Valu, the Eyes and Ears of Pharaoh, Chief Prosecutor in the courts of Pharaoh, will present the full bill of charges against you. I said "part" because Shufoy and Standard-Bearer Nadif, together with the Medjay, are at this moment ransacking your quarters at the Temple of Ptah. I am sure they'll find more evidence.'

Minnakht sat composed, as if in shock. Now and again he'd look to his left and right, whisper to himself and stare up at the ceiling. Amerotke wondered if his wits had wandered, and realised how cleverly the Chief of Scribes had masked his true self.

'Eventually,' Amerotke continued, 'you can present your defence. Until then you will be imprisoned. You have two choices, my lord. You may defend yourself, but I think you will be found guilty, in which case you will be impaled or buried alive out in the Redlands. On the other hand, you can reflect very carefully on what I've said and make a full confession. Your death will be swifter than those of many of your victims.' He raised a hand. 'Captain of the Guard, take him away.'

For a while there was confusion. Minnakht leapt to his feet and started screaming at Amerotke, then turned on Lord Ani.

'Do you believe this, do you believe this?' He turned away, talking to himself, his arms flapping like the wings of a pinioned bird. When Asural and the guards laid hands on him, he struggled for a while but then went slack and was taken quietly out of the hall. Ani, Hinqui and Maben, terrified at what they'd seen and heard, were ready to scurry out after him. Amerotke called them back.

'One further matter. My lords,' he leaned forward smilingly, 'you were all present when Grand Vizier Senenmut spoke about the Memphite merchant – his spy – whose identity the alleged Rekhet assumed. You do remember? I demand to know which of you later gave such information to the Libyan chieftain know as Themeu?' He watched the consternation on Hinqui's face. 'Themeu,' Amerotke continued softly, 'will soon tell us. He'll be held hostage in Thebes until he complies fully with the Divine One's request. It's best if the priest responsible confesses now and throws himself on Pharaoh's mercy.'

Hinqui burst into tears; face in his hands, he rocked backwards and forwards. The sobbing echoed eerily through the silent hall.

'Why?' Ani gasped.

'He was beautiful . . .' Hinqui whispered, taking his hands away. 'I was stupid! I was trapped. He threatened me. I panicked. I told him what I knew . . .'

Amerotke summoned his guards forward. They grasped the still sobbing Hinqui and pushed him from the court. Ani and Maben staggered to their feet, broken men, drained of all arrogance.

'My lords,' Amerotke declared, 'it is best if you wait outside until Standard-Bearer Nadif returns. Maben, I have unfinished business with you and your family.'

'So you have, Lord Judge.' Maben crept forward so as not to be overheard. 'This morning Standard-Bearer Nadif and his Medjay came to our house. They took Lady Meryet into custody; they would not allow me to speak to her.'

'Your sister is safe,' Amerotke replied. 'Now, my lord, I beg you to wait.' He turned to where Qennu still knelt on the cushion. He beckoned him forward, took a small scroll and thrust it into his hand. 'Take this to my house. The Lady Norfret will look after you.'

Qennu went down on his knees again. 'Lord Judge, my gratitude to you—'

'This is not over yet,' Amerotke interrupted. 'Until it is, you must stay with me. Minnakht will now reflect. Lord Valu's men will question him, show him whatever evidence Shufoy and Nadif have found. Now you must go; other matters await.'

Qennu left as Asural came forward.

'The crowds outside wish to come in.'

'The crowds outside,' Amerotke declared, 'can only be here for a trial; this is not a trial. Asural, you have archers?'

Asural nodded with his head to the shadows at the back of the court.

'Make sure they are ready,' Amerotke declared. 'Hotep is a Kushite warrior, a veteran. What will happen here could be very dangerous. Bring him in.'

Amerotke turned to Prenhoe and the line of scribes. Some of them were still writing, copying from each other. Astonished by the revelations, a few had forgotten to transcribe properly and were now asking their colleagues for help.

'What will happen here,' Amerotke declared, 'could become violent. Do not intervene or rise from where you are sitting. You are armed as I ordered you?'

Prenhoe and other scribes fumbled under the cushions and brought out the thin thrusting daggers they'd hidden there, a not unusual precaution. It was known for the condemned or the convicted to try to escape, or even take out their anger and fury on whoever was nearby. Amerotke nodded in satisfaction. The doors at the side of the court opened and Hotep, clad in a loincloth, a white linen robe over his shoulders, strolled in. He knelt on the cushions and stared at Amerotke. Despite his military swagger, this man was frightened and wary. He waited until the doors were closed, sealing off the crowd and their hubbub outside.

'Lord Judge, why am I here?'

'Silence,' Prenhoe shouted. 'It is not right for you to speak first.'

'You asked a question,' Amerotke replied, raising a hand, 'and you shall have an answer. Hotep, you were captain of the guard for the dead merchant Ipuye, yes?'

'You know I was.'

'No insolence here.' Amerotke leaned forward. 'You are, therefore, guilty on two counts. First of murder, and second of betraying your master's trust.'

Hotep would have sprung to his feet, but Asural and three of the guards strode forward and stood behind him. One lowered a spear so that the blade rested on the Kushite's left shoulder.

'The lady Meryet . . .' Amerotke paused for effect. He was about to practise subterfuge in order to shatter this man's confidence. Within a few heartbeats he would know whether he had discovered the truth or not. He was certain he had. 'The lady Meryet has confessed. I shall tell you, Hotep, how you killed your master. On the day Ipuye died, Lady

Meryet and her brother Maben left the House of the Golden Vine to attend the ceremony at the Temple of Ptah. We know what happened there, but as regards Ipuye, there was no interference by the Rekhet; you were the killer, Hotep. Before she left, the lady Meryet handed you a sleeping potion. Ipuye and Lady Khiat rose late. They came into the main part of the house, where the only person waiting for them was Hotep, their captain of the guard. Just before they left the house for the lotus pool, both husband and wife drank wine, water or fruit juice in which you distilled the sleeping potion. Not very much, but certainly enough when mingled with the wine they drank later on to induce a heavy sleep. Unlike poisons, sleeping potions leave little or no trace. You washed the goblets thoroughly, then hurried out after your master to the lotus pool. The ever-faithful retainer, you checked your men, but you had also brought them refreshments: a jug of beer and some bread. Of course the beer was also laced with the light sleeping powder. The sun grew stronger. Outside the palisade your men squatted in the shade, drank their beer and gently dozed. After all, who can blame them? A beautiful afternoon in an opulent garden, a cup of beer, its effects heightened by a sleeping powder. Meanwhile in the lotus pool Ipuye and Khiat poured some wine; that and the heat, not to mention the sleeping potion, had the desired effect, and they fell fast asleep on the couches in the sun pavilion. Once you were sure everyone was resting, you carried out the next part of your plan. You and Lady Meryet had hidden in the undergrowth a ladder pole with rungs on either side.'

'This is not true, my lord.' Hotep's lower lip quivered.

Amerotke could tell from the man's face that it was; the Kushite was truly startled at the extent of the judge's knowledge.

'Also hidden in the undergrowth was a fresh, clean loincloth. You stripped yourself naked, took off the chain around your neck, your rings and bracelet, and hid them carefully away. You then took the ladder, positioned it against the palisade, climbed up and peered over the top. The place you'd chosen provided a vantage point. You could see into the sun pavilion, but because of the trees and lush vegetation, any of your men who might be awake couldn't see you. You dropped down to the ground, went into the sun pavilion, picked up the lady Khiat, took her to the pool and drowned her. Perhaps there was a little resistance, but how long does it take? A few heartbeats? Her head was pressed down underwater, her body floated away. You then returned to the sun pavilion. Ipuye was heavier, but you are a strong warrior, Hotep. You picked him up, walked into the pool and again lowered him gently, turning him over and thrusting his face down. There may have been some splashing; Ipuye might have regained consciousness, but he was weak and heavy limbed due to the wine and the sleeping potion. The water surged in through his nose and mouth and soon he lost consciousness.

'No lapis lazuli was found on the feet of Ipuye and Khiat. I now realise the real reason for that: they were lifted into the pool. You made sure both were dead, then you climbed out and raced back to the palisade. The transverse beams on the inside holding the poles together made it easier to scale. You climbed up, let yourself down the ladder and returned to your hiding place. That was when you made your only mistake. Any lapis lazuli on your feet you washed away easily enough with a jug of water. You also used your old loincloth to dry yourself, wiping off anything that could betray what you had done, then putting on a fresh loincloth. Perhaps you crossed the folds a different way, though I shall return to that. In your excitement, you also picked up your ring and bracelet. Old customs die hard, don't they, Hotep? Instead of putting the ring and bracelet on your left hand, you acted as if you were still a member of the Medjay and put them on the right.

'The afternoon drew on. You took advantage of your men's drunken sleep to go back to the house and clear up any details that might arouse suspicion, then you waited. The sun began to set. Saneb awoke and went into the pool enclosure only to discover his master and mistress dead. He hastened out to raise the alarm. We know what happened next. Saneb, however, was vigilant and sharp eyed. When he was talking to you, he realised that your loincloth was new, clean and fresh. Perhaps the folds were arranged differently from earlier in the day. He certainly noticed the ring and bracelet on the wrong hand and arm and became suspicious. You see,' Amerotke smiled, 'Saneb too had been a member of the Medjay; he would realise that, half asleep or excited, he might put the ring and bracelet on the wrong hand himself.' He paused, tapping his sandalled foot. 'Saneb's suspicions would be easily fanned. After all, he would wonder, if no intruder could break into that lotus pool and commit murder, then the assassin must be someone in Ipuye's household; even a member of his bodyguard. Saneb, however, wasn't interested in justice but in blackmail; he hinted at what he knew so you killed him. Saneb didn't run away. I suspect his remains are lying amongst the reeds of some crocodile pool along with a sack or cloth containing his possessions.' Amerotke paused. Hotep was highly agitated, chest heaving, eyeballs rolling. Now and again he'd glance to the left and right.

'The lady Meryet maintains that you are responsible for the deaths of Saneb, Ipuye and Khiat,' Amerotke continued. 'She maintains that your heart has always burned with lust for her but that Lord Ipuye would never allow his bodyguard to marry his former sister-in-law.' He swallowed. What he had said to Hotep wasn't a lie. He believed it was the truth and that his accuracy of detail would convince Hotep. 'But of course the lady Meryet herself is not innocent,' he declared. 'She wanted Ipuye dead, didn't she, Hotep? She promised you that once he was dead she'd be free to marry you. The truth is, Lady Meryet had hoped to become Ipuye's second wife. She became his lover and visited him under the name Nibit Pi, Mistress of the House, in his Place of Pleasure in Thebes. Ipuye enjoyed her, and promised her that if anything happened to her sister she would be his next wife. And something did. Ipuye left for his Place of Pleasure, ostensibly on business in Thebes. Shortly afterwards Lady Meryet and her sister Patuna went for an evening stroll in that neglected part of the garden near the midden heap. Perhaps they quarrelled, perhaps Lady Patuna knew what her sister had done. Whatever the reason, Meryet decided that Patuna must die. She smashed her skull with a mallet and buried her corpse beneath the compost. She came back, burnt that collarette and marriage bracelet, and left the poem so the story would spread that Patuna had fled.' Amerotke paused. Hotep sat, shoulders tense, his black skin gleaming with sweat.

'I do not believe,' Amerotke's voice grew louder, 'that Ipuye's heart was clean. He may have suspected what Meryet had done but he couldn't accuse her. Instead he did something worse: he totally ignored her and married Khiat. He knew Patuna hadn't fled, that her body lay somewhere in that garden, but he let Meryet spread her lies about his alleged involvement in her death. He knew the truth.' Amerotke pointed further down the hall. 'I have talked to a Priest of the Ear from a chapel in the Temple of Ptah. He heard Patuna's confession. She suffered a strange form of malady and was reluctant to leave her house. Few knew of her ailment. Ipuye certainly did, but he didn't care. He had something he could use to blackmail Lady Meryet, threaten her with. She had no choice but to remain his lover. By declaring that he would only eat what she cooked, Ipuye made sure that he would never fall ill of some mysterious sickness. How the lady Meryet must have seethed! Oh yes,' Amerotke paused in mock surprise, 'didn't you know, Hotep? She continued to see Ipuye; I have seen the accounts of his amorous visitors. Nibit Pi figures prominently there. Lady Meryet, however, was caught. The only thing she really wanted was Ipuye dead, but poison was out: Ipuye made it well known, through his own house as well as beyond, that she cooked his food. So she turned to the captain of Ipuye's guard, a warrior, a former police officer. According to Ipuye, Lady Meryet is skilled in the arts of love. She seduced you and you believed her, didn't you? She laid the plans, gave you the sleeping potion and you arranged the rest. A clever plot,' Amerotke mused, 'Meryet not even being in the house when Ipuye died.'

Hotep made to rise; it was clear he did not know whether to protest or scream.

'Am I telling you the truth, Hotep? Throw yourself

on Pharaoh's mercy! Who knows what compassion you may be shown. Lie? You are a former member of the Medjay. You've seen men impaled alive above the cliffs of western Thebes. Is that how you want to die? Meryet has confessed hoping to save herself; why not you?'

'It's true,' Hotep licked his lips, 'it's true, Lord Judge, but it was her plan. She wanted Ipuye and Khiat dead. She ordered me to kill Saneb. Lord Ipuye did not trust her from the start; that is why he hired me in the first place. He believed the Rekhet did not send that tainted wine, it was a gift from the lady Meryet, who was furious at what he had done. My lord, I have done wrong . . .'

Amerotke stared to his right at the heavy wooden door on the side wall, a grille high at the top. Behind it Nadif's men held Meryet gagged and bound so she could see and hear everything but make no protest.

'Captain Asural,' he called, pointing to the door, 'allow in the lady Meryet.'

Asural strode across, lifted the latch and opened the door. The guards brought Meryet in; she looked dishevelled, hair hanging over her eyes.

'Release the gag,' Amerotke declared. As soon as they did, Meryet ran forward and fell on her knees beside Hotep.

'You fool!' she screamed. 'You stupid dolt! I told him nothing! What he said to you was all speculation! I never confessed.'

Hotep stared in horror at her then back at the judge. He went down, hands to the floor, crouching like an animal on all fours, then looked up. Even Amerotke, watching his eyes, was taken by surprise as Hotep gathered himself, screamed and lunged forward. He had reached the steps leading to Amerotke's throne when the first arrow hit him. Amerotke stood, dagger poised, as the Kushite stopped and turned as if to look for his tormentors. A second arrow took him in the throat, a third in the chest. He staggered to the side, coughed, blood spluttering out of his mouth, and crashed to the floor. Asural raced forward and turned the corpse over, feeling for the life beat in the throat. He glanced up at Amerotke.

'Dead? Take his corpse away,' Amerotke said quietly, trying to control his own breathing. His body was sweat soaked, and he could almost hear his heart thudding.

'You knew he'd do that, didn't you?' Meryet screamed. 'You tricked him!'

'I told him the truth,' Amerotke replied, walking down the steps towards her. 'I told him precisely what happened and why. I told him about his involvement and yours. Lady Meryet, where is the lie in what I have said?' He pointed to the line of scribes. 'They have taken down Hotep's confession. The promise I gave him I now offer you. You have heard the indictment; you will go on trial for your life. You know what the outcome will be. Take her away.'

HRU MIT: ancient Egyptian, 'death day'

EPILOGUE

'Last night I dreamed . . .' Prenhoe, standing behind Amerotke, murmured, 'I was floating on the wings of an ibis bird above the Nile; beneath me sailed a royal barge. What do you think that signifies, Lord Judge?'

'That you want to be an ibis bird,' Shufoy joked.

Amerotke held up his hand. 'Not here,' he whispered. He stared down the dark passageway of the House of Death beneath the Temple of Ma'at. Guards, their faces masked, stood either side of the two cell doors now thrown open. Amerotke, dressed in the full robes of his office, walked towards them. In the first cell Minnakht sat in a corner cradling the death cup. When Amerotke came in, the former Chief of Scribes returned to staring at the floor, moving the cup slowly from hand to hand. Around the cell stood guards wearing the jackal mask of Anubis; they were dressed in leather kilts, spear in one hand, shield in the other. Amerotke nodded and went to the adjoining cell. Here Meryet sat with her back to the wall. She too held the cup of death. She glanced up as Amerotke entered, shook her head, lifted the cup as if to drink then put it down. Amerotke left and went back to stand in the passageway.

'Lord Judge.' The Chief Executioner walked forward, took off his mask and wiped the sweat off his face. 'My lord, how long are we to wait?'

'You know the ritual,' Amerotke replied. 'An hour.'

'It's an hour,' Standard-Bearer Nadif echoed. 'They must drink within the hour.'

The executioner, the Bringer of Death, nodded and walked away. Amerotke stared up at a ray of light from the grating above. He just wished it was over. Nadif and Shufoy had returned from the Temple of Ptah. They had found Minnakht's hiding place. One of those water clocks had been cleverly used to hide both the Books of Doom as well as a generous collection of Minnakht's poisons, each carefully inscribed in their jars or boxes. Other evidence had been found in his chamber, enough to convince the Chief Scribe to confess and throw himself on Pharaoh's mercy. He had openly acknowledged in court, in the presence of Lord Valu the Chief Prosecutor, that the indictment Amerotke had presented was true in every way. He confirmed that he was the son of the author of the Ari Sapu, and described his career at the Temple of Ptah, his deep disappointment at not being promoted. In the end his story had become rambling, but he had confessed and been led away.

Meryet, faced with the hideous possibility of being either impaled or buried alive out in the hot desert sands, also admitted her guilt. She had confessed her hatred for Ipuye and acknowledged Amerotke's indictment was true. Both had received the mercy verdict. They would be allowed to drink a cup of poison which would lead gently to death. Now, five days after the indictments had been presented, Amerotke stood and listened to the distant sounds from the temple above him as he waited for sentence to be carried out. Everything, he reflected, could change so quickly in Thebes. The Libyans had left, openly disconcerted. Hinqui had been banished to a village deep in the south. The news about Minnakht and the lady Meryet had swept Thebes. Others had come forward offering scraps of evidence which Lord Valu would have certainly used if either had elected for trial. In the end it had come to this.

Amerotke heard a sob from one of the cells and again walked down the passageway. Minnakht had drunk his cup and was lying on the ground like a child, hands beneath his face, staring at the doorway. Lady Meryet too was drinking. Amerotke stepped back, closed his eyes and murmured a short prayer. He knew the effect of the poison. The numbness in the legs would spread, and the victims would fall asleep and slip quietly into death.

After a while one of the guards called out.

'It is finished . . .'

AUTHOR'S NOTE

Poisons were more deadly in ancient times because the authorities lacked the means to search for and analyse them. It wasn't until the nineteenth century, for example, that clinical tests were introduced to detect the effects of arsenic. A. W. Blythe's *Poisons: their effects and detection* (London, 1920) is one of the most fascinating studies, though rather dated. Poison in ancient times was regarded with the same horror as we view chemical or biological warfare today. Many of the accounts in my story are based on actual events from ancient history. In the fifth century BC Xenophon describes the devastating effects of poison honey from the Black Sea area. Pliny the Elder also talks about this 'mad honey'. The most famous example of a skilled poisoner is Mithridates of Pontus, who lived in the first century BC. He had access to secret manuscripts from India and elsewhere, and became such an expert that he tried to produce theriac, a so-called antidote to all poisons. Finally, lapis lazuli was used as decoration, as well as to give people a better grip on shiny floors. The crushed blue stone (of sulphuric origin) was mingled with gold dust which made it shine.

Interest in the cultivation of poisons was common in Egypt, as it was in China and the civilisations of the Indus valley. Poison terrorists are also not just a phenomenon of modern times. The Latin writer Dio Cassius mentions epidemics of man-made poisons, people being pricked on the streets with specially smeared pins. Ancient Egypt's flora and fauna, as well as its access to the teeming lush jungles of the south, made it a leading centre for the collection and distillation of potions and powders as deadly as any modern-day toxin.

Paul C. Doherty
July 2006

Website: www.paulcdoherty.com

The Assassins of Isis

Paul Doherty

The location of Rahimere's tomb, somewhere deep in the desert, has long been kept a closely guarded secret. But now, the Sebaus – a sect taking its name from demons – has plundered and pillaged the sepulchre for its most powerful treasure.

The fiery Pharaoh Queen Hatusu must fight to protect the tombs of her kin and tighten her grip on the collar of Egypt. Then Egypt's great military hero, General Suten, is bitten to death by a swarm of venomous vipers, and it appears events have spiralled out of her control.

Meanwhile, a dark shadow lies across the peaceful Temple of Isis; four of the temple handmaids have vanished without trace. Will Lord Amerotke, Pharaoh's Chief Judge, be able to unravel the mysteries before further violence erupts? Or will he find that the perpetrators are in league with forces beyond his jurisdiction?

THE ASSASSINS OF ISIS is the fifth novel in a series set in Ancient Egypt, following THE MASK OF RA, THE HORUS KILLINGS, THE ANUBIS SLAYINGS and THE SLAYERS OF SETH.

Acclaim for Paul Doherty's novels:

'Superb entertainment' *Historical Novels Review*

'The best of its kind since the death of Ellis Peters' *Time Out*

'An opulent banquet to satisfy the most murderous appetite' *Northern Echo*

0 7553 0782 8

headline

The Year of the Cobra

Paul Doherty

Egypt is in danger. The barbarous Hittites are rumoured to be massing their armies. Pharaoh Tutankhamen is seriously ill and the country appears powerless against its enemies. Scheming minister Lord Ay sends Mahu, Overseer of the House of Scribes, to uncover the Hittites' plan. But what Mahu discovers could be more devastating than any attack . . .

When the Masked messengers emerge to guide Mahu many unanswered questions reveal themselves: the truth about Pharaoh Akenhaten's disappearance; the identity of the 'Watchers' and secret knowledge about the Aten; the one God and the coming of a Messiah. Mahu knows that Egypt's future rests on this knowledge, but he also knows that knowledge is power . . .

Acclaim for Paul Doherty's novels:

'An opulent banquet to satisfy the most murderous appetite' *Northern Echo*

'A delightfully dark tale' *Historical Novels Review*

'Doherty dazzles with his knowledge and intimate feel for ancient Egypt' *Time Out*

978 0 7553 0344 1

headline